CU00408519

THE G CLUB

by

Paul Madden

© Paul Madden. 2017

To Lloyd, Tobias & Finley

Acknowledgements

This book would not have been possible if weren't for a huge group of people, who will now and forever be called the G Clubbers. Thanks for all the draft reading, encouragement, photos, edits, texts and phone calls.

Thank you, Sarah, Becky, Fidelma, Lloyd, Marjorie, Liam, Mam, Tara, Emer, Treasa, Ken, Sue, Chris, James, Leila, Nova, Richard B, Gareth, Damian, Tom & the Hey Bitches Book Club. (I hope I haven't left anyone out)

THANK YOU!

Chapter 1

It was almost pitch black. A blue hue from the digital clock in the corner of the room robbed the night of complete sovereignty. It served as a reminder that time, especially at night, goes by very slowly. It was mostly quiet. Stirring birds' noises punctured the silence at the oddest of intervals. It was soothing to Jamie to think that he wasn't the only thing not asleep. He had given up tossing and turning. It was futile, and he knew it. The inside of his head was sore. It wasn't a headache; it was like his brain had run a marathon; mental and physical exhaustion combined. His eyelids weren't heavy, but his lips were dry, and he needed to pee, but he didn't want to make noise.

A nasal snort erupted from the bed as his husband turned over to lie on his back. He opened and closed his moist mouth and continued to sleep deeply. Jamie honed in on Tom's breathing. It was effortless; slow paced inhaling and exhaling. There was no jealousy. He was just glad that Tom was asleep and didn't have to endure this exhausting regime of interminable nothingness. Heat from Tom's body radiated to Jamie's side of the bed. Their bodies didn't meet under their duvet. Their heads were closer together than their feet were, that had been the way for the last nine years of their twelve-year relationship.

An all too familiar sound from under his pillow began to swell. He quickly silenced his alarm and just as his feet were about to hit the floor, another set of feet had beaten him to it. As he rose, Jamie saw the silhouette of their nine-year-old cat George, stretching just before he trotted out of the bedroom. He grabbed his grey dressing gown and followed. George was sitting on the top of the stairs wondering if his owner was just up to use the toilet or were things returning to normal. He tied his dressing gown around his waist and stiffly made his way downstairs, led by George who nimbly dashed down in front of him.

The coffee machine was fired up, ready to deliver some needed caffeinated therapy. While that was happening, a glass of water was poured, and some vitamins were consumed. These supplements were bulk bought when Jamie turned forty earlier in the year. They seemed like a good idea at the time. His friends joked that it was some sort of midlife crisis.

His phone vibrated, so he pulled it from his pocket. The bright screen hurt his eyes. It was a text message, another one on top of the eleven others that he hadn't read. The newest one was from his boss, Jonathan. He opened it and smiled.

Looking forward to seeing you. As you would say to me, "take it easy." J

He replied, his first text in quite some time:

Great advice. See you at 9. Jamie

The sound of soft padded feet cantering into the living room meant one thing, George was ready to be groomed, which Jamie did without thinking. Both men never wanted children but did feel that something living, other than plants, was required in their home. Tom's job as a celebrity hairdresser took him travelling, so a dog was a no no. A cat seemed to fit the bill. Nine years later, it was evident they had an atypically aloof Ragdoll cat.

Entering the bathroom he removed his robe, t-shirt and boxers and Jamie looked at himself in the mirror, but it felt like someone else was looking back. The dark circles under his chestnut brown eyes made his face look more elongated. He hadn't shaved for a month, and he knew that it didn't suit him. He stroked and caressed the mass of patchy brown stubble and hair that had grown over the four weeks he'd been off work and wished he could pull off this look, but stubble and facial hair just made him look dishevelled. Taking a deep breath, he sheared off the excess hair which fell into the sink. He poured shaving oil into his hand and rubbed his face before shaving away the stubble with only a few blood spots. A cleanly shaven face emphasised his tiredness. He questioned should he have kept some stubble, but it was too late now.

He ran the shower, and the hot steam warmed up the air in the cold bathroom. Jamie looked down and was mildly horrified at what appeared to be a larger belly than he was used to. He thought his pubes could've done with a trim too but today was not the day for that. Not moving, he allowed his entire body to be warmed and cleansed. Inside the spacious shower were just steam and thoughts. Shampooing his hair, he noticed it felt longer than he would normally have had it. Tom was supposed to have been back from work earlier to cut it, but his flight was delayed. George was sitting on the toilet seat licking himself clean. Jamie didn't want to leave the shower because it meant putting on formal clothes and shoes, things he hadn't been wearing for a while. It represented re-entering the world.

The shower suddenly ran cold because Tom had flushed in the en-suite. Jamie wasn't worried that he might have made too much noise because Tom would be fast asleep in a couple of minutes, a talent Jamie wished he had.

He grabbed his towel and dried himself. Autopilot kicked in: deodorant, moisturiser & hair product. He used the towel to rub the condensation off the mirror and wrapped it around his waist again. Grabbing his toothbrush, he applied some paste and began to brush. As he got into his rhythm of brushing, he looked up and saw large tears forming in his eyes. They quickly become too heavy to stay put and eventually fell. No sound accompanied them, just the brushing of teeth. More tears formed and fell, no sob or whimper was heard. Jamie looked at himself in the mirror as if nothing unusual was happening. The brushing ceased along with the tears. With red eyes, he rinsed his mouth with some mouthwash and caught another glimpse of himself in the mirror for the briefest of seconds before he switched the bathroom light off.

Jamie got ready in the spare bedroom. He picked out a shirt and matched his boxer briefs and socks accordingly. The dark trousers he chose felt snug. Brown shoes, polished the night before matched the brown belt. At the mirror on the other side of the room, he surveyed his packaged self, which on the surface, appeared to be ready for the outside world. Stepping closer, he swallowed back, breathed a defeated breath and turned the light off.

A short walk down the landing, Jamie crept into their bedroom which felt warm and inviting. His eyes slowly adjusted to the dim light as he searched to see what side of the bed Tom was on. Tom had migrated over to Jamie's side to steal the heat after he had left. He kissed him on the cheek as gently as he could and as he stood up another of his tears fell silently on the pillow.

Jamie exited without stirring anyone, even George was asleep in his usual spot, at the bottom of the bed.

Before he left, he placed his iPhone on the kitchen table and wrote a note on a Post-it, attaching it to the back of the phone. Putting earphones into each ear and the jack into his pocket, connected to nothing, he double checked that the fridge was closed and that the taps, gas and lights were all off.

The first half of his walk was usually solitary, apart from the odd stray cat or fox who seemed to live harmoniously on their quiet road. Jamie eventually joined the melee that was the daily commute into London once he hit the High Road. There he joined the steady flow of commuters all making their way to Greenwich Station. Coffee drinking ones, paper reading ones, jogging, cycling, scootering ones. After making the same trip into London for years, he began seeing the same people. Their morning routines may have been different but unknowingly, they were in sync with Jamie's, and it was comforting to see some familiar faces. That's all they were to him, faces. He didn't actually know them or speak to them, that wasn't the done thing. When he first moved to London, Tom would laugh at him for saying 'hello' to strangers on the street. He soon learned to stop this parochial trait as London hardened him to look on, look through and to get to his destination. Going back to visit family in the small town of

Ledbury, he had to remember to revert to acknowledging everyone he passed.

The platform was busy as the first train into London screeched around the bend. Not many got off, and there was the usual squashing into the already, jam-packed carriages. Even though he considered himself a seasoned commuter, he still preferred to wait and hope that the next train would be less busy, rather than to try to prise himself into a rammed carriage. There was still a bit of the shy country boy left in him.

"Can you move down please?" could be heard along the platform from the more assertive Londoners. The more timid commuters all wondered where they could move to. The doors finally closed and the train slowly departed. Another train was due in seven minutes.

Mid-August delivered a smorgasbord of weather, making it sometimes difficult to choose what to wear. The morning was warming up nicely as the sun continued to rise. Jamie reached into his bag and put some sunglasses on, which hid the dark circles.

An announcement was made that the next train was approaching and everyone on the platform became tense; ready to jostle to get onboard. The Southeastern train eventually came to a stop, and the doors hissed open to let some passengers off.

Jamie managed to get on and positioned himself at the other side of the train, while others tried in vain to look for a seat. There were only two stops for Jamie, so standing for such a short time wasn't a problem

A couple of years after they met, Tom's grandfather passed away. They were incredibly close, and Tom was left quite a lot of money which paid for him to complete his training at a top hairdressing academy and for the deposit on a small, yet functional house in the trendy London suburb of Greenwich. Since then, their property had increased in value, and Jamie knew that without Tom's grandfathers' generous will, they'd be living somewhere further outside of London which would've meant earlier alarm calls and a longer commute.

As the train sped up, slowed down and swayed left and right, the standing passengers moved in unison. As he swung left and right, Jamie noticed a wisp of pure white hair. He tried to see what the white hair was attached to. The train was approaching Deptford and began to slow down. Stopping abruptly, the standing passengers all shuddered. A few people disembarked, and a quick reshuffle of those left standing took place. As a suited businessman with trainers moved down the carriage, Jamie had a more unobstructed view of the owner of the white hair. It belonged to an elderly lady.who was holding on for dear life while all the other seated, able-bodied commuters did everything in their power to avoid looking at her, afraid they would see this old lady, be struck by pangs of guilt and would feel compelled to give up their seat. Jamie felt annoyed and wished he had the London gumption to have asked one of them to give up their place. He then wished that someone, maybe the businessman with trainers, would've been brash enough to ask someone to let this lady sit down.

No one did. Jamie discreetly kept looking at her. As she held on to the bright yellow bar, she seemed to be mouthing something silently. She looked sad to him but not just sad; she looked on edge. He could feel his heart swell but felt powerless and guilty. London Bridge station, the next and final stop for him, could not come quick enough.

A passenger with an oversized bag turned around and hit the woman in the stomach. She bowed slightly in pain and looked at the person.

"I'm so sorry," she said in an incredibly polite and apologetic way.

She wasn't being sarcastic, which angered Jamie, who was wishing he had the guts to say to this man to be more careful or something emphatic. He had seen people doing this in the past, and for just that moment, he wanted to be that person. The oaf-like passenger had massive headphones on and was staring down at an iPad, completely oblivious to what had just happened and to this lady's apology.

Jamie began to feel hot and bothered. These trains weren't well ventilated, and at that stage of a Friday morning commute it was standing room only, but it wasn't just that. There were rushes of emotions soaring through him: anger, embarrassment, shame, frustration, compassion, all blended together. As the train chugged towards London, Jamie got notes of each these emotions like he was some sort of emotional sommelier.

Without him realising, the train doors had opened, and masses of people were disembarking. He looked around and couldn't see the old lady. Jamie just hoped that she had gotten a seat at last. He alighted and was in the middle of a swarm of commuters moving simultaneously towards the escalators and stairs. Shuffling forward he decided to take the stairs. He could feel the air cool as he left the warm London morning and entered the cavernous station. As he came to the last few steps, he heard a soft thud. The people in front of him all bumped into one another and then halted. Faced with the back of peoples heads he couldn't see what seemed to be the matter. After a few seconds, people on his peripheries began to squeeze and move forward. They were all too busy to be waiting around for someone else. Eventually, the huddled mass slowly dispersed and as he came to the last step, he saw the lady from the train sitting on the ground. She looked flustered. There were a few people around her asking if she was alright. She was embarrassed and wanted them to go about their day.

"Thank you, I'm fine, really," she told them.

Commuting re-commenced all around while she attempted to stand up. Stiffly she made it to an upright position. Jamie was torn and wondered should he also ask her if she was alright, or commute on with the herd. Shamefully, he walked on and pulled out his wallet to use his bank card. He joined a queue behind people who are being held up by someone whose ticket wasn't working. This hold up had incensed everyone in the line. He felt awkward. With his earphones in not listening to anything, he tried to act nonchalantly. To exaggerate this fake breezy attitude amidst the seething commuters, he looked around and saw the lady from the train, who hadn't moved far from where he had left her.

"Fuck sake!" he said underneath his breath and made his way over to her. As he approached, she began to fall again. He ran and grabbed her before she hit the ground. She put her hands out to hold on to him, pulling his unconnected earphones from his ears.

"Are you ok?" he asked.

"Yes dear, I'm fine. Thank you."

Jamie brought her upright and looked around for somewhere to sit. He spotted an empty bench and nodded to them. She held on tight, as they slowly walked over and sat down.

"How are you feeling?" Jamie enquired.

"I'm absolutely fine. No need for all the fuss."

Jamie noticed her soft Irish accent. "No fuss at all. Where are you off to?"

"I've got an appointment, but I've no idea where I'm going."

"Are you meeting anyone?"

"No, I'm on my own. I just need to find this place." She showed him a piece of paper that she had been holding in her hand. It was a letter, folded very precisely, from a private clinic that Jamie was familiar with.   It had the address, appointment time and a small map to help her find her way. Jamie was taken aback by it and said that he knew where it was.

"Are you sure you are ok to walk there?"

"Of course, I'm fine. Now you just point me in the right direction, and I'll be on my way."

Jamie paused for a moment and stood up, about to point to the exit near to where she needed to go.

"I know this place, and I can walk with you for a bit."

"There's really no need and I'm sure you are a busy young man, with places to go and people to be seeing. You're probably off to work, dressed the way you are."

"Well, yes I am, but it's no trouble at all. "

The woman stood up, not as steady as Jamie would've liked. He thought about extending his arm, but it felt wrong.

"It's this way," pointing towards an exit.

In silence, they walked side by side until they eventually reached the ticket barrier. Jamie tapped his card and walked quickly through. He looked behind and saw her pulling out a large shiny black purse with gold coloured fasteners. She was taking her time to open it. She looked like she knew exactly where she had placed it, but a crowd had formed a sort of orderly scrum behind her. Jamie was feeling uncomfortable and inside his head was repeating:

"Why has she stopped? What's wrong now?"

She looked at the ticket for a moment and then at the barrier, but instead of walking forward she sidestepped to her right and presented her ticket to the staff member who let her through. She replaced, not her ticket, but her Freedom Pass, which entitled her to free travel, meticulously into her purse, closed it and put it back into her black handbag.

As she made her way towards Jamie, he surveyed her from head to toe. She was a lady who was in her mid to late seventies. Her hair was white, rather than grey with blue piercing eyes. Her wrinkled face had a pursed mouth that had been adorned with red lipstick. She was wearing a pristine beige coat and on her feet were shiny high heels. They weren't too high, but were black and well kept. The shoes seemed too heavy as she made her way over to him. Just as she approached him, she had another wobble, but Jamie's quick reactions managed to keep her off the ground.

"I think you need a coffee or something sweet," he suggested.

"No, I'm grand. Honestly, there is no need to worry."

"My mother didn't raise me to abandon a damsel in distress," trying to make light of the situation.

"Well, it has been a long time since I had my breakfast and all this travelling is quite exhausting."

"A hot beverage it is then. Do you have a preference of where we go?"

"You are going to be late for work."

"I can be late for once. Anyway, I haven't completed my good deed for the day until I know you're at your appointment."

"Is it ok if we find somewhere outside of the station? It's very dark in here."

Jamie hadn't noticed how dark it was until they had made their way on to the sun drenched St. Thomas Street. It was busy, so they walked at a slow pace in silence. They eventually crossed the busy junction and Jamie lead her into Borough Market. He stopped to think about where they should go as she walked towards a trendy cafe like she was a regular. The door was opened by one of the staff who then brought her to a vacant table. Jamie chuckled to himself and followed her in.

"Would you like a list of the teas and coffees available?" asked the waitress, in a French accent.

"I'll have an Americano with some pouring cream on the side, please," Jamie asked with confidence.

There was a pause, and both Jamie and the waitress stared at the lady who now had reading glasses on to peruse the menu. She whispered over to Jamie, hoping the waitress wouldn't hear her.

"I just want a normal cup of tea, if that's ok?"

The request was sweet and endearing and both the waitress and Jamie couldn't help but smile.

"An English breakfast tea please, oh and two pain au chocolates. Thank you."

The waitress left them alone where they both found each other looking and wondering what to say.

"What are you listening to?" pointing to his earphones which were tucked into his shirt.

Awkwardly, he began to wrap them up and placed them into his pocket.

"I'm listening to nothing."

"Nothing? she asked in disbelief. "And they say I'm mad."

"They? Mad?"

For a split second, they looked directly at each other but said nothing.

"I'm Jamie by the way,' as he extended his hand across the table to break the silence and the awkward moment.

"I'm Teresa."

"Nice to meet you, Teresa."

"Have you travelled far?"

"Greenwich, so not too far."

"Me too."

"Do you do this journey every day?" she asked in disbelief.

"I do. You get used to it."

"I don't think I could."

The waitress arrived at the table. Teresa concentrated on how the young French woman presented the drinks and pastries. Jamie observed her watching the waitress. He poured in the cream and stirred his coffee. Teresa added a teaspoon of sugar and a good helping of milk.

"That's exactly what you need, some sugar," he exclaimed

She sipped the tea and a small smile emerged from behind her cup.

"And what do you do?" she asked politely.

"I'm a therapist."

"Which sort are you?"

Jamie never really liked telling people what he did. Being a psychotherapist meant that half the people he told wanted to divulge their problems, even if he had just met them and the other half became cagey, thinking he was analysing every movement and ruminating over everything they said.

"I'm a psychotherapist for a mental health charity.'

She put her cup down with purpose. "Well, it's your sort that I'm up here to see," she eventually admitted. "They think I'm depressed and they want to start me on happy pills. So, they want me to see someone to talk about my problems." Teresa said 'problem' like it was a dirty word

Taken aback by her frankness, Jamie wasn't sure he should ask any further probing questions, especially in a cafe.

"When you say 'they' who do you mean?"

"My daughter and her husband. Well, lately I haven't really been myself. She told me to go to the GP who said I could be depressed and she has now paid for me to see some fella in a swanky clinic."

"Has your daughter noticed anything different about you?"

"She's very busy. It's just from what I tell her when she calls."

"When was the last time you saw her?"

"Christmas Eve. She's very busy. Works in the City."

"Are you depressed?" he asked, drinking quickly after asking because he couldn't believe the question came from his lips.

"Well, how would I know?" being slightly defensive. In a calmer voice, she said "I've a lot to be thankful for. I've got my health and my house. I play bridge twice a week and I'm involved in a local social group, what have I got anything to be depressed about?'

Jamie felt it wasn't the place, his job or right to spout off about depression to this sweet lady. They both began to eat small pieces of their pastries.

"This is a nice place."

"I'm lucky to have the market across from where I work. When it comes to lunch time I have lots of options."

She seemed to enjoy the chocolate pastry and began humming very softly as she chewed. Jamie thought he recognised the tune.

He spoke the lyrics:

"Sweets for my sweet, sugar for my honey."

She giggled. "Very good. One of my favourites. A classic really. You should listen to music rather than listening to... nothing."

"I do love music. I just left my iPhone at home." As he said it, he knew it sounded ridiculous.

She looked at him with a face of incomprehension. "So you left your phone at home and plugged your headphones into...your pocket? "

"I wasn't really with it this morning," trying to get off topic. Jamie checked his watch.

"I need to get going. Are you feeling any better, has the tea helped?

She looked disappointed and panicked. "What will I say to this fella? I don't know what to say."

Jamie felt for this lady going to a counsellor with no one accompanying her.

"Tell him what you've told me. That was easy, wasn't it?"

"Yes, but it's different. We were having a cup of tea and chatting."

"It's just like that, minus the tea. Actually, if you are going to that private clinic, you might get tea and a biscuit."

They both smiled. Jamie stood up and went over to the counter to pay the bill. She continued sipping her tea. A waiter was clearing away the table as Jamie returned. Teresa began to put on her coat and grabbed her handbag. The door was cordially opened for them as they re-emerged on to the sunny pavement.

"That's where you need to head towards," Jamie told her as he pointed towards a very modern, glass fronted building.

"Thank you for your kindness and for the tea. You're a credit to your parents."

He shuffled on his feet, uneasy with the ending.

"Take care of yourself."

They shook hands and Jamie headed in the opposite direction.

He grabbed his earphones from his pocket and placed them into both ears. The jack was placed back into his jacket pocket, connected to nothing, again. He thought about returning to work and glad that he was doing it on a Friday. It was a nice touch by his manager to suggest it. Very few clients were seen on Friday's. It was mainly a day to catch up on notes, have supervision and meetings. Jamie was never late and detested tardiness; however, it was now 9:30 am, but he wasn't rushing today.

Southwark Street was bustling at that time of the morning. He passed the Rastafarian Big Issue seller who was forever smiling. Someone had left him a coffee and a fruit bowl. He thought about Teresa and the morning's excitement. He wondered how she would cope with her appointment and thought how cruel it was for her to be doing it alone. His professional hat slipped on and he wondered was she depressed and why that might be, but his predominate thought was why was she going to her first appointment with a private psychotherapist alone.

The open plan office afforded him no privacy as he entered his place of work. Heads turned and those not on calls were saying 'welcome back'. Colleagues who were on the phone made various hand gestures, facial expressions and mouthed words of welcome. Jonathan, his manager, appeared to have been waiting for him but tried to look casual as he loitered by the entrance.

"Did you get my text?" Jonathan asked

"Aww...no I left my phone at home. Is everything ok?"

"Yeah, I was just checking in and wondering where you were and if you were ok. There's nothing pressing at the moment. Do you wanna catch up, maybe, once you've settled back in?" His boss seemed a little awkward.

"Yeah, sure. Let me get rid of my bag, log on and check how many emails are waiting for me."

Jonathan went back to his office and Jamie headed to his desk. It was a neat, clean desk with nothing out of place apart from a Leaning Tower-esque pile of letters addressed to him. There were various unopened greeting cards at his keyboard which he quickly placed inside a drawer without opening them. After a few attempts with numerous variations of his password, he logged in and found 841 unread emails. He looked around and saw that everyone was busy. Written on the team's whiteboard was a reminder that the weekly meeting was at 11 am.

After deleting the non-essential emails, he made his way to the only private office on their floor. Jonathan was on the phone but gestured for him to come in and take a seat. He sat self-consciously waiting for the call to finish and felt very young like he was in the headmaster's office. Jonathan was lying back in his chair. His shirt was gaping, and his stomach was bulging through. An older, shorter stockier man, Jonathan was a good boss. He was fair, firm and always tried to do his best with the limited resources available. This was Jamie's third year working for the charity. Being a therapist at a young persons mental health charity wasn't his first choice, but after he left a secure, pensionable, health service job to start up his own private practice which failed, it was the next best thing. He wasn't skilled to do anything else. His dream was to have his own practice and to work for himself. When he started out, it took a while for paying clients to make their way to him. He soon realised that with room rental in London and all the other costs involved, that unless he saw A-List movie stars, a private practice wasn't going to pay the bills.

Jonathan finished his call.

"So, how have you been?"

"Fine, I guess. It's good to be back and to have some structure in my day."

"I bet. We've taken care of your case load and I'm suggesting a week or so of catching up on letters, referrals and stuff and then maybe think about seeing some clients after that. How does that sound?

"Yeah, great…whatever. I don't want to be a burden."

"You're not being a burden. I'm here if you need anything…just ask."

"Thank you. Was there anything else?" Jamie asked nervously, really wanting there to be nothing else so he could get out.

"Unless you've got anything you want to discuss?" Jonathan asked slightly uncomfortably.

"No. I'm fine thanks, I'll head back now."

Jamie headed back to his desk and started going through the hundreds of unread emails. Being meticulous in his work, this task, while boring, was something that he did without much thought or energy. A few colleagues popped up at various moments to welcome him back.

When it was time for the staff meeting, everyone migrated towards the conference room, where the bakers in the office displayed and handed out their wares. Full from his second breakfast, he just grabbed a glass of water. Jamie had been dreading his first day back and in particular this meeting, which was chaired by his boss. However, there was no mention of him or his return. It was just an hour long meeting about everyone's client load, fundraising and the Christmas party. The majority of the staff, a group of eleven, sighed at the prospect of even contemplating a Christmas party in August. Rebecca, the newest member of the team, was beaming at the idea of it and of course, was first in line to volunteer to organise it. No one else had put their hand up.

The meeting was dismissed and everyone filed out of the stuffy room. Just as he was about to exit, Rebecca turned around.

"I know we aren't supposed to say anything...but I'm here if you need anything."

She awkwardly hugged him while he just stood there not moving or hugging back. Rebecca checked no one was looking and made her way back to her desk. Jamie felt awkward, but also intrigued about the edict that must have been circulated to the team and who might have sent it.

While he was checking, sorting and deleting emails, he could feel eyes watching him. When he looked around, he was sure people suddenly got on with something very important, hoping they weren't caught staring.

Letters were next to be tackled, and there was a lot to get through. He half opened the first one but stopped. He needed a break and fancied some sushi. If he went now, he would beat the

Friday lunchtime rush. Grabbing his jacket and earphones, he made his way back to Borough Market.

The market was busy all year round and for workers in the various buildings that surrounded it, a place to be avoided at peak lunchtime. Jamie went straight to his usual eatery with the same staff who knew his order. It was those moments that made London a smaller, friendlier place for him. The glass atrium on the edge of the market was warm with just the slightest of breezes coming up from the Thames. From one of the benches, he watched all the comings and goings. There were those who could afford to eat at this chic market and those who wandered through, getting free samples of cheeses, charcuterie and food from all around the world. Opening his bento box, he added the wasabi, ginger and soy sauce meticulously over the pieces of sushi, placed the box on his lap and picked up his chopsticks.

"Still listening to nothing?" asked a familiar voice.

Jamie looked up, with a piece of sushi in his mouth and saw Teresa. He swallowed and smiled awkwardly.

"Do you mind if I join you?" she asked with confidence.

"No...please...sit," trying to swallow what was in his mouth

She sat beside him on the large wooden bench. They looked an odd pairing. She was much smaller than him. Her feet barely touched the ground.

"Sushi? Fancy!" she said in an inquisitive way.

"Trying to be healthy. Trying. Can I ask how your appointment went?"

"It wasn't very nice. You were right though; I did get tea and a biscuit. He asked lots of questions and spent most of his time writing down the things I was saying, which made me feel uneasy. He said he thinks I'm depressed and suggested I take the pills my doctor gave me and see him once a week."

"Ok," Jamie sensed a 'but' so he didn't say anything else.

She looked around cautiously. "I think it's an awful waste of money. I bet he's not cheap, him in his smart suit and pretty young receptionist with the fancy tea and biscuits.

"I bet," said Jamie, colluding with her slightly.

"He said that my daughter will pay for the sessions. He had an email from her."

"That's nice of her."

"It is, but I can't justify her spending that amount on me."

There was an awkward silence. Jamie filled it by having another piece of sushi. He silently offered her some. She declined it politely.

"No thank you, I'm full from all the tea and biscuits," she said sarcastically.

The market was getting busier. A cooking demonstration was taking place across from them. Someone was showing passersby how to make fresh pasta and throwing dough balls at a large group of Spanish students, who tried to catch them in their mouths.

"You're a therapist, do you think I'm depressed?"

Jamie choked on the food he was about to swallow. He quickly grabbed a bottle from his bag and took a large gulp.

"I suppose you don't get many people asking you that on your lunch break?" she asked with a straight face.

"No, you're right," he said trying to compose himself. Another silence permeated the space around them.

"Well? What do you think?"

"Oh, you really want me to answer that?"

"Well, yes. Honestly now, in your honest opinion, do you think I'm depressed?"

"Teresa, I couldn't possibly answer that. I've just met you."

She insisted by saying: "Do I seem depressed?"

"It doesn't work like that, but clearly people who know you well and care about you are concerned, is that fair to say? The fact your GP has given you some pills and your daughter is arranging private therapy doesn't mean you are definitely depressed but that maybe it would be useful to talk to someone to see if you are." Jamie wasn't sure if she wanted to hear that.

She sat quietly for a while, looking ahead. Both her hands were on the bench as if she was high up on a beam, looking down at the world. In a childlike way, she kicked her legs forward and back.

Jamie softened a bit. "Everyone gets depressed at some point in their lives. If something bad has happened, a bereavement or relationship ending, then being depressed about those sort of things is a normal response to sad events."

Teresa was listening to Jamie, sitting quietly, looking forward. She had a ponderous look.

Jamie continued, tentatively. "If someone is depressed for no apparent reason or for a long period of time or..." he paused. He was nervous about continuing.

She looked round at him and insisted, "Go on, I'm listening."

"If someone was harming themselves or contemplating killing themselves..."

"Like suicide?"

"Yes, suicide...then they could be severely depressed."

She appeared to be taking it all in but in no rush to comment. Out of nowhere, she began to hum. It took him a while but Jamie got the tune.

"*Are You Lonesome Tonight*?"

"You know your stuff, young man!"

"You seem surprised."

"Well, I'm older than you and that song, well, there's hair on it it's that old."

"Still a classic."

"Aw yes!" she said with a smile and a shrugged shoulder.

Jamie had nearly finished his lunch. He knew he had to go back to the office but felt guilty about leaving her like that.

"Teresa?"

She turned to look at him.

"I need to get back to work. I'm really sorry."

"Of course you do, sorry for taking up your time."

"It's no trouble at all. Good luck with everything."

He stood up, grabbed his bag. She looked up at him.

"You've been very kind to an old woman today."

He was touched by the sincerity in her voice. "Take care."

He walked towards the exit feeling bad, but for what, he wasn't sure. He placed his rubbish into the large bin outside the market and looked up and saw her still sitting there. She looked tiny on the large bench as she continued to look down at her shoes, kicking her feet out and back in again. In a moment of guilt and embarrassment, he walked back to the bench. As he approached, she looked up at him.

"For what it's worth, can I suggest two things?

"Certainly."

"Firstly, don't make any big decisions about anything, I mean, whether you should see this therapist or not. Take some time."

"Ok."

He looked a tad flustered. She prompted him.

"And the other thing?"

"The other thing?"

"Yes, you said you had two suggestions for me."

"Shit, yes, sorry, sorry for swearing...this is more important than the first bit. Do something nice today."

"Something nice?" She was puzzled.

"Today must have been tough but you are still here - you've gotten through today. I think that deserves a treat. Don't you?"

"A treat, what do you mean?"

"It doesn't have to be anything big; it could be a hot chocolate, a nice walk, a bath - something to reward yourself for getting through today. It's really important. Promise me."

She looked at him with the warmest of smiles. With her blue eyes sparkling, she extended her hand.

"I promise."

They both shook on it.

"Good."

"Get back to work."

"Ok, gotta run. Take care."

For the rest of the afternoon, Teresa occupied his mind while he opened letters and sorted them into piles. Uncharacteristically, he took his time with his paperwork. Every so often he looked around to see if anyone had noticed his slow pace, but everyone seemed to be on a go slow. It was Friday after all.

At exactly 4 pm Jonathan made his way to Jamie's desk.

"Right, you are finished for the day and you have strict instructions to go and meet your husband in The Duke, right this very minute."

Jamie was stunned into silence but started to pack away his things while staring at his boss.

"I'm going to do what I'm told and I guess...I'll see you on Monday?"

Jonathan had a massive grin on his face. He felt he was doing a good thing for one of his most diligent workers. It amused him too, seeing him squirm and succumbing to some TLC. Once Jamie had left, he glided back to his office, still smiling to himself.

Two quick Underground journeys and Jamie was in Piccadilly Circus. He always felt so cosmopolitan when he climbed the steps from the station and saw the massive neon signs, a far cry from the sleepy hamlet where he grew up. The air was charged with excitement. There were masses of people, cars and buses trying to get through the city. He made his way up Shaftesbury Avenue and to The Duke of Wellington pub.

A little apprehensive, he stepped inside and immediately spotted Tom at the bar. His tall, dark haired husband, with the broad smile Jamie loved so much, had seen him come in and gestured for him to look to his left where all their closest friends were. There was no yelling 'surprise', it was more of a communal hugging and nodding. Jamie was embarrassed and touched in equal measure. Tom, laden with drinks, kissed him on the cheek and shepherded him into their gaggle of friends. When the drinks were evenly dispersed, Tom ceremoniously stood up, towering over the group and raised his glass of red wine. The others mimicked him.

"We love you!" Tom declared out loud.

"We love you!" repeated the group.

They all took a drink and sat down. Jules, Jamie's best friend, squeezed him tight. He gave a mock, stern look but she just laughed it off.

"Oh shut up you, you'd do the same," she protested.

"You know I don't like a fuss. I went into work today, and nothing was said. I've got a hunch that Tom sent my boss an email warning him."

"Why do you think that?"

"It was just odd. An office full of therapists and no one was saying anything, and my boss sent me here, an hour before I was supposed to finish."

"He just wants you to be ok, and you are impossible to look after, so shut up & drink up."

They clinked their glasses together and downed their contents.

Four rounds in, Jamie felt that he should go and buy another. He had been told not to, but he stole away from the group and pushed passed the sea of gay men. Each man in this particular establishment had a different take on facial hair. Jamie thought about what he had shaved off that morning and felt jealous of their virile displays. He got to the bar and placed his order with a very tall, thin barman. He was slightly tipsy but tried not to let it show. Turning around, he surveyed the table he'd just come from. Jules was hugging Tom. She always got like that when she had a few drinks. Jamie used to share an office with her in a previous job. They were destined to be soul mates in the most platonic of ways. No one ate and drank like her and stayed thin but behind all the beauty, drinking and eating, she loved him and he her, and there wasn't anything they couldn't say to each other, well, most things.

Tom's colleague, Max, stumbled up to him at the bar, offering to help him with the drinks. Max's tall stature, olive skin and perfect stubble caught most of the men's attention. He knew he had this power and one would expect him to be full of himself, which he was, but he was also quite insecure and sweet as anything and this endeared him to Jamie. He was aware that Max had been in the bad books with Tom recently, due to a spree of sickness and calling in at the last minute to say he wasn't coming to work. Tom reckoned that Max was partying too hard. He was the youngest of the group and at thirty, exhibited more energy than the rest, with an insatiable appetite for gay London life.

"Alright my love?" Max said with his East London accent.

"I am, baby girl!"

"You know if you ever want to talk about anything, you can. I may only be a colourist, a damn good colourist might I add, but I listen to people all day. There is depth here," pointing to his heart.

"Thank you, Max!"

Jamie kissed him on the forehead. The drinks started to line up on the bar, ready to be transported to their table. Max grabbed as many as he could and before he walked back, leaned into Jamie to whisper something.

"If you ever, like, need to talk but, like, not talk...just say." Max winked at him, turned and headed towards the table.

Jamie was intrigued by the offer of talking but not talking. It was the first thing that seemed to make sense in a long time. He paid the barman and made his way back with the rest of the drinks. The group cheered in unison. Once all the drinks were handed out, he headed to the Gents.

"Quick, how do you think he is?" Tom asked Jules.

"Fine, you know what he's like. Doesn't like talking about things. How do you think he's doing?"

"He seems fine, but he's so hard to read. All he wanted was life to continue as normal and that's what I'm trying to do."

"Nice touch with that email to his work."

"I bet he's figured it out. I knew the last thing he would've wanted was for people at work to be making a fuss."

"Shut it...he's coming over!"

They both began to laugh and drink quite convincingly.

The bar was full with very little room to move. Long gone were the days of three nights on the trot, getting the last train home or even worse, the dreaded night bus. All their glasses were now empty, and there was only one thing for it - food. Leaving the bar, they were greeted by the warm air that was full to the brim with excitement. Friday night in Soho was something to behold. There were people everywhere. Some were going places, others going nowhere. Masses of people travelled to the heart of London to be a part of its' vibrant nightlife. Jamie loved the fact that people wore what they liked, had their hair the way they wanted and did as they pleased and no one cared. They made their way down Old Compton Street to get some food from Ed's Diner. At that time on a Friday night, they knew that they wouldn't get seats. Jamie and Max were the first people to emerge with food. For a few moments there was just eating; lining their stomachs a little too late. Jamie eventually broke the silence.

"Remember, back in the pub you said that if I need anything?"

"Yeah? I'm a good listener. You know what our job is like, I bet Tom is the same. Yes we are cutting and colouring, but we are like you, therapists," Max answered with burger and chips in his mouth.

"You mentioned talking and not talking...what did you mean?"

Max took a moment to finish what he was eating, aided by some water. "You know."

"No, I don't, Max," getting a little impatient.

Just then, the rest of their crew appeared, all laden with food. Dan and Brian, who Jamie hadn't really spoken to all night came over and began their night feast. Max had a big grin on his face. Jamie tried to concentrate on what Dan was saying.

"So great to see you, Jamie. When Tom invited us, well, we wouldn't have missed it."

"Thanks guys, really appreciate it."

Dan and Brian were a couple they met on holidays. It was one of their first trips together. They were a little older than Jamie and Tom and kept themselves to themselves which Jamie appreciated. He knew there would be no prying from them tonight. They joked about being older, worried about missing the last train home and dreading the inevitable hangover.

Jamie finished his food and went over to Tom where he linked his arm. Tom rested his head on Jamie's.

"Can we go?" Jamie asked.

"Two seconds, let me finish this."

Jamie continued to link Tom's arm as he looked around. Life was happening, everywhere. The streets were alive with groups of people, couples, gay, straight, pan, undecided, families, tourist groups, hen parties, stag parties. Like worker ants, he watched them get on with whatever they needed to do. Part of him was happy that life continued as normal, but there was another part of him that wanted to scream with all his might, to make them stop and take notice.

When Tom finished his food, he squeezed his rubbish into a nearby full bin and put his arm around Jamie. Exiting Soho, they made their way to catch the last train home.

Chapter 2

The sound of soft padding around the bed was heard from under the duvet followed by a pause. Frustrated, the padding resumed, but this time it returned to Jamie's side of the bed and stopped again. Jamie wasn't awake or asleep but in that middle place. There's a limit to the amount of patience a hungry cat has, and eventually, George jumped on the bed and sat on top of Jamie's chest. The hungry feline began to knead his chest and purr loudly. He was hungover, but George's purring and kneading were comforting. After a few minutes, George had had enough and just lay on his owner. Jamie got the message and pulled himself out of the warm bed. He looked back and could only see the outline of his husband. He did the dutiful thing and brought water, some painkillers and made him swallow them but let him return to sleep. He fed and groomed George as per their daily routine and sat in his dressing gown with a cup of coffee staring out at what appeared to be another sunny Autumn day.

The second cup of coffee was made while he checked his phone. Facebook reported that he was out in Soho the previous night. Jules was a persistent social networker and had tagged him in some photos. Usually, this didn't bother him, but he quickly untagged himself. Instead, he took a picture of his full, steaming coffee cup and added Rihanna's song *Cheers*, which got an instant like from Jules. There were texts from everyone, all saying they got home ok. Max's message was different and just said:

Here if you need to 'not talk'. Max x

Jamie heard two thuds from upstairs. Tom was up and worse for wear. Slow, zombie like footsteps got closer and closer, and eventually, Tom appeared in the front room, wrapped in their duvet.

"Make it stop...make the room stop spinning."

Jamie chuckled and moved down on the couch for Tom to fall, where he wrapped Jamie up with the warm duvet. They held each other and didn't move while George sat on the end of the sofa preening himself.

Jamie began to remember a time when he was five years old. He had taken all the blankets that weren't on beds and made a tent outside, using clothes pegs to secure them to a metal fence. He had also rounded up all the cushions and pillows he could find and laid them on the ground. It was a perfect summers day to be inside the makeshift tent. The occasional summer breeze made the sheets flutter. He remembered his mother bringing him and the neighbours' kids a Sparkler ice lolly as they sat in the tent. His mother had to wake him up at dusk because he had fallen asleep and they had no cushions left in the house.

The warm feelings that memory gave him vanished into thin air as Tom began to snore. Jamie slowly removed himself from Tom's sleepy hold and returned moments later dressed in shorts, flip flops, a baseball cap and hoody. He closed their front door as quietly as possible and made his way to Greenwich Market to pick up some pastries for breakfast.

Greenwich looked beautiful in the sunshine, and everyone appeared better for it. There was a stress-free feeling in the air like everyone was on holidays. Entering the market, he saw all the traders were doing good business as he made his way to their favourite French Pâtisserie stall. The owner spotted him in the queue, and once he got to the front of the line, Daren kissed him on both cheeks.

"Long time, no see my friend. Where have you been?" asked Daren as he picked up two pain au chocolat for Jamie and some rustic bread.

Hungover and shocked by this seemingly innocent question Jamie lied. "Work has been crazy busy. Lots of weekend working."

"You work too hard. Weekends are for fun and good food," Daren exclaimed, presenting him with the freshly baked goods.

"You're right. Hopefully there'll be no more working weekends. How's business today?" changing the subject.

"Great. Expecting a good day."

"Well, thanks and see you next week."

They kissed again; both cheeks.

On leaving the market, he had a deja vu moment. It made him smile because for the briefest of moments he felt like himself, something he had struggled to feel for a while. As he walked home, he tried to hold on to it but it was futile. He just thought it was nice that he felt it for however long it lasted.

Entering the house he smelled fresh coffee brewing. Tom had pulled out the cafetiere. The papers had been delivered and were placed neatly on the table. Tom kissed him on the cheek and took the brown bag from under his arm. The oven was on to slightly warm the pastries. Tom, a bit like George the previous day, thought that things were back on track and that their Saturday routine of coffee, cuddles, papers and pastries had resumed. Jamie could sense Tom's excitement and relief, but rather than fighting it; he went along with Tom's upbeat-ness as he felt his husband deserved it.

A few hours of coffee drinking, paper reading and some sleeping went by when Tom exclaimed that he was going to cut Jamie's hair. Jamie couldn't think of anything better as they made their way to the upstairs bathroom. Jamie removed his t-shirt and was poised over the sink as Tom slipped into work mode and began to wet Jamie's hair. Shampoo was applied and rinsed; then it was conditioner and more rinsing. With a towel used as a turban, they returned to the kitchen where Jamie had a head massage, one of his favourite things. As his husband massaged his damp scalp he was without thought; nothing was going around in his head. He completely zoned out and enjoyed what seemed like all thoughts being manoeuvred out of his busy brain like knots from a stressful back. He loved the fact that he married a hairdresser; no inane conversations with a yappy, chappy barber, no queuing and no noise. While it was a necessary chore, to have one's hair cut, he preferred the silence and comfort of home and his own private stylist. Tom understood all these demands and was equally happy to wash, massage and cut in silence. It still made him smile when he recalled the time Jamie told him about having his weekly Saturday night baths when he was a child. He would be dried and put into pyjamas, crawl along the sofa and lay his head on his mother's aproned lap, where she would run her fingers through his hair. Jamie told Tom that she would say that she was looking for nits but they both had an unspoken agreement which was that they both loved that special time; a mother running her fingers through her son's hair and a son feeling the physical and emotional warmth from a doting Mum.

The massage was never long enough, but his hair had to be cut. Tom returned with a portrait mirror he placed in front of Jamie and produced his bag of tools. Tom played music from Jamie's Playlist on their iPod as he began to do his thing. This monthly routine continued in comfortable silence as Tom concentrated and Jamie continued to empty his head. There was no need to talk about the style, Tom knew best, and

Jamie trusted him implicitly. Brown hair fell to the floor, the electric shaver whizzed on, then off again, and Tom went from side to side examining his work.

As a song finished, there was the three-second gap between tracks. Without warning the new song started with a soft drum and the single strum of a guitar. Both men stopped and caught each other's eyes in the mirror. Tom didn't know what to do: keep working or say something. Jamie wanted to skip the track and say nothing as if nothing was the matter. Tom could see tears starting to form in his husband's eyes. Internally Jamie was trying to suck these tears inward, to somehow absorb them into himself, to look like nothing was happening. His arms were under the black hairdressing cape, so he was unable to erase the tears with his hands. As the song continued and Kirsty MacColl continued to sing *Days*, both eyes were glistening with a tear filled blob. Tom was working and looking at the mirror then quickly away, to give Jamie the illusion that he hadn't noticed anything either. Then the chorus started.

The tears couldn't be held in anymore. Jamie's face, which up to this point remained still, was contorted with sorrow as he sobbed uncontrollably. Tom put down his tools and crouching down, took him by the hand, motioning him to stand up, which he did reluctantly. He enveloped Jamie in a large embrace that allowed him to sob without the world seeing it. The song continued while the tears were being absorbed into Tom's t-shirt. They didn't move, sway or talk. They were waiting for the song to end, which it did, shuffling onto something more upbeat. Jamie released himself from Tom's arms, rubbed his eyes and sat back on the chair. Tom, unsure whether to say anything, started to comb the slightly dishevelled hair back into place. Looking like he was concentrating on his work he looked at the mirror to see a broken man. His eyes were puffy and red. The three-minute song had zapped his energy. Jamie refused to look at his reflection and just stared downwards.

The haircut came to an end, and Tom seemed pleased with his work. He looked at his subject from all angles, impressed and relieved that it was done. Jamie was feeling trapped underneath the cape and the watchful eye of his husband. This usually enjoyable experience couldn't finish quick enough for him.

"Perfection!" Tom reported as he released the knot from Jamie's cape.

Trying to walk off to the bathroom to shower off the loose hair and to get away from Tom, Jamie mumbled a thank you. In a moment of desperation, Tom grabbed his hand that stopped him from moving away.

"Pet, this can't go on forever. I don't know what to say, what to do to make you feel better…"

Jamie interrupted and erupted. "You can't! No one can! That's the point of it - it's pointless. That's why I want to not talk about it because there's nothing to say. There is nothing to do. There is nothing you or anyone can say or do that can help." Beginning to sound more angry than upset, he continued. "I have to go through my day like nothing has happened...that I'm ok, that we're ok. Going out for drinks with friends as if life is fucking fantastically brilliant. Well, it's not! It's fucking awful, but getting through the period of time that my eyes are open I have to make the world, make you, make me even, look like the old me. I have to dodge the 'how are you holding up?' 'I'm thinking of you' bullshit from colleagues and friends when I just want to stay in my room and not come out."

Tom went in to hug him again, but Jamie pushed him back.

"Don't do that. I'm fine," Jamie ordered him.

"You're not fine and that's ok."

Angrily Jamie snapped back. "Just stop it and can you please just stop this."

"I'm not doing anything hun."

"You promised you wouldn't do this."

"Do what? Be a supportive partner?" Tom replied, a little annoyed now.

"Yes, all of this. You said you wouldn't do this and look at you - you're doing exactly what you said you wouldn't."

"I can't help it. There is only so much of this I can take."

"Oh poor you having to put with me and all this. Poor Tom having to live with the crazy man who wants to get on with life."

"I didn't mean it like that," Tom interrupted.

"What did you mean, Tom? What!? Is this all too much for you? Is it?

Realising that this was getting a little too heated, Tom put up both hands and tried to calm things down "Come on Jamie. You know what I mean…it's just that…"

Jamie cut right in, "Just what? Come on! Let's see your years of training as a hairdresser sort this one out!"

Deflated, Tom replied, "I don't know what to do anymore. I knew this was going to be tough, but I didn't think it would be like this; us fighting like this."

Patronisingly Jamie kept going: "Oh sorry Tom. I'm sorry I'm a mess, I'm sorry I ruined your weekend, I'm sorry that I've made life difficult for you and that life isn't full of haircuts and 'been anywhere nice on your fucking holiday's love?' "

Tom grabbed his house keys from the bowl at the centre of their table and made his way to the door feeling the need for space and fresh air.

"Perfect! Perfect Tom, just leave."

"I can't do this right now, J. I love you, but this is harsh, and you are out of line. I know you're hurting, but this can't go on."

"Well, I'm sorry for my mini-tanty Tom, how inconsiderate of me and how fucking inconsiderate for my Mum to die on you."

Suddenly there was silence in the house. Tom's hand was on the front door, about to make his escape. They were both stunned that the words were uttered, that the actual announcing of it somehow made it real. Tom turned to Jamie.

"She is gone, and I can't tell you how sorry I am, but we, you and I, are still here." He doesn't wait for a response as he exited their home, closing the door gently.

Feeling like his feet were glued to the floor, Jamie didn't know whether he should prize them off the ground to run after Tom or to go to his bed and dive underneath a duvet. He chose the latter and went straight to the bedroom. For a moment he thought he could sleep, wake up and it would all be over. However, his mind was racing, which meant that wasn't going to happen. Frustrated he threw on his hoody again and left George in the house on his own.

He felt uneasy about how things were left, but this was trumped by his anger. Entering Greenwich Park, Jamie went to their regular haunts, joining the steady flow of tourists who were making the most of the park and the Autumn sun. He scoured the paths and all the benches, but Tom was nowhere to be seen.

After an hour of walking, Jamie came across an empty bench where he perched himself. He exhaled loudly and checked his phone.

There were no missed calls or messages from Tom, which annoyed him. Alone on the bench, he fought with himself. Should he call him, he thought. Screw him; he walked out first. He took out his phone and began a text message to Tom.

Where are you?

He stopped and erased each character in anger. Exiting from the new message, he saw the text from Max. He re-read it and wondered what it meant. Feeling the way he did, he didn't care because at that very moment it sounded perfect to him.

I'd like to 'not talk' now. You free? J

He sent the message and shoved the phone back into his pocket, placing his head in his hands. The sound of vibrating startled him and he immediately reached for his phone.

Cool. I'm 'not talking' now if you want to come round. Tom coming too?

Jamie replied.

No. Just me. On my way.

Jamie made his way out of the park and got on the train to nearby Canary Wharf. He had been to Max's apartment before but never without Tom. In transit, Jamie kept checking for messages of concern or an apology, but none came through as the train pulled into his stop. He headed towards an apartment block and was surprised to see Max waiting outside. They hugged, and air kissed.

"Where's Tom?"

"To be honest, I'm not sure. We had a bit of a bust up."

"It'll be fine, he'll get over it," Max proclaimed with very little empathy.

"Where are you going?"

"Where are *we* going, is the question you need to ask yourself."

"Where are we going, then?"

"A friends place in the block across from mine - let's go."

They began to walk towards another block of plush apartments. Max's boyfriend, David, was a wealthy investment banker, hence the area Max lived. There was no way he could afford living in the heart of London's business district on a colourist's salary. David spent most of his time in New York which gave Max lots of freedom to work and party hard. Jamie felt weird being with Max without Tom but he was still angry about the fact that Tom hadn't called or texted him.

"What were you girls arguing over?"

"I'd rather not say."

"Fine by me...I get it, you don't want to talk, and that's why I've brought you here." Max said as he pressed the buzzer.

A few seconds later there was a distorted radio squeak from the intercom system where music could be heard and then a high pitched voice.

"Who is it?" asked the mystery voice.

"It's Max from across the way, and I've brought a friend."

"Max, who?"

"Oh, it's ColourMyWorld85," Max informed the confused voice.

The sound cut off immediately. Jamie looked at Max as the door was buzzed open.

"Let's go," Max commanded.

They entered the building where a lift was open. Max entered the floor number, and the door closed.

"What are you taking me to, Max?" asked Jamie with a little concern in his voice.

"Relax. This is exactly what you need right now. It's - 'not talking'."

As the lift door opened, the music that was heard through the intercom was pulsating from the direction Max began to walk in. He knocked on a door which was immediately answered by a middle aged man wearing white gym shorts and nothing else. They both air kissed and began to stare at Jamie.

"He'll do, what's his name?"

"It's Jamie. Jamie this is William."

Jamie went to shake his hand, and both Max and William laughed hysterically, leaving Jamie to feel very self-conscious. When they eventually stopped laughing, William dawned a straight face and extended his hand.

"Nice to meet you, Jamie. Welcome to my humble abode." William gestured for him to enter.

Cautiously he entered a fantastically, minimalist pad. There were two closed doors on his left as he made his way down a smartly lit hall which opened up into a spacious kitchen, dining, living area where there were three other guys, also in shorts, on a large leather L-shaped couch. They were all on their smart phones, giggling and hadn't noticed the new arrivals. The music was quite loud and the space dimly lit.

"This is Max and his friend Jamie," William informed the others.

Like meerkats, they looked up in unison, smiled unconvincingly and returned to what they were doing. This gave Jamie a chance to check them out. Two of them were Latino; the olive skin, great pecs, long dark lashes, brown eyes and perfect stubble gave it away. The other guy was very young, eighteen at the most and was from Manchester, based on his strong Mancunian accent. This was an odd space for Jamie to be in. He was no prude but parties like this, and he was only guessing that this was indeed the start of some sort of sex party, was not his thing. Tom and he would joke about being an old married couple where the only cravings they had were cups of tea and custard creams. They had a

WhatsApp group where Max would report back on the weekends' sexcapades, which sounded like the last days of the Roman Empire.

Max and William began to chat on their own. Awkwardly, Jamie checked his phone. Still no messages.

"Fuck him,' he whispered.

He felt eyes watching him, so he looked over at the couch and saw one of the tanned guys staring. Confidently, he just winked at Jamie. Bashfully, Jamie looked away and checked Facebook. Without warning, a kiss landed on his right cheek and then his left.

"I'm Jesus," said the winker and kisser.

"I'm Jamie, pleased to meet you,' he replied while extending his hand to offer a shake.

Jesus stared at his hanging hand in disbelief.

"How are you?" asked Jamie, putting his hand away with great speed.

"I'm good. Such a long week at work I really need to unwind."

"Yeah, me too, it's been one of those weeks." Jamie heard himself give these glib answers. He felt totally out of his depth.

"And what do you do, Jamie?" Jesus asked, batting his long dark lashes.

"Oh, I'm a…a therapist. I work with young people with mental health issues."

"WOW! I bet you are reading my mind now. What am I thinking?"

Jamie giggled, "it doesn't work like that, unfortunately."

"I can read your mind, Mister Jamie."

"Oh yeah? What am I thinking?"

"You are thinking..." he paused with great purpose, rubbed his hand up and across his tanned chest.

Jamie's eyes followed Jesus' hands, and unconsciously he licked his lips.

"You want a drink?"

Jamie snapped out of looking at the body before him, "that's exactly what I was thinking."

Without asking what he wanted, Jesus, spun on one foot, stopped and strutted towards the white high gloss kitchen and prepared Jamie's drink.

Walking over to the window, Jamie took in the magnificent view of The O2 and Canary Wharf. He couldn't hear anything, but he saw a city in constant flux; cars, trains, people, cable cars and boats, all on the move. Minutes later, Jesus returned with drinks.

"Bottoms up," Jamie announced and suddenly regretted it. He felt he was so uncool.

Jesus found it endearing. He raised his glass and before he consumed it's contents, winked at Jamie again.

Max grabbed Jamie's arm and pulled him to one side.

"You ok? Having a good time?"

"Yeah, I guess. Not sure there's any actual alcohol in here, but apart from that, yeah, why?"

"Just chill out, that's what you need after..." Max stopped with a look of horror.

"After what, Max?'

"The argument and stuff."

"Stuff? Really? Stuff? Oh just fucking say it, Max!"

Maybe it was the alcohol that he'd consumed before meeting Jamie, but he decided to go for it, to name it.

"Yes, your parent's passing. I know there was no love lost with your Dad, but I know how close you were to your Mum. That's gotta be tough. Is that what you guys were arguing over?"

"Yeah, sort of. I'm sure Tom tells you things..."

Max was about to defend his work colleague, but Jamie didn't give him the chance to.

"...it's ok. I'm sure he has told you I just didn't want to discuss it at home or with anyone. I felt the best way for me to get through this was to get on with life. I'm sure he thought I was doing great and that apart from seeming a little tired, that I was coping. I know he feels because of the kind of job I do, that it should make me better equipped to deal with this, but I don't think it does. It's like you cutting and colouring your own hair."

They both chuckled nervously and took a sip of their drinks.

"I've been trying not to let him see me upset and with him being away a lot with work recently..."

"Tell me about it," Max interrupted.

"...I've had more time alone which is good and bad."

Max sensed something odd in what he had just heard and probed a little.

"Good and bad? What do you mean?"

Jamie wondered for a second should he continue talking or just shut up.

"Good, in that I can come home and lounge around or take a long bath, have a few extra glasses of wine and not feel like I have to put on a performance of the old me."

"And the bad?" asked Max.

Jamie looked down at his glass. Max's face was expectant; he wasn't letting this go.

"Promise you won't tell Tom?" pleaded Jamie.

Max put up his right hand as if he was swearing an oath in court.

"I don't know why I did it, but I started to download Grindr on my phone when Tom's away." Jamie scanned Max's face for any sign of disgust or judgement. He saw neither and continued. "I've been just chatting to guys. First of all it was for company. Even saying that out loud sounds ridiculous."

"No, it doesn't."

"The company of strangers who don't know me or my sad sack story, who would never know what's happened to me. It sounds pathetic but when I'm home alone and bad feelings are hanging around, it sort of makes them go away."

"I didn't know you guys had an open relationship?"

"We don't."

"Oh…okay."

"On Thursday night, Tom had promised he'd cut my hair but you guys were delayed at the airport for ages, so I downloaded it again and I almost met up with someone."

Shocked, Max's mouth was slightly open. This didn't phase Jamie.

"I realised I was using it a lot and yesterday morning, afraid that I'd use it on my commute or lunch break or even on my first day back at work, I left my phone at home."

"Did anything happen with the guy?"

"No, nothing. He called me a time waster and blocked me."

Max looked like he was concentrating hard. He was trying to be supportive and come out with something meaningful. Jamie looked quizzically at him and waited.

"I don't know what to say. Maybe you need more time or to let off some steam."

"Maybe."

"You know my lifestyle, I can't judge anyone, so I'm not going to start judging you but, everybody deals with their own problems differently. I think life's too short so we must make the most of it and what it can offer and this is why I've brought you here."

Max raised his glass with confidence, "To your Mum and to fun!"

A little unsure of the sentiment behind the toast, Jamie clinked Max's glass anyway and they both emptied them in one go.

An incessant quacking noise began to bellow from someones phone and there was great excitement from the boys on the couch. All three scantly clad guys made their way quickly to the kitchen to replenish their drinks. Jamie turned around and noticed an odd look on Max's face.

"What?" he asked.

"You ready to not talk?"

"Yes, please!"

"Then let me take your glass."

Max joined the boys in the kitchen, and Jamie asked to use the bathroom. He was told that it was the door on the right. Feeling the effect of having offloaded, Jamie made his way to the bathroom. His back muscles felt relaxed, and his mind was definitely going down in gear. With a stupid smile on his face, he opened the door and unexpectedly saw four naked men he hadn't seen before on a bed, in various positions, all having sex. None of them noticed him enter. The heat and aromas from the room were intoxicating, and it took him by surprise. Jamie quickly closed the door shouting "sorry." He went into the next room, and while standing using the toilet, he checked his phone once again to find no messages or missed calls. His cheeks were red from the awkward encounter next door. He turned off the phone and shoved it into his back pocket. After flushing, he returned to howls of laughter. Max gave Jamie the wrong door on purpose, and they all found it hilarious. He wanted to feel annoyed, but he just began to laugh louder and harder than them.

"Cheers!" they shouted in unison.

All the guys stared at Jamie, then at Max and start snickering. He thought nothing of it and downed the drink. Jesus selected a song and cranked up the volume. Without instruction, they all began dancing together as if the beat commanded it.

"I love this version," shouted Jamie as he tried to impress the group with his love for Madonna.

He noticed that Jesus chose the live version of *Future Lovers / I Feel Love* from *The Confessions Tour* album. Max, knowing that Jamie had an encyclopaedic knowledge of Madonna's music and the ability to talk about it for hours, threw him a look as if to say "not now." Jamie got his meaning and embarrassingly kept quiet. As the song continued, the group closed in. Jamie was feeling hot from the proximity of all the naked chests. A droplet of guilt slowly dissolved as he put his hands in the air to show he was moved by the music and that he was not caring, that he was done with thinking and to assert he didn't want to feel anything except this pulsating beat. Hands belonging to someone held his hips and he felt a crotch pressing against him. In two beats of the song, both bodies moved in time, thrusting slowly in the same direction. The hands grabbed the bottom of Jamie's t-shirt and he allowed it to come off. The drink gave him confidence and lowered his inhibition to be exposed amongst these gym fit gays dancing by the window that looked over the city.

The group was even closer now. When Jamie opened his eyes he saw other eyes, then pearly white teeth, nipples and six packs. It was sensory overload and blood pumped all round his body in time with the music. He reached behind and pulled the thrusting crotch into him. The song broke and everything was in slow motion. The body that was up against his exerted tingling feelings of epic proportions. Even his hands that were caressing his own body gave him this heightened sensation. Jamie screamed along with Madonna, "Come with me!"

The tight-knit group all screamed. The Donna Summer, *I Feel Love* section of the song began to mix in and everything just kicked off. Jamie felt sexy, desired, horny and at one with the mass of flesh and the throbbing beat of the seventies classic. He felt the group move, guided by chests and hands touching his and leading him away from the window. Everyone's hands were everywhere, in the air or touching the nearest chest. A random hand ran down Jamie's stomach and he noticed that he was sweating. The group were making their way down the hall. The door of the bedroom flew open and they all fall in. Everyone found it hilarious; some struggled to breathe, they were laughing so hard. Looking up, he saw thrusting hips; the guys from earlier, all kissing each other. He began to feel hotter and his chest tightened. The fallen group were all lying across him. He began to panic and struggled to stand up because of all the sweaty bodies. For a split second, he saw nothing but continued to hear everything. Then his sight was restored momentarily, where he saw Max and William kiss passionately. A hand began to undo his belt. He looked up and saw Jesus staring at him and he realised that's who was struggling to undo his buckle. His sight kept coming and going. Jamie tried to scream out but with the mix of panic, the heat and the men on top of him, he couldn't. Jesus came close to his face with a seductive smile and everything went black.

He felt sleepy, safe and free from worry. There was an innocent smile on his face which was lying on something soft. He felt a warm touch to his bear leg. He inhaled and his smile broadened.

"It's time to wake up," instructed a kind, familiar voice.

He opened his eyes and saw that he was laying on all the cushions from his home. Old blankets with coloured lines were blowing gently in the breeze above him. He turned to look at the owner of the hand...

Can you hear me?" asked a harsher, stronger voice. "Nothing. Ok, this is a John Doe. Approximate age is mid to late thirties. Unresponsive for several hours now. He was brought in by the police and ambulance crew and was found at Canary Wharf tube, naked, disorientated and incoherent. This is a suspected GHB overdose. Make sure he is hydrated and monitored closely please." The voice then petered out as it walked away.

"Jamie? Jamie, can you hear me? It's me. Please wake up," Jules pleaded.

It was Sunday morning and she had made it to the Accident and Emergency Department of The Royal London Hospital. Jamie could hear her, but couldn't see anything and felt unable to move. He heard her speaking to a nurse who had a French accent.

"Is he going to be ok?"

"Yes. He will be fine. He's stable and we are just waiting for him to gain consciousness. Don't worry, we see this all the time," said the French nurse in an unexcited manner, like she was bored of seeing patients in this state.

"Do you know what happened?"

"Are you his next of kin?"

"Yes, I'm his wife," Jules lied convincingly.

"What do you know?" asked the nurse who was now unsure of what to say.

"I got a call from a mutual friend saying that Jamie was being put into an ambulance. He asked me to come to his place to pick up his belongings and then I came here. I'm so worried."

"It appears your husband has had a G overdose."

"What?"

"GHB or G...it's an illegal drug."

"Drugs? Jamie? No!"

"We can't be certain, but it's a classic presentation. Of course, we will need for him to wake up to find out for sure."

"I can't believe it, I'm not doubting you, but it's so not like him. Thank you," she noticed the nurse was trying to leave the room to attend to a commotion that was occurring near the entrance of the department.

Jules was unsure what to think or what to do? There were dozens of missed calls and texts from Tom on her phone but none from Max. She paced the curtained area trying to stay calm, believing this would enable her to think straight. Without warning, Jamie sat up in bed with a red face, looking petrified. Jules quickly got hold of the cardboard bowl on his bed and placed it in front of him as he vomited violently. Jules screamed for help until the French nurse returned. Jamie eventually laid back looking grey and exhausted.

"That's good, that needed to happen," the nurse said to Jamie as she checked his temperature with the back of her hand while staring at the monitor he was attached to. Jules scanned the nurse for any signs of worry. She remained pokerfaced which did nothing to comfort her.

"Now, I need to pre-warn you. He is going to start to shake which might be a little distressing. This is normal, ok?"

"Ok…should I do anything?"

"No, you did brilliantly already," gesturing towards the full cardboard bowl on the bed.

They both laughed nervously. Maybe Jules misjudged her for being a cold health professional or maybe it was a French thing. She pondered this as a way of distracting her from her current predicament.

Alone with Jamie, her phone vibrated once more. She pulled the curtains closed in a futile attempt to muffle the sounds of a busy London hospital. Without looking at the screen, she knew already that it was going to be Tom.

"Hey Tom, how are you?" trying to sound nonchalant.

"Hi Jules. I'm a bit worried actually. Have you heard from Jamie?"

"Don't worry Tom; he's at mine." She could hear him breathe a sigh of relief.

"Thank God! Did he tell you?"

"What?"

"We argued earlier."

Delighted with this she answered, "Yes, he told me. Don't worry; it'll blow over."

"I've been calling and texting him, now it's going straight to answerphone and my messages aren't even being delivered."

"He turned his phone off, and he's just in the bath now. Don't worry he'll come round."

"I'm off to Paris in the morning. Tell him I've left enough food for George and," Tom then fell silent.

Jules' heart swelled. She felt bad lying to him but she knew Jamie would've done it for her. She heard a sob on the other end of the line as Tom tried to get through the call.

"...tell him I love him and I'm sorry."

"Of course I will. Don't worry...he'll be fine. Take care."

"Thanks Jules."

Jules hung up and sat on the bed cradling the phone in her lap, looking exhausted from very little sleep, the stress of seeing her best friend in such a state and having just lied to Tom. She turned to her unconscious friend in the bed.

"You owe me big time, mister!"

His hand twitched. She didn't see it but heard a sound behind her. She jumped straight to her feet and scanned the bed. Nothing. Sweat was forming on his brow, so she got some paper towels from the dispenser on the wall and wiped his face. He moaned quietly.

"You're ok, I'm here," whispered Jules.

Jamie heard a new sound. It was a rhythmic, mechanical rushing of energy which stopped and started at varying intervals. On top of this, there was female humming, but he couldn't work out the tune. From his laying down position it was soothing to know she was close to him. He heard his friend from a few doors down walk in.

"Sorry Jamie," David said in a very insincere way.

"Good boy, now go out and play and stay out of trouble," instructed Jamie's Mum.

"What are you sewing, Mrs Anderson," inquired David.

"Just new trousers for Jamie, they're a little long."

It was summer and the doors in the house were all open. A cool breeze flowed through every room.

"Anything yet, darling Jamie?"

"No Mum," Jamie replied.

"It'll come back," she reassured him. She put down what she was doing and came away from the sewing machine to the sofa where he lay, brushed back his long fringe, kissed each eyelid gently and placed a third kiss on his forehead. Jamie smiled awkwardly and tears fell from his eyes at the same time. He loved how his mother looked after him when he wasn't well but he was scared that his eyesight wouldn't return after falling off his bicycle and hitting his head. David had kicked a football at his tyre which caused the accident to happen.

"Don't worry my love. You're ok; I'm here."

Jamie's eyes opened suddenly and he was shaking violently in the bed. He didn't know where he was, how he got there and was struggling to breathe calmly. Jules disappeared from the curtained area screaming for help. Seconds, maybe minutes, he couldn't tell, a nurse appeared with Jules.

"Jamie, my name is Claudia, you are at The Royal London Hospital and you are ok. We've got you. Just relax," spoken with real compassion and authority which took Jules by surprise.

"Jamie, I'm here too. Everything will be ok, try to relax."

With that Jamie's body went limp and he fell back on the bed. Still panting and with a petrified look on his face, he stared at Jules with tears streaming down his face.

"What have I done? Help me!" he whispered.

Jamie fell asleep, worn out by the exertion and some strong pain relief administered by the nurse.

Hours passed painfully slow for Jules who had nourished her worry with awful sandwiches, mediocre tea and too many Skittles. Jamie was now dressed and sitting at the edge of the bed waiting to be discharged. They hadn't really spoken as he was still emotional and any utterances from him ended in full scale dramatics. Jules patted him on the back or squeezed his leg which said multiple things. Claudia appeared, closing the blue paper curtain behind her.

"I'm not sure what you remember if anything at all, but you might want to start taking these until you figure a few things out," she said all this looking at him directly while also checking Jules' face for any reaction.

"What is it?" he asked intently.

"PEP," she stopped abruptly, waiting to see any telling facial expressions.

Jamie looked confused and upset in equal measure and just began to cry, staring down at the floor.

"What is it? Jules asked, taking charge of the situation.

"It's medicine we give to people in similar…situations, if we think they might have been exposed to HIV. It basically reduces their chances of getting it." Claudia had had this conversation many times, but she wasn't generally telling the wife of a patient.

Jules knew that she should act shocked, but she was tired and had forgotten that she had lied to the nurse. Jules walked out of the curtained area with Claudia where she explained how Jamie, her husband, should take the medicine. Moments later, she reappeared and stood in front of her friend.

"Let's get out of here," smiling broadly.

"Thanks Jules," mouthed Jamie, through more tears.

They got a black cab straight to Jules' flat in Battersea. Jamie slept for the entire journey and was slightly miffed when he was awoken by Jules nudging him to get out of the car. Like getting an elderly relative out, Jules opened his car door and awaited for the feeble Jamie to emerge. With no tumbles, they made their way to the front door. She opened it and allowed Jamie to go up the stairs first, following behind, expecting him to fall back.

Jamie just stood in the middle of her living room, while she closed the door. She went to the kitchen to get him some water. He struck a pathetic pose as if he'd just landed from another planet. Knowing her friend well, she didn't mother him.

"Ok, here's some water. Take your first pill and then get some sleep."

Looking dazed and confused, he did exactly that and got into Jules' bed. She closed the sliding door, blocking off her bedroom, leaving a slight gap so she could check in on him. As quietly as she could, she went to the kitchen and made herself a proper cup of tea. While the kettle boiled, she texted Max.

What the hell have you done?

She returned and peeped in at Jamie, who was fast asleep. Slipping off her shoes she sat back into a comfy chair, sipped her tea and waited like a nurse on a night shift.

Chapter 3

Clock watching was so tedious. Jamie did little else since he got into work. At eleven, his phone vibrated to remind him to take his pills. He hadn't missed one, however, hours later, he sometimes doubted if he had actually taken them at all. He took the PEP pills twelve hours apart, strictly following the instructions.

This weeks staff meeting was a blur for him, and if his life depended on it, he couldn't recall one item that was discussed. He spent his time reading and re-reading the week long text conversation he had with Max, who was still in France with Tom. Frustratingly, they were both sharing a hotel room, so communication had been through text messages, which were too infrequent for Jamie's liking. He had spent his days texting him to get to the bottom of what happened. Max, when he did reply, was flippant and gave no details, eventually signing off with a suggestion of meeting when they arrived back from Paris.

He was still on desk duties, and he had cleared the back log of referrals and emails. These tasks were a good distraction from checking his phone or checking his body for signs and symptoms of all sorts of infections which he had Googled the nights before. The only positive news this week was that he would be back seeing his clients on Monday.

Like with Max, there'd only been text communication from Tom. Paris Fashion Week was always a full on affair for him, and at this stage in their relationship, the lack of phone calls usually wasn't a big issue. They were aware it was all work and no play. Jamie sent the first message when he woke up at Jules' on Sunday. Thankfully she had charged his phone while he slept most of the day. Tom's reply was gushing, packed with relief that they were back in touch which made Jamie feel Judus-like. The rational side of his brain told him that there was nothing wrong between them; that Tom didn't suspect anything. The irrational side of his brain, which had been in full flight this week was convinced otherwise and constantly tormented him with harsh comments and judgements on his behaviour as he injected meaning into every word, punctuation, and emoji Tom had used and turned it into tailor-made torture. In elusive, calmer and more lucid moments, Jamie thought how cruel the mind could be on itself.

His phone vibrated on his desk, which was standing upright against his screen. It was from Max saying they had arrived in London and that he was getting the Tube to meet him. He grabbed his coat and announced that he was going for lunch, checking if anyone needed anything. Only Rebecca piped up.

"Surprise me," she said.

He felt so sorry for her. They had long heart to hearts over a few lunches that week: boyfriend troubles. She was the youngest and newest member of the team, and he felt protective of her. This was her fourth guy this year. She had been incredibly unlucky, meeting the worst men possible.

Jamie dashed to Borough Market. He wasn't hungry, and his stomach was in knots. He just needed and urgently wanted to know what had happened at the weekend. Max's lack of cooperation angered him, but he knew that if he went in too strong, knowing Max, he could withhold the vital information in some sick and twisted game. Jamie grabbed a coffee and waited in the glass atrium at the edge of the market. There was nowhere to sit today, but Jamie wouldn't have been able to sit still anyway as he paced up and down. Eventually, he recognised a face but was shocked that it had a massive grin on it. Max went to hug him, but Jamie discreetly stopped it from happening.

"What the fuck?" Jamie exclaimed.

"What? Oh, for God sake, calm down dear!"

"Calm down? Calm down? I've hardly slept this week. Does Tom know anything?"

"Of course not, I'm not an idiot."

"Did he say anything?"

"Nothing. He mentioned you guy's had an argument and that was it. It was hectic so we were working all day and sleeping once we'd finished."

"What the hell happened? You know I'm on PEP?"

"PEP?"

"Yes, because apparently, I had a G overdose."

Max smirked. This infuriated Jamie

"How could that have happened, Max?" asked Jamie sarcastically, steeped in rage.

Max was now tired of Jamie's histrionics and quipped back. "You need to calm down Jamie. You contacted me, remember? You wanted to 'not talk' and, well, I thought this was what you meant or what you needed. You complained that you spend your days listening to other peoples problems, no one ever listens to yours. Then your parents die, and you ban people from helping you, so you bottle it all inside. I get that. I really do. I just thought you could do with escaping, that's all."

"You drugged me!"

"Now wait, I put a small amount of G in your drink. There was no way you would OD on that. I do this stuff all the time, so I should know."

"So I was in safe hands? I could've died!"

"Unless…"

"Unless what?"

"Did anyone else give you a drink?"

"Yes, the Jesus guy."

"Bastard, William said he didn't trust him. I bet he put some into your first drink. I've hazy memories of that night but was there a big gap between drinking his drink and the one I gave you?"

"No, not really…twenty minutes?"

"That's it then. That's probably how you ended up in that state. Honest mistake."

"What? I can't believe you. I can't believe you are just shrugging this off."

"Oh, when you've been to the number of parties I've been to, it's like someone sneezing. Has that cleared everything up for you, Anxious Annie?"

"No. The last thing I remember was someone trying to take my belt off. Did anything happen?" Jamie paused and looked around, then got close to the side of Max's face and whispered, "was I raped?"

"What? Oh my God, no. I'd never let that happen."

"Are you sure?"

"I'm totally sure. I remember we fell over in the bedroom and you panicked and began screaming Tom's name, which was a total buzz kill by the way. You managed to get out of there and down the lift. We waited for the lift to come back up and saw all your clothes on the elevator floor. When we found you, you were naked and screaming for help, screaming for Tom, screaming for your mother."

Jamie put both hands up to his open mouth. He looked like he'd seen a ghost. He was completely mortified and in total disbelief that he was that person. The relief that nothing sexual had happened was overwhelming.

"Great package, by the way," Max said, a failed attempt to ease the tension.

For a moment Jamie felt the anger being replaced by a tidal wave of relief. Light headed, he grabbed Max's arm to steady himself. He thought it might have been the pills.

"Steady mister. You ok?"

He had thought the worst; that he'd been raped. He had gone over and over the scenarios on a loop for the last week. How he would have told Tom. Would he tell him? What if he contracted HIV?

"I just need a minute."

"Drink some of that coffee."

Jamie removed the top of the takeaway cup and took a large mouthful followed by a few controlled breaths.

"I've been so worried about this; you have no idea. Please, please don't tell Tom. It's the last thing he or I need," Jamie pleaded, feeling less angry now.

"Cross my heart," Max promised, doing the actions across his chest at the same time.

Suddenly Jamie felt a soft touch on his back and heard an apologetic voice.

"Excuse me, would you like some sushi?"

He turned around and saw Teresa with a Feng Sushi bag. For a moment he didn't know what to say. She stood there comfortably in the silence and placed a piece of sashimi into her mouth.

"You were right about the pastry the other day, so I thought I'd give this a go. Very fishy but I like it...I think. Do you want some?" she asked with a semi-full mouth.

Max shuffled up to Jamie and asked quietly, without trying to move his lips "Do you know her?"

"This young man came to my rescue the other week," Teresa answered in a matter of fact way.

Snapping out of it, Jamie cleared his throat.

"Max, this is Teresa. Teresa this is Max, a friend of mine."

"How do you do?" Teresa asked, unable to shake hands with one carrying the bag of food and the other holding chopsticks like a novice.

Max was stunned and looked at both of them, and it jarred with his sense of style.

"Jamie, I better go and leave you…to it."

"Sure. Thanks - sort of."

Max made his way out of the market.

"And how have you been?" Jamie inquired, sounding like he hadn't a care in the world.

"Me? Well, I'm good thanks."

"You know there's a good sushi stall in Greenwich market; you didn't have to come all the way here."

She laughed. "Oh no, I had another appointment and thought I'd pop here for something to eat. A treat, as you would call it, after that ordeal."

"So you went back? Still not going well then?"

She looked at him intently as if she was about to ask the most important question she'd ever ask: "How would you know if it was going well?"

Jamie paused to think but struggled. "Good question with not a straight forward answer."

A group of school children pushed passed Teresa, and she was slightly knocked off balance. Jamie grabbed her.

"It's packed today," she commented, not really caring about the unruly youths.

"It is. Full of children with no manners, do you want to go for a walk?"

"A walk? Well, I'd love that."

"Come on; let's get out of here."

Jamie guided Teresa out of the heaving market which wasn't an easy task with hundreds of people trying to get their lunch from the various stalls. Passing each one, Teresa commented on how great each particular cuisine smelled. They eventually escaped the hordes and arrived on to the banks of the Thames.

"That's better," Jamie said as he surveyed the space they now had to walk and talk along the vast river with its skyscraper garnished banks.

"Do you want some?"

"Yes please."

"Use your fingers. I don't mind. I'm going to have to because I can't use these things," as she put the chopsticks back in the bag.

Jamie took a piece and swallowed it whole. With his stomach unknotting, his appetite had returned. Teresa instantly lifted the bag up for him to take more.

"So what do you make of it?" Jamie asked with a half full mouth.

Teresa hesitated. She looked like she was worried she'd offend Jamie. "It's ok. A bit too fancy for me."

"At least you tried it."

They began to walk along Bankside. For a while there wasn't any talking. Jamie was so relieved that nothing, apart from being drugged, happened at the party and that Tom didn't suspect anything.

Teresa was walking along like she was on holiday, looking at all the architecture, the people, taking in the air and enjoying not being hassled by the crowds. The silence didn't bother either of them, but eventually, Jamie broke it.

"So, do you want to tell me what happened today with your therapist? You don't have to if you don't want to. I completely understand."

"My therapist? I sound like one of those neurotic Yanks from the films," she sort of laughed at herself. "It's just the same as before. I'm there, with my cup of tea and he's sitting at his desk, writing things. He writes when I'm saying things and when I'm not saying things. There are lots of silences, and he stares at me, tilts his head this way, then that way and asks me what I'm thinking. I want to tell him that I think this is all a great big waste of time, but I don't. I'm sure he's very good at what he does, but I'm not sure why I'm there or what I should do."

"Why do you go then?"

"Oh, I don't know. My doctor says I should talk and the fact it's being paid for, I think, why not? My doctor said that expressing myself might help me - what way did he put it?" She stopped walking and took a moment to think. "Yes, understand why I'm feeling this way," she recalled, saying every word very distinctively.

"What way is that?"

"It's really hard to put into words."

"Try me. Pretend for a second that you're describing it to an alien who has just landed from Mars and the first thing he wants to know, the only thing he wants to know is exactly what happens to you when this feeling occurs."

She looked at him like he was mad. Her face softened, and Jamie could see her struggling to start.

"There are people worse off than me."

Jamie interrupted quickly. "That will always be true, but I'm more interested in you. So think about when the last time you felt this particular way."

"I have a nice life. I want for nothing, but out of the blue and I can be anywhere, at home, at my social club or walking in the street and I suddenly feel like something really terrible is about to happen. It just comes over me. It's like pure dread."

"That doesn't sound nice at all, Teresa."

"It's not. Sometimes I think I'm about to have a heart attack. I worry that someone will see me and I'll be taken away."

They stop without deciding to and both take another piece of sushi from the bag.

"Is that…?" Teresa then drew a blank.

"The Globe Theatre? Yes, it is."

"In all my years in England, I've never seen it. Plays weren't our thing. We loved musicals. We loved music."

"Is this…?" Jamie didn't know how to ask it.

"My husband," she said with an endearing smile.

"Do you speak to him about these feelings?"

She looked at Jamie completely deadpan. "He died five years ago. He would've been seventy-six this year," she said politely.

"I'm so sorry to hear that."

"Heart attack. Out of nowhere. We got up one morning and while having our breakfast and listening to The Beatles, he just…" she stopped, struggling to find an appropriate end to the sentence, "…he just went."

Jamie could see her eyes welling up. She was in a kind of daydream, recalling all this. He didn't force her out of it because she looked like she was happy, even with the tears forming. She swallowed back the emotion.

"He was a good man."

"With good taste in music, The Beatles?"

"Oh yes. He certainly did."

They walked without talking for a few minutes. There was no eye contact but no awkwardness. Street entertainers with various skills dotted the path outside the imposing Tate Modern Museum. Teresa got closer to see their shows. Jamie saw a childlike amazement appear from beneath her wrinkled face as she watched them. They went through the tunnel at Blackfriars Bridge which was filled with a saxophone playing the lead from *Baker Street*. Teresa dropped a pound into the musician's hat and mouthed a 'thank you.' As they walked on, the music quietened. Leaving the tunnel, they were back out in the open.

"What's a happy memory for you? The happiest. Don't try and think about it too much, the first one that pops to mind?"

She stopped, making the people behind swerve around her.

"Don't over think it," Jamie said gently.

"Ok. I've got it. Saturday nights when my daughter was young, we would turn the TV and radio off, and I would sit on the sofa with Bill, and we'd listen to my daughter playing the piano."

"Was she any good?"

"Of course she was, I taught her," she said sternly, but in jest.

"I didn't know that."

"Yes, I taught music all my life. I'd teach her a couple of evenings a week, once she'd finished her homework. She was a quick learner."

"And had a good teacher," Jamie interjected.

"I was alright."

"So tell me about these Saturday nights. Remember, I'm still a Martian. I know nothing of such things."

"My daughter would be out of the bath, I'd have blow dried her hair, and she'd be in clean pyjamas. Bill would have been showered after a days working. We'd sit down and have our tea: always chips, beans and eggs on a Saturday. I'd pour him a beer and myself a wee glass of wine. We just always ended up going to the sofa, the two of us and our daughter would start playing. He'd put his arm around me, and we'd sip and listen, watching our baby at the piano. When she was young, her feet wouldn't even touch the pedals. She could read music but on Saturday nights she would play songs Bill and I loved, all from ear."

"Sounds like a lovely evening in," Jamie commented, enviously.

"Oh, it was. They were simpler times when children are at that age. It's small things that made our hearts flutter. Now, life is less about those things and more about busyness and not sitting down. It's about doing things. Back then, it was Bill, our little girl, me and the stand-up piano in our front room. I'm sure we drove the neighbours made, but we never had any complaints."

"What was your favourite song she played?" asked Jamie.

"That's easy. It was *Imagine* by John Lennon. I just love that song and it was in a film that Bill once watched about the Vietnam war. It was the only film I ever saw him cry at. After it was over, I could see him sobbing his little heart out. I asked him if he was ok and he said that he was fine and that he just had a bad headache.

"Were you all Beatles fans in your house then?"

"I guess we were," she answered with a smile on her face.

Passing the Oxo Tower, Jamie saw one of two jetties that jutted out from the busy walkway towards the middle of the river. They served no real purpose apart from being away from the crowded path. About to pass the second jetty, he motioned for her to follow him down one that had no one at the end of it. With a quizzical look, she followed him. They got to the end of the jetty and looked back at all the people walking along the river. Jamie placed both hands on the railing and breathed in and out, loudly. Teresa gingerly looked over the railings and saw the rushing Thames swirling and moving.

"Much of a singer?" Jamie asked.

"Me? no. Not really. Why?"

"Remember when we first met I suggested something? A treat?"

"Yes," she answered with confusion in her voice, wondering where this was going.

"I am going to suggest something else. The next time you feel that feeling again, the dreaded feeling, I want you to do two things."

"Ok."

"I want you to first think of those Saturday nights."

"Right."

"And I think you should have a mantra. Something to sing."

"A mantra? Like what?"

Jamie was silent for a moment. She could see him really thinking hard and after a few seconds, he finally shouted aloud, startling her slightly. He then sang a song from a Beatles song.

"What?"

"Call yourself a Beatles fan?" Jamie teased her.

"The Beatles didn't sing in gobbledygook. Did they?"

"It's from one of their songs called *Across The Universe*."

She began to laugh out loud, which was infectious and Jamie giggled along with her.

"I *do* know that song but I am not going to tell you what I thought the words were."

"I don't know what it means, I think it's Sanskrit, but it's followed by a line which they repeat a good few times."

"I'm impressed you know that song."

"To be honest I know it through another singer, so don't be too impressed." He put both his hands on the railing again and looked straight across the river. He spread his legs and gestured that she copy him.

Self consciously, she looked around but eventually, she put down the bag and did the same.

"Ok, are you ready?"

"Ready for what?"

"One - two - three..." stopping his singing abruptly, he stared at her.

"I feel silly."

"Me too but let's be silly together."

He started again and eventually, they both sang the chorus.

They both looked at each other.

"That's it," he said

"That's what?"

"Try this the next time you feel that dread begin to take over. Sing it inside your head or out loud, but make sure you are thinking of sitting on that sofa."

"What's it supposed to do?"

"I'm hoping that the dreaded feeling will go away when you do it."

"I'll certainly try," she answered slightly bemused by the public singing.

"That's all I ask, that you'll try," he said with much kindness. "I need to get back to work."

"I'm so sorry for taking you away from your friend and taking up your time."

"It's my pleasure. Don't worry; I enjoyed the walk. Do you know how to get to the station from here?"

"Yes, I do," she answered confidently.

"Well, mind yourself and don't forget the happy thoughts and song."

"I won't."

Jamie reluctantly took his leave from her and got back to the office. He felt a massive weight had been lifted after hearing what didn't happen from Max.

When he got back to work, he placed a packet of salt and vinegar crisps on Rebecca's desk. He saw her boots from under the frosted glass of their boss' office and guessed a serious meeting was occurring so he stuck a Post-it on them which said *Eat me*.

An hour or so later, Rebecca reappeared. Jamie could tell that she'd been crying. Head down; she made her way back to her desk. She saw the crisps, her favourite flavour and the Post-it, giggled and then sobbed. Jamie coughed to get her attention and mouthed to check if she was ok. She rubbed her tears and nodded quickly. Their boss appeared from the office and signalled Jamie to follow him. Jamie did as he was told.

"Close the door behind you."

Jamie complied and sat down. "What's up?"

"Nothing at all. Just checking in to see how you are and how you feel about seeing clients again on Monday?"

"Yeah, I'm good thanks. Referrals all sorted and just itching to get back in the hot seat again."

"That's good to hear. Have you had supervision since you got back?"

"Mmm…no, not yet? Is that a problem?" Jamie asked, slightly concerned.

"No, not really. I just think it would've been useful to have seen Helen before you saw your clients again. Have you thought about how the sessions will continue and any impact your…situation might have on them?"

Jamie hadn't thought of it at all but he could see that his boss had and that it might be a potential issue.

"To be honest, I just can't wait to get back to the clients. It's been far too long and you know how much I live for the work. I think it will be really good for me, and them, I hope," Jamie said reassuringly.

His boss was looking to his right, thinking about what was being said to him.

"Ok, but just be mindful of yourself and them and book in for supervision ASAP. Helen has some availability later in the week, ok?"

"Ok. Anything else?"

"How's Rebecca doing? I know you're close."

"Man troubles but I think she is a great asset to the team. New blood."

"Hmmm. Ok. Why don't you go home early."

"Ok, I'm not going to look a gift horse in the mouth. See you Monday and have a good weekend."

"You too."

Jamie grabbed his stuff, logged off his computer and checked he had all his belongings. On his way out he passed Rebecca's desk. She was on the phone with a client. He kissed her on the head and she leaned back into him, smiling. Heading to the train station, he picked up some flowers. They never did the cliche 'I'm sorry' flowers but they did take turns to ensure there was a fresh bouquet on their large dining table. His train just pulled into the platform as he ascended the stairs in one of those rare, perfectly timed, commuter moments. He quickly texted Tom to say he was on his way home. Searching his iTunes library, he located Rufus Wainwright's version of *Across the Universe* and pressed play. He thought about Teresa and wondered what she was doing now and hoped that if she did feel, what he believed were panic attacks, that what he had suggested would help her. He thought of Max and the life he led. For the first time, he felt almost judgemental towards him. Before all of this, it was all light and fluffy, listening to the rundown of his weekend antics. They used to laugh about what he got up to when he filled them in via WhatsApp on Monday and sometimes Tuesday mornings. He felt differently about it now and for once, saw the human cost of such weekends and it's unspoken collateral damage.

Before this, these people he would hear about were faceless. Now he was sort of one of them and the idea that what happened to him was being talked about so frivolously, upset him.

The announcement on the train signalled they were nearing his stop and all judgemental thoughts cleared. He just couldn't wait to see Tom. Planning to be as normal as possible, he told himself not to be over the top, but secretly he couldn't wait to hug him and be hugged back. For the entire week, millions of scenarios played out in his tired mind. What life would be like if Tom had left him? Where would he live? Could he afford to live in London? Could he cope with sharing a house or flat with strangers? If Tom did divorce him, were parties like Max's what he would have to attend to somehow fit in?

Opening their front door, the house instantly felt like home, something it hadn't done for the entire time Tom was away. He saw George at his bowl eating and a suitcase in the hallway. Tom was in the kitchen cooking. No words were spoken as Jamie stood behind and wrapped his arms tightly around him while Tom stirred a saucepan. Jamie inhaled his scent as if he'd never smell it again.

"Hey you." Tom said lovingly, "miss me?"

Jamie didn't let go or say anything; he just nodded his head.

"I think I need to go away more often," he joked.

Jamie just hugged him tighter.

"So Max rang," Tom said innocently.

Jamie panicked, opened his eyes and held his breath.

"Yeah, he told me you're having secret liaisons."

Jamie let go of him to try and gauge Tom's facial expression. They stood looking at each other. No ones face gave anything away. Eventually, after what felt like an eternity, Tom finally spoke.

"Didn't think old ladies were your type?"

"Oh Teresa?" The relief was seismic. "Just a lovely lady I met at the train station. She's very sweet."

"Once she knows your taken and all mine," he said in jest before kissing him on the lips.

Jamie didn't reply. He kissed and hugged him until the water boiled over and Tom had to quickly turn the gas down.

Their evening was distilled domesticity: Tom served up a delicious Thai green curry, while Jamie arranged the flowers he bought and poured two large glasses of Chablis. Jamie asked Tom about his work trip and Tom gave him all the gossip from what seemed like an eventful Paris Fashion Week. Jamie could listen to him talk about his work all day. He loved that about him, how he talked so passionately about it. While he listened, all the stress from his week dissipated. Jamie always wanted a partner who would not expect the same in return. Professionally, the line of work he was in meant that confidentially was of utmost importance and something he took very seriously. They wouldn't have lasted this long if Tom was one of those people who asked about his day or demanded to know what went on in sessions. He was also amazingly discreet on those rare occasions when they bumped into one of his clients. Tom never asked questions and would always politely excuse himself and look into a shop window or walk slightly ahead. The other reason he cherished this lack of professional interest was the fact that Jamie really didn't want to talk about work outside of work, he always thought that's what supervision was for. Tom knew the names of Jamie's co-workers and had met some of them, but that was as far as it went.

After dinner, Jamie washed up and when he was finished, joined Tom on the couch, where they caught up on the week's TV soaps. Snuggled on the sofa, with George at their feet asleep, Jamie wanted this feeling to last, to permeate every pore and enrich his very being. After a few more Friday night shows, Tom eventually nodded off with his head on Jamie's chest. Jamie stealthy turned the volume down on the TV, looked up at the ceiling and tried not to think. This worked and eventually, he too fell asleep.

Eleven o'clock and they were suddenly startled by a noise coming from the kitchen. Tom was in a daze but Jamie was immediately on his feet.

"I bet you that's Rebecca," he lied convincingly.

He knew that his phone was not telling him there was a new text message. It was the alarm he had set to remind him to take his PEP medication. Dashing to the kitchen table to silence it, he nearly slipped, a combination of being in his socks and the shiny floor. He grabbed his phone and eventually turned off the incessant alarm. Relieved that Tom was still lying down and now switching channels to see what was on, he noticed a few messages. One from Rebecca, thanking him for the crisps and another from a number he didn't recognise.

Hi Jamie, Max gave me your number. Maybe we can meet again sometime soon. Jesus xxx

Jamie dropped his phone and with delayed reflexes from being asleep, he tried to catch it but ended up tossing it down the kitchen floor. He jumped to retrieve it and instantly deleted the message.

"Rebecca?" inquired Tom.

"Yes, bless her."

"Let's hit the hay."

"Come on then, sleepyhead."

They gravitated upstairs slowly. Brushing their teeth at the same time and looking at each other in the mirror, they heard George jump on to their bed. Every pre-sleep task felt arduous. Climbing into bed, trying not to disturb their feline bedfellow, they kissed each other good night and fell fast asleep.

The following morning, Jamie began to wake up. His eyes were still closed but he heard neighbours' doors opening and closing.

Sometimes there were conversations longer than the obligatory salutations. He recognised some of the instigators of these chats. The clock in the bedroom told him it was 11:11 am. He couldn't believe he'd slept that long but was also startled to see that the bed was empty. Donning his dressing gown, he made his way downstairs. There was a noise at the front door and halfway down the stairs, Jamie spied Tom going to see who it was. Tom took a parcel from the postman along with some letters. Jamie just stood there, still tired, as he rubbed the sleep from his eyes. Tom didn't know he was being watched and Jamie saw him put the parcel at the door while he flicked through the post. One particular letter was immediately stuffed into his pocket while he placed all the other mail on the table in the hall under the large mirror. Tom was startled by the sight of his husband on the stairs.

"You scared me! Good morning sleepyhead. Someone needed that?"

"I certainly did."

"Coffee is on," Tom said, as he made his way back into the kitchen.

Their Saturday morning was just like the previous one without the haircut, the tears and the argument; a welcome relief to both men. Jamie could sense that Tom was trying so hard to appear like he wasn't trying for their weekend to be as it had been before his mothers passing. Jamie was completely aware that Tom, before saying or doing anything, inputted his next move or conversation through an internal process, in a bid to see if this would upset his partner; was it something that could trigger emotions? To the outside world, they looked like two men in a relationship having a relaxing time. They were both far from relaxed. They were both struggling. They were both just getting by.

Sunday lunch was an impromptu gathering at Dan and Brian's, or so Jamie thought. Tom had arranged this on Friday evening. It wasn't that Dan and Brian wouldn't offer to cook for them. They did this every couple of months and it was always something they looked forward to. It was that Tom had urged them to have Jamie out of the house on this particular Sunday afternoon. When discussing it with Tom on the phone, Dan never asked too many questions. He could sense that this would be a huge favour.

Tom and Jamie, before boarding the bus to Blackheath picked up some wine and flowers from the market. Red wine for their hosts and white wine for themselves. Arriving on time, they were greeted warmly by Dan. Brian was shouting his salutations from the kitchen. The guests popped their heads in and smelled wondrous aromas but could see a stressed Brian, so they left him to it. They joined Dan in the living room and weren't sitting long when they had glasses of white wine in their hands. They conversed on the week that had been. Jamie didn't share too much about his week for obvious reasons. They laughed about how long their hangover took to leave them after the night in Soho. Finally,

Brian appeared and apologised for his stressed out state and ushered them to the dining table.

"Cheers boys," Brian announced as they clinked glasses. "So Jamie, how have you been?"

Tom looked at Brian. Dan looked at Jamie while kicking Brian under the table.

"What?" asked Brian innocently. "Am I not allowed to ask how my friend is doing?"

It was awkward but Jamie felt like he had to say something.

"I'm doing ok, Brian. Thanks for asking." Everyone seemed relieved. "I've had good days and not so good days but I suppose that's to be expected."

"I bet," answered Brian.

"How was Paris, Tom?" Dan asked, changing the subject.

A lot of time was spent dissecting Tom's week. Dan was an accountant and Brian worked as a town planner, so Tom's job seemed so exciting in comparison to theirs.

Two courses down and a few bottles of wine later, they were all loose tongued, full bellied and relaxed. Tom helped Dan clear away the plates as their respective partners talked intensely about the video footage of Madonna dancing on a table in Cuba for her birthday. Passing plates to Dan who carefully placed them into their dishwasher, Tom broke down in the kitchen. Dan continued what he was doing, not because he didn't care or the fact that he wasn't the touchy feely type, he just allowed Tom a few moments of release. Once all the dishes were packed away, Dan nodded towards their back door. Armed with wine glasses, they escaped to the garden.

"This will get better; you know that?" Dan said reassuringly.

"I know, I know. It's just so hard to be around him at the moment."

"What do you mean?"

"I know he's hurting really bad. All I want to do is to wrap him up and hug it out of him but he wants, demands the opposite. So while I see him breaking apart in front of me, I am supposed to stand back and be normal. It's tearing me apart, Dan. It's exhausting."

"I can only imagine."

"Thanks for agreeing to have us 'round for lunch."

"It's no trouble, but can I ask why the insistence that it was today, not that we don't want you guys around. You just sounded so desperate on the phone."

Tom took a large mouthful of wine and tried to hold back his tears. Dan took a sip from his glass and discreetly checked to see that their partners were still at the table. Tom could see him doing it and felt reassured.

"Every Sunday afternoon Jamie would call his mother on the landline. It's the only reason we have it. It was their weekly ritual and this is the fifth Sunday where there's been no phone call. The fifth Sunday since she died and I just wanted him out of the house and away from the weekly reminder of their only contact."

"I get it. You are really thinking of everything Tom. This will all pass."

"But when?" asked Tom with desperation etched on his face.

"Dessert anyone?" shouted Brian from the kitchen.

Tom was too upset to answer.

"That sounds great," answered Dan, for the both of them. "I know it's not my place, but have you thought of suggesting counselling?"

Through his tears and amidst a gulp of wine, Tom chortled,"that's the hilarious paradox of this whole scenario. It's the first thing I thought about and it'll be the last thing I'll suggest. He doesn't want to talk about it. Isn't that fucked up? What he's probably telling his clients at work to do, he won't do himself."

"Physician, heal thyself."

"That's a more eloquent way of putting it," Tom joked to lighten the mood. "When his Dad died, there was none of this."

"Hardly surprising, though. This is the same father that refused to come to your wedding?"

"The very same one."

"You are in a unique position, to have both your parents still alive and you've a great relationship with them. Jamie had a difficult upbringing, to say the least. He was never going to have a loving parental experience and now that will definitely not happen and I imagine he's grappling with that."

"You're right, you're right. I just feel helpless."

"Incoming," said Dan, without moving his lips, warning him that his husband was walking towards them.

"What are you two birds gassing on about?"

"Boring work stuff," said Dan.

They stood around in silence. Those with wine took a sip from their glass.

"Dessert is served," Brian shouted from the open kitchen window.

They all made their way inside and devoured Brian's infamous chocolate cake.

Retired to the comfortable seats and armed with coffees, they lounged for a few hours. Too tired and a little too drunk to be bothered with a bus ride home, Jamie suggested getting a taxi instead. Tom thought he'd never ask and quickly got out his phone to arrange it. They said their goodbyes and expressed their thanks for a stupendous Sunday afternoon. Tom hugged Dan for what seemed like a longer period of time than normal.

"Thanks for listening," whispered Tom.

"Anytime," Dan whispered back.

The Taxi was outside already. Jamie rested his head on Tom's shoulder as they were driven home.

Too full to do anything interesting and too tired to even feign an interest in something exciting, once home they got straight into their PJ's and lounged on the sofa. George joined them on the couch after he was fed and watered.

The weekend concluded all too quickly for them, but it was one that was without outward signs of sorrow or tears. As Tom lay in bed, he was thankful for that while he dozed and began to snore. Jamie stared at the wall and thought that today would've been the fifth Sunday without talking to his mother. Tears dampened his pillow.

Monday morning came all too slowly for Jamie, who didn't sleep well. Both men were up and getting ready at the same time. This was an exception rather than the rule due to Tom's early flight to Manchester. Tom shaved and showered while Jamie prepared breakfast. They passed on the landing as Jamie took his turn to occupy the bathroom. He felt excited about getting to work and back to seeing his clients because he liked to feel useful and had felt far from that since he'd returned.

Both dressed and ready to leave, they kissed each other and said goodbye to George, who was already asleep on their bed. Jamie started to walk to the train station as Tom hopped into the taxi that had been waiting outside their house.

After a typically horrendous Monday morning commute, Jamie was released from the rammed carriage and strode to work with a coffee in his hand. He was the first one in, so he turned on the lights, started up his computer and stared out the window, sipping on his brew. His phone beeped. He flipped it over and saw a message from TalkTalk, their home phone provider. He opened the message to read it in full. It was an automated message thanking him for his custom over the past five years and that they were sorry to see him leave and if there was anything they could do to make him change his mind, to call them at once. Jamie reread the message trying to understand what was going on. He knew he didn't need the landline anymore and had planned to call the company when he was ready. Annoyed, he threw the phone down on the desk. How dare Tom do that, he thought. How insensitive of him to do this behind his back. This was the last thing he needed before seeing his first client of the day. His phone vibrated again. It was from Tom.

Have a good one and good luck with the first client. T x

Jamie deleted the message angrily and didn't reply. He felt agitated and adding coffee into the mix wasn't going to help things. In an act of pointless passive aggression, he downed the flat white in one final mouthful.

Colleagues started to make their way into populate the office. There was small talk backwards and forwards about their weekend. Jamie found it irritating and grabbed the files he needed and went to one of the therapy rooms. The large white room was quiet and away from the office. He sat on the large couch rather than his designated chair and opened up the files he needed. His first client was a sixteen-year-old boy called Dwayne. He had been seeing him for two months before his mother died, so he had another month or so before he had to finish with him. In the era of financial cuts, having three months of therapy was as much as this current government would fund, which left Jamie and his colleagues sometimes just scratching the surface of the problems they were presented with. Jamie looked at all the email correspondence since he was off to get an idea of what Dwayne had been told. Rebecca handled contacting his caseload for him. He loved the softness of her emails.

Jamie has had a bereavement in his family and will be out of work for a few weeks.

There was no hiding from it, which annoyed him. Lying and saying he was off because of a health matter was now, not an option. It just meant he would have to sit there with the knowledge that his client knew and Jamie would wonder whether it would be brought up.

Rebecca knocked on the door and entered the room.

"Dwayne is here, bless him, he's never late, is he?"

"Nope, never."

"Your other two clients for the day have cancelled and haven't rescheduled but there are a few assessments we could get in for you if you want to try those?"

"Yeah, sure."

"Ok, good luck."

Dwayne was always twenty minutes early for every session. There were two ways of looking at it. Polite, not wanting to be late or very anxious and afraid of being late. Regardless, Jamie would only call him in at 9:30 am on the dot, keeping the boundaries of their therapeutic relationship. He switched off his phone and tidied away all the notes, placing them beside his chair. He ensured the box of tissues were placed in easy reach, on the couch. Double checking the clock on the wall, he opened the door and called his first client in.

Dwayne was a tall teenager, taller than Jamie. His posture made him appear like he was carrying the world on his shoulders, which wasn't too far from the truth. A permanent look of sadness embossed his brow but he mustered a smile and his large dark eyes shone momentarily to indicate he was happy to be back seeing his counsellor. He took off his jacket and sat on the right-hand side of the couch. Jamie sat on his chair, across from him.

"How have you been Dwayne?" Jamie started off gently.

"How have *I* been? Should I not be asking you that?"

"Well, I'm not on the couch. You are Dwayne. So what's been going on?

"What's been going on?"

"Yes Dwayne. Has school or home life gotten better or worse since we last saw each other? Or is there anything you'd like to talk about today?"

"Who died?" fell out of Dwayne's mouth.

Jamie was completely taken aback and wondered whether he should answer it or not. At that moment he understood why his boss was so insistent on him seeing his supervisor before he resumed seeing clients again. Thinking that this line of questioning wasn't going away, he answered honestly.

"My mother…and father, Dwayne."

"Oh my god, I'm so sorry."

"Thank you."

"Were you guys…close?"

"We're not here to talk about me. How have *you* been?" asked Jamie, trying to get the session back on track.

"I've felt really sad," Dwayne replied.

Jamie relieved that the session was starting to move forward, probed further.

"Sad?"

"Yeah, sad. When I heard that someone had died belonging to you, it just made me sad. Sad to think that I wouldn't see you and that you might be hurting."

"I really appreciate that Dwayne, I'm fine, but we are here now and we'll get back on track with our sessions. Is that ok?

"I guess so," he mumbled.

Silence fell on the room. Jamie examined Dwayne's facial expression but noticed his feet had begun shuffling. He was holding on so tightly to all his training and the professionalism he believed he possessed. A part of him wanted to run out of the room but he tried to ground himself by feeling his feet on the floor and placing both of his hands on his lap. He inhaled and then exhaled. Dwayne remained silent and Jamie started to panic. He scrambled for something to move the session along but nothing came to him.

"My dog died a couple of years ago," Dwayne said without invitation. "He was old though."

"What was his name?" asked Jamie with great relief.

"Jake. He was a border collie."

"Great breed. What was so great about Jake?"

Dwayne looked at Jamie with his sad eyes and considered for a second his answer.

"Everything." His eyes began to well up.

Jamie didn't offer anything. He wanted Dwayne's answer to fill the room.

"I'd wake up to a wagging tail or my face being licked. He would be so sad when I went to school but would be doubly happy to see me come back home. When I began to get depressed, he'd know. I don't know how he did, but he did. I'd be up in my room under the blankets not wanting to talk to anyone. He'd make his way up the stairs and walk with his head a little lower than usual and his tail wagging left to right. He'd lick my face and jump onto the bed with me and just lay there. My house was full of people but I felt alone. Jake would make me feel like I wasn't on my own. I never felt alone with him on the bed with me."

"He sounds like an amazing dog, Dwayne."

"He was. He was the best," he replied, fighting back the tears.

Jamie began to feel emotional too.

"What do you miss about Jake the most?

He looked up. Jamie could tell that Dwayne was really thinking about it. Eventually, after many moments had passed Dwayne came up with his answer.

"Our routine. You know that we don't have much money, so we never went on holidays or out anywhere like my school friends. So Jake and I had our routine which probably sounds dumb and boring but I knew where I stood with him. I knew what would happen if we went to a certain park or when I got home or went to bed, he would always do the same thing and that made me feel safe."

"Feeling safe is important, isn't it?"

Dwayne nodded and rubbed his eyes. Jamie realised that that's why he was so angry with the TalkTalk text. He knew there would be no more phone calls to or from his mother and being practical; it was a waste of money having the landline connected when it was only used for one purpose that was no longer required. He just wasn't ready to cut that cord just yet. He needed time. He was angry because it was taken out of his hands but being in the therapist's chair, he was able to see that Tom thought he was doing him a favour by dealing with it for him.

"What do you miss the most about your Mum and Dad?" Dwayne asked gingerly.

Jamie wondered whether he should've answered this but thought since Dwayne had been open about something so personal, it would seem a tad unfair if he didn't reciprocate.

"Knowing that she's not there if I needed her. I'm a lot older than you Dwayne but you never don't need the knowledge that if something goes terribly wrong, you have a parent who can make things alright, even if you're a grown up like me."

"That's really sad, Jamie."

"It is, but we somehow have to dust ourselves off and get on with life a bit like you and Jake. You'll never forget him and nor should you, but he'd want you to be happy and get on with your life, wouldn't he?" Jamie asked, not really believing what he had just said.

"I suppose so."

The rest of their time finally steered away from the topic of death and loss and focused on Dwayne's depression and anxiety which had slightly improved. The next appointment was booked and Jamie brought their fifty-minute session to an end. He stood up and went to the door to open it. Dwayne walked by and without warning, hugged Jamie. Internally, he panicked and worried about becoming too emotional in front of his client. He was moved, not just by the impromptu hug but by the entire session. Jamie was also self-conscious of what his colleagues would think if they saw his client hugging him. Jamie allowed the hug to happen and put one arm around him.

Dwayne let go and walked on without saying anything as if that embrace never happened. Returning to the room, he fell on the couch exhausted. Secretly he was glad that his other two clients had cancelled. He didn't think he would've coped with another session. Eventually, he pulled himself together and wrote up his notes. Reemerging from the therapy room, he went straight to his desk to find a message from Jules checking was he free for a drink later. His immediate thought was to get home as quickly as possible and get under his duvet, but, he fought this off and accepted her invite.

After work Jamie decided to walk to Soho to clear his head. It was a walk he enjoyed as it passed so many well known London landmarks: Big Ben, 10 Downing Street, Trafalgar Square. It amused him that these iconic buildings were on his doorstep and that he was walking by them. Halfway down Old Compton Street his phone vibrated. He read a message which instantly changed his mood. Jules had just cancelled at the last minute with the feeblest of excuses. She had done this quite a bit until Jamie, with the help of Tom, stood up to her and they had a massive argument. They got over it and she hadn't done it for a very long time. Whether it was for a genuine reason or not, she had form and he was enraged. Stood in the middle of the street he had two options: to go home or have a drink. Deciding on the latter and since he was there already, he walked on.

In a cocktail bar on Wardour Street, he ordered a Cosmopolitan. Slightly self-conscious, he sat at the bar and drank slowly. For Soho, it was still rather early and the bar was quiet. The handsome bar staff were preparing all their drinks and fruits in advance for all the concoctions they would have to create later. When his glass was empty, it was promptly replaced by another because it was Happy Hour. It wasn't in his plan but he thought why refuse a free drink. The bar began to fill up slowly and the music got louder.

The effects of the strong cosmopolitan started to kick in. On the bar stool, he felt alone but less worried about it. His chest was sore. It was a physical pain that felt connected to a well of tears just below eye level. He began to think that other people were watching him, so he looked at his phone to distract himself and to feel less socially awkward. Not replying to Jules was punishment enough he thought as he texted Tom to say he was going to be late. No other messages, missed calls or emails. The French barman looked at the empty glass and asked if he wanted another. Jamie looked at his watch then looked at the handsome man in front of him with the sexy accent.

"I've got work tomorrow so maybe some sort of mocktail?"

Moments later, he was presented with an non alcoholic cocktail.

"Merci," Jamie said embarrassingly, not drunk enough to avoid blushing cheeks.

"Santé," replied the barman.

Jamie sipped and checked his phone. Again, nothing. He caught a glimpse of himself in the mirror behind the bar and had a word with himself about what the hell he was doing, which ended up with him telling himself to shut the fuck up.

"Hola chico!"

Jamie looked around and due to the dark bar and feeling a tad tipsy it took him a second to focus on the face from where the voice was coming from.

"Jesus?"

"Si, it's me," he said jokingly.

"Coming to date rape me again, are you?"

"Now, now, now, don't be like that. I'm sorry. It was an honest mistake," he pleaded, mockingly with his hands in the air.

"Who cares anyway. What do you want?"

"A drink, is that ok?" Jesus asked coyly, then signalled to the barman that he wanted a Diet Coke. Nothing was said while his drink were being prepared. Jesus raised his glass towards Jamie.

"Here's to a fresh start. Sorry."

Jamie reluctantly clinked his glass. Jesus sat with good posture on the stool next to him. Jamie was slightly slouched now and feeling even more self-conscious. Jesus sipped at a steady pace and didn't check his phone, but was happy observing the goings on in the bar. Eventually, the silence was broken.

"Good day at work?" Jesus asked.

"God awful, hence I'm here,' Jamie barked. "And what is it *you* do?"

"I'm a Junior Doctor."

Jamie, while not impressed by this, was surprised by the answer. He certainly wasn't expecting that.

"You're a counsellor if I remember correctly."

"Yes, you've remembered correctly."

"I'm genuinely sorry about the other night. I wasn't sure if you'd taken G before and I lost track of time, but lesson learned."

"I ended up at A&E and I was given PEP, you'd think that someone in your position would be a little more careful." This verbal attack didn't perturb Jesus one bit.

"Like I said, I'm sorry. It wasn't my intention for you to have to go through any of that."

Silence descended on the pair. All the other groups were drinking and chatting. Jamie was now staring at his empty glass, as Jesus confidently signalled for two more. Jamie shook his head.

"I insist."

"No, I need to go home."

"Are you sure?" asked Jesus staring into Jamie's eyes.

"I don't want another drink but..." Jamie paused and looked around the bar "do you have any G on you?"

Jesus' smile widened.

"I thought you'd never ask. I think you actually need it and I'm a doctor."

"Doctors orders," Jamie joke saluted.

"Have you had any alcohol this evening?"

Jamie thought for a second and lied, "No just mocktails, it's a school night."

"G is dangerous if taken with any alcohol, I don't want you going to hospital again or worse."

Jamie just wanted to feel nothing and thought that the cosmopolitan from earlier would have worked it's way out of system already.

Two drinks arrived. Jamie picked his up and Jesus instructed him to lower it. Jamie complied and Jesus poured a liquid in. He took the other drink as Jesus added some G to his own glass.

"Bottoms up," Jamie said about to down the contents of the glass.

Jesus held his arm. "Slowly, slowly."

Embarrassed, Jamie took a small sip and placed his glass back on the bar. "I don't normally do this. I have a husband you know. I'm just going through some stuff at the moment." He tried to sound less serious but didn't succeed.

Jesus said nothing and just nodded. Jamie's phone vibrated in his pocket. He saw Tom had replied but ignored it.

"So where are you from?"

"I'm from Barcelona, you've been?"

"A few times."

"Do you miss home, your parents?"

"I do, that's why I try to visit them as much as I can and to escape the terrible British weather." They both laughed.

"Bad weather, bad food and boring men. Why come at all?"

"It's not all bad," Jesus replied seductively.

Jamie wasn't that naive to not notice the line but he didn't ignore it nor act upon it. He began to feel different. The dark bar had become brighter. The people nearest to him including the barmen appeared in sharper focus. He felt relaxed, which was what he had hoped the drinks would've done for him. Jesus seemed closer now. His facial features enhanced, he noticed his black eyelashes that stood watch over his dark chestnut brown eyes. The pattern of his stubble seemed more defined, trimmed perfectly. Jesus' eyes were locked on Jamie's. Jesus took another drink while Jamie saw the slow licking of Jesus' lips. His Adam's apple rose and fell in smooth, slow motion underneath his tanned skin.

"Feeling good Jamie?" Jesus asked while flashing his bright white teeth.

"So good, gracias."

Jamie leant forward as if he didn't see clearly. Leaning a little too far forward, he had to place both hands on Jesus' lap to stop him from falling over on the high bar stool.

"Take it easy," joked Jesus.

Jamie took his time to regain his balance. He felt the muscly thighs inside Jesus' jeans. He swore he felt heat rising from his crotch. He was aroused and he saw that Jesus was too. Jamie finished his drink and placed the empty glass back on the bar. Jesus mimicked this but being more in control, placed the glass back more gracefully.

"So what now?" Jesus asked.

"What now indeed! You live far from here?"

"I'm ten minutes in an Uber. Wanna call over?"

Without hesitation, Jamie replied, "Sure, let's go."

Jamie grabbed his bag and coat and was halfway out the bar leaving Jesus to pay for the drinks. The doorman wished him a good night but was ignored because he was distracted by the lights of the cars that passed him. He fumbled but eventually, he got his coat on. Jesus found him on the street, in the middle of the pavement, transfixed by the lights all around him, as if no one else was there. Jesus opened the door of the car that had pulled up just outside the bar.

"Your chariot awaits."

Jamie broke from gazing up at the sky and looked at him with watery eyes. Turning to his left, he saw a bald doorman looking at him with a concerned expression. Jamie looked back and got into the car. Jesus closed the door and dashed around to get in. He sat so close to Jamie that his nose almost touched Jamie's cheek. Jamie felt a rush of blood go right through his body and settle in his groin. While still looking at Jamie, Jesus gave the Uber driver the instruction to go.

Chapter 4

The sound of the house phone startled Jamie. Only half his face was visible as the other half was buried in the pillow. Both eyes suddenly opened but he appeared to be paralysed. His brain was slowly switching on. The phone continued to ring. He bolted out of bed and scrambled to the other side of the room, lifting the receiver. His heart was pounding hard. Before he heard anything, he struggled to figure out where he was and what time it was. The darkness outside made the call seem ominous.

"What's wrong?"

"Jamie is that you?" his mother enquired.

"Yes Mum, what's wrong?" slightly irritated by the fact that no one else called this number.

"It's your father; he's taken a turn for the worse."

A slight pause brewed. Jamie was no longer interested in the emergency. He slumped down on the floor.

"Okay," Jamie eventually said, feigning interest.

"Yes, well I think it means I won't be able to make it next week."

"You are *actually* joking?" Jamie was angry.

"There's no one to look after him, and he is really poorly, Jamie. If you were here, you'd see he's so frail now."

Jamie felt that was an attack on him and fired back. "Well, I'm not there, and now you aren't going to be here. Wonderful news!"

"Jamie, don't be like that. I know you don't really care, but I think this is it for him" her voice began to break.

"Then, that's that." Jamie hung up the phone with force.

He continued to sit on the floor, legs crossed with his head in his hands. Tom was propped up on his elbow underneath the duvet looking on silently. He knew that this was not going to be a good day. Not only had they a lot on, it being a week before their wedding, but he was now going to have to deal with an angry and heartbroken fiancée who had just found out his mother was not going to be at his wedding. After a few minutes had passed, Jamie rose and got back into bed with his back to Tom who was weighing up whether letting him be or hugging was the appropriate thing to do. Eventually, he decided to hug Jamie, who was in a foetal position. His body was cold from being out of the duvets protection. Tom hugged and spooned him. There was no resistance from Jamie. In the silent embrace, Tom could feel Jamie's body shudder as he struggled to keep the sobbing at bay. Tom placed his hand on Jamie's chest as if doing so would ease the pain from his hurting heart.

Jamie suddenly jumped out of bed and ran towards the corner of the room.

"Where is the phone? I need to call her back!" he screamed hysterically.

"What phone?" asked Max.

Startled by Max's presence, Jamie gestured to the corner of the room where there was a phone connection in the wall, but no phone. He stood wearing only his boxer shorts and looked like a toddler that had woken up in a strange house; tired, agitated and trying to fight through it but ultimately feeling lost and vulnerable.

"Maybe you should get back into bed," Max suggested, who was sitting on the only chair in Tom and Jamie's bedroom, reading a book.

"Where is the phone? Where is Tom? What are you doing here?" Jamie asked with little breath between each question. He was irritated by Max's calm demeanour. It gave him the impression that Max knew more than he did and that he was relishing it. Max closed the book, put it on the table beside him and looked up at Jamie.

"I think you should rest Jamie; it's been a long night."

Jamie looked even more confused as he looked at the corner where he believed the phone should've been and then back at Max, who was sitting in his bedroom.

"I think I'm losing it. This must be some sort of nightmare."

"It's all real Jamie. I'm here. You're here. There is no phone here, but I could call Tom and ask him if you'd like?"

"Tom? Where is he and why are you here?" Jamie demanded to know.

"Charming. Tom had to go to work early, and I brought you home last night," Max said smugly.

Jamie didn't move. He covered his slowly opening mouth with both hands. Max lay back in the chair; he knew the penny was dropping very slowly and that when it did, it was going to be entertaining. Jamie sat down on the floor and began to rock back and forth.

"What have I done? What have I done?" he asked himself.

Max began to feel sorry for him as he witnessed a grown man slowly break in front of him. He decided to ease Jamie's torment.

"You did nothing," Max tried to lighten the mood.

Jamie looked up. Only his eyes were visible. His hands were clasped around his mouth.

"You went back to Jesus' place, and before anything happened, you passed out. Jesus called me and explained what had happened. I brought you here in a cab."

"Does Tom know?" could be heard through Jamie's hands, his wide open eyes not blinking in horror, afraid of what was going to be said.

"He thinks you and I bumped into each other in Soho and we got pissed. I slept in the spare room and only came in here when I heard you whimpering. Tom left hours ago for work, where I should be really, but here I am again, rescuing you...*again*."

Jamie hid his face. Max picked up his book and looked for the point where he had left off. Every couple of sentences he would lower the book and check in on his patient. Jamie was relieved yet confused. He began to stare at the corner of the room.

"I need to call her back," whispered Jamie.

"Call who back?" Max asked, without lifting his eyes from the page.

"I need to tell her it's ok, that I understand." replied Jamie.

"Who?"

"She knows it means a lot and that I just snapped. I was tired. I am tired."

"Jamie, I think you should get back into bed. You're not making sense."

Jamie crawled across the floor to a pile of his clothes. Going through all his pockets, he searched for his phone. With each empty pocket, he became more agitated. Max stood up and went over to try and usher him back to bed. Jamie swung his arm out to break Max's hold on him.

"Leave me alone. You don't understand," Jamie urged through gritted teeth.

Max pulled out his phone. "I'll call Tom and ask about the phone, okay?"

Jamie sat on the bed defeated, "Okay."

Max dialled Tom's number and walked out of the room. He paced the landing willing Tom to pick up. Eventually, it went to his voicemail.

"Tom, it's Max, can you call me back ASAP?" He ended the call and turned to go back into the bedroom when Jamie, dressed in a hoody, tracksuit bottoms and flip-flops emerged at speed and ran down the stairs. Max dropped his phone and lunged to try and stop him but failed.

"Come back, Jamie!"

"I need to call her back and tell her it's ok."

Jamie began to walk in the direction of the town centre. There were lots of people walking on both pavements going in the same and opposite directions. All this movement made him feel on edge. Jamie felt his crotch quickly because he thought people were looking at him due to his zip being undone. There was no zipper on his tracksuit bottoms, so it wasn't that. He felt his hair with his hands and tried to smooth down some of the parts that he felt were out of place, but this didn't work. He flipped up the hood on his sweater and ploughed on with determination and fear.

Approaching a pedestrian crossing, he saw a group of people waiting for the green man. He stopped and waited, checking from underneath the hood at the people beside him. A young girl in shorts and t-shirt stared at Jamie while holding her mother's hand. The mother became aware that her daughter had gone quiet and looked down. She saw her looking at this hooded stranger and yanked her closer. A police car approached the crossing and began to slow. Jamie shoved his hands into his pockets and glanced forward. His heart began to speed up. He felt sweat forming on his brow and proceeded to bite his lip. Quickly, he stole a peek at the police car. The officer inside was looking at him. Jamie quickly looked away. The police car eventually stopped. Jamie stepped back from the crowd and pulled the hood further down on his face. A beeping noise started, alerting the pedestrians it was safe to proceed, and the group moved on leaving him exposed. Jamie froze for a moment and then jerked into action. He followed the crowd across the street. Every few steps he would look behind him. Every glass shop front was scanned for any trace of him being tailed. Once he was on the main street, he began to search up and down both sides for a phone box. He felt more and more people were in his way, so he walked on the double yellow lines of the road to avoid them. Due to the narrow roads and them being very busy, he was being beeped at by drivers who came dangerously close to him. Suddenly he stopped. Then came a loud, hard, deep horn. He whipped his head around and saw the black covering of a lorry's wing mirror rushing towards him. He ducked down and fell back on the road. As the truck carried on, fellow pedestrians came to his aid checking if he was ok, helping him back on his feet. Jamie didn't say anything and just ran off. The good Samaritans communicated in silence that he was rude and ungrateful and after their passive aggressive tutting and gasping had concluded, continued with their day.

Jamie couldn't find any public phones on the high street. He thought the only place left to look was the market. So he turned abruptly and careered through the people behind him with flailing arms like they were curtains. On entering Greenwich Market, he walked around the boundary of it thinking that logically, a phone would be here if anywhere. After two full circuits, he realised his search was pointless and sat heavily on a nearby bench, resting his hooded head in his hands. He felt hot and exhausted. With both hands, he pushed the hood off his sweaty head and lay back on the bench with his legs outstretched. In three breaths he passed out.

For over an hour Jaime had the bench to himself. No one wanted to sit beside a sprawled out hobo. Passers-by stopped and stared, and at one point there were a group of Spanish students who successfully took selfies of themselves with Jamie. They were eventually moved on by two community Police officers. Once the students had gone, they gently nudged Jamie. Nothing. Then the officers in tandem tried to shake him. Jamie slowly opened his eyes. The delayed reaction came, and they sought to calm him down. He was completely disorientated with no clue where he was or how he had gotten there.

"You're in Greenwich Market, sir. You are safe," said the female officer.

Her colleague had turned his back and was speaking on his walkie talkie.

"Is there someone we can call for you? Tell them that you're ok?" she continued.

On hearing the word "call", Jamie burst into tears. He suddenly remembered what had happened in his house, looking for the phone and Max being there. The officer placed her hand on his shoulder to calm him down. She gestured to her colleague to bring some tea back from one of the stalls. Jamie just looked around trying to get his bearings. The officer, seeing that this might take some time just sat down beside him and said nothing. She checked her notebook, and every few lines would glance at Jamie to see how he was.

Just as her colleague was arriving back with a styrofoam cup filled to the brim, a group of elderly ladies were passing by in high spirits. The tea bearer stepped back in a display of chivalry, nearly spilling the hot brew over himself. One of them stopped as her friends walked on.

"Jamie?" she asked in a soft, concerned voice.

He looked up and focused on her.

"Do you know this gentleman?" inquired the female officer.

"Well, yes I do, I suppose. His name is Jamie. Oh, I'm Teresa by the way," she said very apologetically. Teresa saw that Jamie wasn't himself so without thought or judgement she called out to her friends who had stopped to wait for her. "I'll see you girls next week if that's ok?"

They walked on neither sad nor happy about the sudden change of plans. She stepped over to the edge of the bench where Jamie was.

"Thank you so much, officers. I'll take it from here. I don't live far, and I'll put on a cup of tea and some sandwiches for Jamie, and he can get some rest."

"You sure you're ok with him?" enquired the male officer, a little put out that his tea was surplus to requirements but also worried for her safety.

"I'm sure, thank you though," she said politely, yet with authority.

The officer began to drink the tea and watched Jamie get to his feet and follow Teresa.

The short walk to Teresa's house was a slow paced one. Jamie was a few steps behind her for most of the way. Just before every road crossing, she would stop and half turn around to look at him. She hummed various melodies until they reached her house. Jamie focused on her sweet voice like she was the Pied Piper of Hamelin. He was becoming more aware of his surroundings and what was going on but there was still part of him that was dazed and a few steps and thoughts behind.

Stopped outside a house with a duck egg blue front door, she smiled as he approached her. Eventually, after more humming and with some rummaging for her keys, she found them. She opened the black metal gate and carefully opened the door and walked in. Turning to invite her guest to enter, she saw Jamie looking up at the house.

"Do come in," she said.

He didn't move. For a moment he was unsure if he should or even if this scene was real. The urgent need to find a phone had passed yet the residue of it was still around. Looking at her fixing her coat and hearing the melodies he felt whatever happened next, he was going to be safe at least. He walked in, and she closed the door gently behind him, placing her bag on the table by the door where she took off her coat. Passing him in the hall, she informed him that she would make some tea. She disappeared into the kitchen leaving Jamie to walk down the hall that was bedecked with photographs. Some were black and white and faded, but he could make out Teresa on her wedding day. She was very pretty in her long plain white gown. Her new husband in a policeman's uniform on one arm and white Calla lilies in the other. She was much smaller than he was but they looked right. Walking along he saw her age, photo by photo. Then the two became a three. Regardless of the change, there was togetherness and happiness oozing from each frame. The last picture which matched up to the Teresa he knew, was at what appeared to be a retirement dinner for her husband. He was standing in a dark suit, taller and greyer. Treasa's arm was linking his and in her other were calla lilies.

"Sugar?" was heard from the kitchen.

"No thanks," he replied awkwardly. He heard her repeat it to herself quietly as if she was remembering a large order at a restaurant. He checked himself and tucked his t-shirt in, flattened his hood and rolled up his sleeves before entering. The wooden kitchen was clean and tidy with everything in the right place. There were coasters beside a stack of placemats at the ready, near the large table at the other end. The kitchen towel hung from the beige Aga along with oven gloves. The display cabinets housed wonderful crockery, crystal glasses and a large decanter. The warmth of the Aga, the quaint kitchen and seeing Teresa zooming around preparing the tea was like medicine for him.

"Where shall I sit?" he asked politely.

"Wherever you want Jamie and welcome to my home," she said with great pleasure.

The table had six chairs, which was in the conservatory part of the kitchen. He sat at the top of the table and before Jamie could pull in his chair, a placemat and coaster were put in front of him, followed by a large cup of tea and some ham and cheese sandwiches. He didn't take a sip or nibble until she joined him.

"I hope it's ok," she said apologetically.

He drank some tea and made a noise of contentment which pleased her enormously. They both took a sandwich each and ate quietly.

"So, how have you been?" asked Teresa. She decided not to start by asking why the police were there.

"I've been good thanks, you?" he replied coyly.

"Fine, not a bother on me."

Then there was an awkward silence. Jamie could see her trying to come out with the right turn of phrase that wouldn't offend him. She took a gulp of tea hoping that Dutch courage was contained within the blue Denby cup.

"Why were the police there? Is everything…okay?" she said squirming inside. She wasn't a nosy person at all and hated that in others. She was just genuinely concerned.

Jamie, not surprised by her question and ultimately half expecting it, had a quick think.

"I'd a rough night last night and woke up craving some food. I must have sat down on the bench and just dozed off."

"I know that feeling. Not the rough night, even though I've had a few in my time, but the dozing off. Sometimes I'll get in from my walk, and I'm exhausted. The minute I sit down, I'm gone."

They shared a silent chuckle. Jamie hoped that she believed him. She hoped she hadn't offended him as she got up from her chair and made her way to the fridge, informing him she had some Swiss roll and that she wouldn't take no for an answer. She turned on some music while she beavered away. Jamie was surprised that she had an iPod and a speaker. Very modern he thought. The first song that came on wasn't one he knew, but he liked it and loved that Teresa was harmonising to it. Turning around to ask him if he'd like some ice cream, she saw his hand tapping the table and told him that The Andrew Sisters were a class act.

"Let's use the good sitting room, shall we?" she asked, standing with two plates.

Jamie had never heard of a good sitting room but followed her anyway. It was a room just off the kitchen which up to this point was closed. It was a very smartly decorated living room with a large leather sofa and matching chairs. Every table had an ornate lamp and some piece of crystal on it. There was no television, but it did have an old fashioned Hi-Fi system with quite an extensive CD collection underneath it. Jamie recognised albums based solely on seeing the design on the spine of some of the CD covers. A black, stand-up piano stood adjacent. He could tell it was cared for as its surfaces shone from being polished, daily he guessed. On top of the piano was a tiny easel which displayed a single CD. It had a black and white image on the front, with the silhouette of a lone figure who looked like he had wings. He went in closer to inspect. It was an album by Neil Young entitled *Harvest Moon*. Above it, hanging on the wall was a frame that contained the same albums cover as the background and had the lyrics of the title track printed on it. Along the bottom of the border it said:

Our Fifty Years Married Song.

Jamie imagined that this room was used for guests to be entertained. While it looked spotlessly clean, it seemed to him that it was rarely used. Coloured photographs of the family were placed strategically throughout and on the wall above the fireplace was a large university scroll. Teresa saw that he was reading it.

"That's my daughters," she said with great pride.

"Impressive."

"She was top of her class. She worked hard for it; got that from her father."

They sat and ate quietly, washing their dessert down with the tea until Jamie asked her about her daughter. She informed him that she was her only child and that she had married a few years ago. They lived in West Sussex and that they both had good jobs in the City. She talked about all the hours she worked and gave Jamie the impression that her daughter was financially well off with a big house and lots of foreign holidays. She looked so proud speaking about her. Jamie was reading between the lines and saw a widow in a lovely house not being visited by her only child, but he wouldn't bring that up.

The daughter's absence was like a scent that enveloped her, and after speaking her up to her guest, it had started to suffocate. She got up and took the plate from Jamie's lap and went into the kitchen to get more tea. He sensed that she enjoyed having company, but at this point, he felt she needed some space, so he didn't offer to help.

Teresa got out more Swiss roll from the cupboard and chopped a few slices. Armed with a plate and teapot that was still warm from the Aga, she came back into the sitting room to find Jamie had dozed off. Not annoyed by this, she stepped back into the kitchen as quietly as she could and placed the teapot back on the oven and put the cake in the fridge. She returned with a checked woollen blanket and gently covered him with it and left him in the room on his own. She had a contented smile on her face as she placed all the dishes that needed to be washed beside the sink, thinking it better to wash them after Jamie had woken up.

A vibrating sound came from her handbag in the hall. She retrieved it and answered it so quickly she was unable to see who it was from. It was her daughter, which took Teresa by complete surprise. Jamie woke to hear a very one sided conversation that sounded more like a cold caller. Teresa's daughter was ringing to find out how the counselling sessions were going but not in any way that would lead one to think the daughter was concerned about her mother. It was more akin to ensuring that her mother was aware that the sessions weren't cheap. Jamie squirmed inside as he heard Teresa replying 'yes' and 'no' to what seemed like a conversation fraught with tension. The ending was abrupt, and Jamie guessed that the daughter had hung up before Teresa had finished a litany of bye-byes.

There was silence for few seconds until Jamie heard the gentle folding of her mobile and he imagined her, in the hall, holding the phone in her hand, observing it before carefully putting it back into her bag and getting on with her day.

Jamie felt uncomfortable as he made his way back into the kitchen. The sight of him kicked her back into hosting mode where she offered another cup of tea and whipped out the Swiss roll from the fridge.

"I hope I haven't taken up too much of your time today, Teresa?"

"Don't be silly. I was kind of glad I met you, I was trying to get out of that meeting all week," she replied with a cheeky smile on her face.

"How come?"

"My social group is organising the Christmas dance, and well, I just wasn't feeling in the mood for it."

"They're talking about a Christmas party in my office at the moment. I'm certainly not feeling festive."

She raised her cup and said "Bah. Humbug!"

He joined her and clinked his tea cup off hers. She explained that every year the Greenwich Seniors held two dances for their members. One was during the summer to coincide with the Proms, and the other was their Christmas Dinner Party. She used to be very involved with the organising of these events and had developed a good circle of friends, but she just wasn't feeling the same this year. She and her husband both loved the event because it was a chance to show off how good they were at dancing. She told Jamie that people would make space for them when they saw him chivalrously extend his hand to her, inviting her to dance with him. It never ceased to make her feel young. Everyone talked about them and how they could watch them move around the floor for hours.

Teresa wanted to make sure she wasn't sounding big headed and told Jamie that she was completely oblivious to all the eyes that might have been watching. She said they were in their own little world. Her husband was light on his feet and lead her perfectly around the floor.

"It was our thing, dancing. At home he would put on a record or CD, and I'd be in the kitchen trying to cook the dinner, and he would just come in behind me, and we'd dance for a few moments," she recalled with fondness.

"That sounds so lovely," Jamie commented, not wanting her to stop.

"We used to joke that we'd both get the bus pass and do nothing but travel and dance. He would say that retirement would be our harvest time, reaping the benefits of working hard all our lives and that we'd enjoy our twilight years in each other's arms, dancing and laughing. When we met, he promised he'd work hard and that when we got to 75, we'd slow down and enjoy what time we had left in comfort. He just wasn't able to stay around for that special dance he'd promised."

Jamie could see her welling up. He didn't say anything as she stood up abruptly. She excused herself and disappeared into a bathroom that was in the hall, outside the kitchen. Jamie was heartbroken for her and in a moment of awkwardness began to wash the dishes they had used.

With no sign of Teresa, he dried them to fill the time. When all the cleaning was done, he crept very quietly to the bathroom door. He understood that she was upset, but he was worried that she might have slipped on the floor. As he neared the toilet door, he heard something, a whispering noise. His first feeling was relief that she hadn't slipped, but then, as he put his ear to the door, he recognised what she was saying and that in fact, she wasn't whispering, she was singing very quietly, the chorus of *Across The Universe*. Teresa sat on the lid of the toilet seat with wet tissues in her hand as she dried her eyes and repeated the chorus.

Jamie quickly tiptoed back into the kitchen, drank some tea and waited for his host to return, which she did in a gust of apologies and energy as if this would make him forget the last ten minutes.

They continued chatting, mainly about music this time, until Jamie informed her that he better get back home.

"Is that the time already? Your wife is going to wonder where on earth you are."

Jamie wasn't sure if he should correct her. He was happily married, and the people in his life knew he was gay, but he always struggled with strangers. Inside him, there was still that young boy that was scared of rejection. He may have been proudly married to a man but that uttering of the word husband meant coming out, again. Usually, it was to a hotel or restaurant when he was organising a surprise, which was less of an issue. When he would have to get builders or plumbers to call to the house for work to be done, he used 'other half' or 'partner' and hoped for the best.

"I'm gay, Teresa. I'm never sure when I should bring that up in conversation. My husband is Tom."

Teresa was a little flustered for a moment, and he saw this. It seemed like forever, but she did reply.

"You're an awful waste of a man," she sighed jokingly.

Jamie was relieved because he didn't want to have been this sympathetic to a homophobic pensioner.

As he was walked down the hall, he sensed a change. Her walk seemed slower, and her shoulders were more sunken, it was as if she had aged in the ten or so footsteps to the door. Jamie began to feel responsible for this transformation.

She stood in the doorway as he turned around to bid her farewell.

"Thank you for your hospitality," Jamie said with heartfelt sincerity.

"You're more than welcome, anytime."

Jamie had begun to turn and face the direction for home when he returned to face Teresa, who was about to start closing the door. She saw this, and this stopped her. He hadn't said anything but had a look on his face that said he was trying to come up with the right phrasing or the courage to speak out. Teresa thought she'd help.

"Did you forget something?"

"Do you want to meet for lunch on Friday?" he eventually asked.

Teresa wasn't expecting that. She dreaded the hourly sessions at her therapist's office and thought that lunch with Jamie would be something to focus on while she sat there wondering what on earth she was doing.

"That would be lovely. Is 1 pm ok?"

"It's a date," Jamie said with a cheeky smile.

"See you then."

Jamie's twenty-minute walk home was in stark contrast to his journey through the streets of Greenwich earlier that day. He was feeling lighter in himself and had forgotten about the previous night or even his interaction with Max that morning.

It was now evening, and the roads were rammed. The pavements were busy with commuters returning home after a tough day in London. He checked his watch, and for the first time today he knew what time it was and where he was. Tuesday evening was takeaway night as he re-entered his house and heard the shower running upstairs. A selection of takeaway menus were fanned out on the coffee table in the living room for them to decide where in the world they were going to dine from. A bottle of white wine and two wine glasses were placed on the kitchen table and beside these was an official letter from TalkTalk, the home phone provider. Jamie could see their logo on the top part, the rest of the letter was folded. Like he had been punched in the stomach, Jamie slumped down on one of the kitchen chairs.

The house went silent when Tom turned off the shower. His footsteps were then heard going from room to room, getting dried and dressed. He eventually came down with damp hair and was about to walk into the kitchen but stopped when he saw George sitting at the doorway being deathly still. He hadn't heard Jamie come in, but he suddenly became aware that he was no longer alone. Walking in slowly he saw what their cat was guarding. At the table, Tom saw his distraught husband sobbing. The table below him was damp from tears that looked like they'd never stop. Jamie looked up, and Tom saw a red faced man who looked lost, whose tears were blinding and exhausting him. Now both George and Tom were at the doorway looking on. They didn't know how they should approach it. Act normal and ignore it, that seemed harsh. Run over and hug him so hard that in some way he absorbed some of his hurt and tears, he felt that approach would suffocate him. George flicked his tail and looked at his floundering owner as if to say 'do something.'

Jamie picked up the letter from TalkTalk and slowly stood up causing the chair he'd been sitting on to make a screeching sound. Standing up Jamie looked more pathetic. Tom could see that he was using all his might to hold in and muffle a mighty sob that seemed to be brewing up from deep inside him. Jamie face contorted and reddened and became even wetter but eventually, his mouth opened.

"Thank you!" was all he said followed by eruptions of pain and anguish. Tom ran to him and enveloped him his arms. His right around his back and his left hand on the back of Jamie's head. Tom knew he didn't need to say anything, just hold. He could feel Jamie weakening with each sob. George was now on the kitchen table, calmly watching the two men standing, holding and not speaking.

He knew what he was being thanked for. They joked that they were the only people they knew who had a landline in their home. Tom saw the bill come through the door, which was addressed to Jamie and even though Tom never used it, he felt that cancelling the bill and removing the landline phone from the house without Jamie noticing would've been helpful. Tom had discussed this with Jules over text messages for days.

The ritual of Jamie calling his mother was very much alive for both men. The last five Sunday afternoons had caused Tom to panic as he fretted over how Jamie would be or react when he felt it was time for "the call."

For Jamie, the routine of life had delivered a blow of reality with each Sunday that had passed since he buried his mother. A routine is a routine because of repeated actions. Losing someone doesn't alter the schedule discreetly. Instead, the routine does its thing; an urge to do something out of habit. Sometimes Jamie registered the feeling and without thinking began to move to go and make the call. Jamie wanted to make a plea and fight the case that he'd always done this on a Sunday but that didn't matter. It left him alone, and shell shocked like he had been told again, for the first time of his loss. It hurt because he was reminded. He was disappointed in himself for being so stupid and thinking that he might have forgotten about it but most of all he felt guilty that for some part of that day, he lived life like it was normal.

Finally, Jamie's sobs became less violent and frequent. George was now lying on the table looking on. Jamie announced he was okay with two pats on Tom's back which triggered Tom to release his supportive grip. Jamie tried to dry the shoulder of Tom's t-shirt which was wet but Tom placed both his hands on Jamie's face, kissed his forehead and ordered him to shower and that he could choose where they dine from. Jamie shuffled out of the kitchen, placing the letter from the phone company in the bin.

Chapter 5

Like clockwork, Teresa arrived at the market at 1 pm. Her session finished ten minutes prior and like every other one she'd been to; she couldn't wait to leave. Jamie greeted her with tea and a sandwich. She offered money, but he wouldn't accept it. They went over to the glass atrium to eat and drink, and because they were both starving, they did so in silence, on one of the few unoccupied benches. It didn't take long for him to have finished both halves of his pastrami on rye while Teresa had completed only one. She put the other half neatly away in her handbag, telling Jamie she'd have it for her tea later.

"Shall we?" asked Jamie.

She stood up and they both, without discussion began to walk out of the market and onto Bankside, along the Thames. It was a little windy, but they had dressed appropriately.

"Need I ask?" enquired Jamie.

She didn't reply apart from rolling her eyes and smiling.

"Same?"

"Yes." She told him how she dreaded going to see her therapist and how she couldn't really talk to him. She described a well-dressed man with tanned skin and gelled back hair who sat behind a large desk. She joked that she had never seen him without a pen in his hand and expected a caricature drawing at the end of each fifty-minute session because of his incessant scribbling when she was hardly saying anything, certainly nothing worthy of writing down.

"What were you talking about today?".

"Well, to be honest, I hadn't slept very well last night, so I was a little bit grumpy with him. I think he sensed it, so he asked me a few questions."

"Anything in particular?"

"Not that I was aware of, well, I think he was trying to get me to talk about my husband, which I just didn't feel like doing, not to him at least. He is very word light this man, so I never know what he really wants."

A few joggers were making their way towards them, chatting amongst themselves with minimal regard to what was in their way. Jamie stopped and ushered Teresa back to the railings that ran along the river. She turned around to look across the choppy Thames. He began to walk on but saw that he was doing it alone so returned.

"You ok?"

"I'm fine, just a little tired."

"Any more of those funny turns?"

"To be honest, I feel one coming on now," she said with an embarrassed and frightened face. Her eyes were darting from side to side to see if anyone else was watching as she held on to the railings. Jamie grabbed the railings too, looked out and began to inhale loudly and with great effort, signalling her to do the same. She could see his eyes were closed. Her breathing was shallow and fast, so she tried to loosen the scarf that was around her neck, but was unable to really concentrate and hadn't the dexterity at that very moment to perform such tasks. Jamie opened his right eye to take a peek and saw her panicking. He loosened her scarf for her and looked straight into her eyes.

"All we need to do is breathe. This wobbly moment is going to pass. Breathe with me."

He returned his hands to the railings, stood tall, looked out across the river and began his exaggerated breathing. Feeling relief from the scarf now draped down her shoulders, Teresa felt she'd nothing to lose and so mimicked him. It took her a few breaths to close her eyes, but eventually, nothing but concentrating on her breathing filled her head. The wind had picked up which blew her tears across and eventually off her face. Shaking her head in defiance and doubling her efforts, she heard Jamie humming *Across The Universe* which made her smile and join in.

Joggers, tourists and workmen went by, but they were too busy to take notice. A city like London affords people the freedom to generally do what they like, once it wasn't too intrusive, which this certainly wasn't. A relaxed expression began to spread across Teresa's soft face. Jamie quickly opened his eyes and saw her, head tilted up, eyes closed, looking serene as the wind blew at her hair.

He let out an audible sigh to signal he had finished. Slowly opening her eyes, she turned to him, smiled and silently mouthed a 'thank you.'

"You know, I've been trying this out, this breathing thing and when I remember or before the dreaded feeling has caught a good hold of me, it does work," she said proudly.

"I know it works, but sometimes, the feeling sets in too quickly, but that's ok."

Walking a little slower now, down the bank of the river, they joined the tourists taking in the sites of this bustling part of the city. Behind them was St. Paul's Cathedral, they could just about see the House's of Parliament in front of them. They were about to pass the jetty they had ventured on the last time they went for a walk. It was occupied by a photographer working with a newly wedded Asian couple. The wind was playing havoc with her veil. The groom did his utmost to hold it behind them as they posed, smiled and looked lovingly into each other's eyes. Teresa commented on the dress and how happy they looked. Unable to walk down the jetty they had a rest on a nearby bench.

"It's all ahead of them," she said, transfixed by the newly weds. Jamie was looking at a TV crew dismantling cameras to his left as they headed back into a nearby studio.

"It sure is. I remember the day going by so quickly."

"Mine too."

"How did you both meet, if you don't mind me asking?"

"I don't mind at all," she replied, focusing on Jamie and leaving the windswept couple to have their moment.

July 1964 and it was a glorious summers day, one of those days you always remember because it was so hot, with no clouds in the sky and that occasional welcomed breeze. Everyone was pleasant, helpful and happy. Teresa had just turned twenty-three and her birthday present from all her family was a trip to England. No fancy hotels or B&B's, the trip alone was more than her family could afford hence she stayed with relatives in Broadstairs, a much loved Kent coastal hotspot. She was from Meath, a county in the middle of Ireland and had been to seaside towns before, but Broadstairs was picture postcard worthy.

She had arrived the night before after the mammoth journey across the Irish sea. Sharing a bedroom with her cousin Lily meant little rest but plenty of talking throughout the night. Her slightly older and more worldly cousin helped her with her outfit. This was Teresa's first time to wear a miniskirt, something that would've been the talk of the town back home, but not here. It was a multicoloured, floral pattern which she wore with a white buttoned top, flat shoes and a cardigan which would go straight into her bag after they left the house.

Her cousin was more daring, wearing an even shorter mini skirt and flowing top with flared cuffs. She tied two ribbons, one yellow and the other red, around each leg, from her ankle to just below the knee, tying it off with a small bow.

Cheekily, Lily did something with the belt around Teresa's mini skirt that shortened the length. This made her feel slightly embarrassed. While the tucking and pulling were going on, Lily explained that without this, how would she find herself an English husband. They giggled like school girls to the annoyance of Lily's mother, who was a cantankerous old woman who constantly harked back to the good old days of Ireland. When the music and laughter got too much, she would shout up the stairs "empty vessels make the most noise," which only made everything funnier.

They presented themselves in the front room. Lily's mother looked up from her knitting and made a sound that was indecipherable. Neither of the girls knew if it was of disdain or delight. Lily just grabbed her handbag and informed Marie or Mrs McBurney, that they'd be out all day. Teresa's hand was grabbed, and she was dragged to the front door. Lily knew there'd be lists of do's and don't's pinging off her mothers lips and she already knew them but she just didn't want to hear them as she felt that it would have had some negative impact on the day that lay before them.

The beach was full, the donkeys were in full employment, and the ice cream van couldn't churn out quick enough. They strolled along the beach at a slow pace, looking at all the sunbathers and swimmers, checking out the people outside their beach huts and those under the veranda who found the heat all too much while The Beatles' *Hard Days Night* was being played from various portable radios.

Amongst the rows of windbreakers, demarcating each families section of Kent coast, Lily spotted a family decamping rather quickly. Teresa just turned around to see her cousin running ahead, with a group of young men seemingly running after her. When she caught up with Lily, she began to hear what all the fuss was about. The family were leaving because one of the children had been stung by a bee and from the looks of him, was allergic to bee stings. Lily had cunningly noticed this and was there to claim their spot. The three men were arguing with Lily saying they saw it first but she wasn't having any of it. Standing a little back from them, Teresa looked on in admiration at her cousins' brazen approach. The mother and child pushed passed her, leaving a clumsy Dad to try and take down the windbreaker, the deckchairs and somehow get these back to their car in one go.

Feeling uneasy with the tension and not helped by the heat, Teresa lent a hand to the floundering father and began to pack up his things. He thanked her while wiping beads of sweat from his brow. She offered to carry some of his things back to the car, but he said that she'd done enough.

Lily was still standing her ground and not giving in to the group of men. They all looked like copies of each other in their flared jeans. Two of them, the most vocal out of the group, were wearing white shirts with very few buttons buttoned and their sleeves rolled up while the other stood awkwardly silent, dressed in a blue shirt. They caught each other's eye and communicated that they were both feeling embarrassed and just wanted to sit down to enjoy the day.

Finally, a truce was agreed which meant that they would share the space. Lily put down two towels, and the three guys just sat on the sand beside them. They didn't possess any towels, or wind breakers, just a few cans of larger, some sunglasses and a portable record player. Lily flicked off her shoes with abandon, used her bag as a pillow, slowly put on her sunglasses and laid back not before hiking up her skirt slightly which got the boys whistling. Lily tried to disguise a smile by biting her lip.

Teresa tried to copy her confident cousin and nearly pulled it off except that when she flicked off her shoe, it landed in the lap of the blue shirted young man. She was paralysed by the mortification of it but he simply and calmly walked over and placed it beside her.

"I believe this belongs to you," he said with a cheesy smile.

"I'm so sorry. Thank you. Sorry again!"

"It's quite alright. I'm Bill by the way."

She removed her sunglasses rather clumsily and saw an outstretched hand. She delicately clasped it and said, "I'm Teresa, how do you do?

"You're a Paddy?"

"So what if she is?" Lily inquired, not impressed by his casual racism.

"Lily!" Teresa said, trying to calm her.

"Sorry, I didn't mean anything by it. I just love the accent," Bill qualified.

The other lads were cheering on their mate.

"You'd wanna watch that lad, he has a soft spot for Irish girls," piped one of Bill's friends.

He threw them a look. "Would you like to go for a walk, Teresa?"

The sound of her name from this tall, dark haired, English man made the hair on the back of her neck stand on end. She had never experienced such bravery from a man before. His blue eyes, squinting in the sunshine dazzled above a smile that made her feel safe. He might as well have been from another planet, as her experience with men thus far was a world away from this suave approach. Her dancehall days in Ireland were marred by the local men needing too many pints to work up the courage to even ask her for a dance. She loved nothing more than to be on the dance floor but because they were so intoxicated, it never turned out the way she dreamed.

Lily's sunglasses were lifted off her face as she observed what was going on. She wasn't jealous at all and would say weeks later that she knew that Bill and his two mates had indeed spotted the family leaving before her, she just fancied one of them and thought it was a good way to start a conversation.

Teresa agreed to a walk along the waters edge with Bill. A few steps away from the safety of her towel and cousin, the boys jeered him on. Lily playfully told them to shut up. The cool water of the English channel felt good on their hot feet as they meandered up and down the beach. Walking in-between other strollers and children racing in and out of the water, they disclosed more and more about themselves. In fact, it wasn't until they had been up and down the same stretch three times that Teresa realised that she had talked about herself. She apologised for yakking on, but he was ever so polite and said that he loved listening to her and not just for her accent.

She had filled him in on her history, and she was determined to hear his which he did modestly. She found out that he was an only child, like her and that his father was a police officer and his mother was a teacher. He was from Charlton in London and was thinking about following his father's footsteps to join the MET. He loved music, dancing, cars and going to the pictures. He seemed to idolise his mother, which for an Irish girl, was always a good sign. It was easy talking and listening to him. There was no pressure to be a certain way or to say things to seem cool. It was so relaxed and the time just flew by without them noticing it.

They had lost count of the number of times they had walked up and down. They eventually saw Lily and Bills' mates waving from the exit of the beach. She was holding her belongings aloft, indicating it was time to go. As they approached, they all had smiles on their faces. Lily declared that it was time they were bought some ice cream. The men were compliant which amused both girls. Lily really did know how to get what she wanted. She marched the group up the street and to an incredibly busy ice cream emporium.

Morelli's was absolutely jammed packed inside, with a queue that stretched down the high street. Lily knew from experience that they weren't going to get a seat, so she shooed the men to join the queue and instructed them to bring back something cold and tasty. She grabbed her cousin, and they just laughed as they waited on a bench nearby. Lily wanted all the gossip on what was discussed. Teresa regaled her on the afternoon with Bill and the highlights of their chat. Lily also had a productive afternoon as she got James' number and was going to go to London the following weekend.

The sun was fading, but there was still heat in the day as they sat on the bench letting the world go by. Teresa could've been in Monaco. She felt, for the first time, that she was glamorous and grown up. She kept thoughts of returning to Ireland at bay for they would do nothing but suck the technicolour of life from that very moment.

The girls heard a cough. Opening their eyes and raising their shades, they saw the three guys licking at large ice creams. James presented Lily with a large cone that was sprinkled with a multicoloured collection of toppings and dripping in reddy translucent syrup. She wasn't pleased nor silent about it. Reluctantly she snatched it from his hand and tried but failed to enjoy it without it dripping down her top. Bill presented an immaculate vanilla ice-cream with a large chocolate flake in it.

"I hope it's ok?" he asked

"It's perfect, thank you," she replied.

Lily nudged her to stand up which she did uncomfortably. Bill invited her over to the railing that ran along the path which overlooked the beach, the pier and the sea. The sun was calming as it started it's decent. They quietly ate their ice-cream, taking in the beautiful view. Bill noticed that an elderly couple on a nearby bench had caught her eye. They were both hunched over eating their ice creams. They had thick rimmed glasses on, and the lady wiped some of the white drips from the man's cone that made their way to his chin. Teresa smiled.

"When we get married, that'll be us in 50 years time," Bill said with confidence and charm.

"And that's how we met," was how Teresa ended the story with a slight sigh of fondness and sorrow.

"Wow, that sounds like a movie."

"I suppose it was," she chortled. "Do you mind if we keep moving, I'll seize up otherwise."

They both stood up and silently resumed their walk, allowing the story to percolate. Any other conversation would've sounded banal in comparison to Teresa and Bill's first meeting, but Jamie knew he had to get back to work. Before he did, there was something they needed to do. Ahead of them, he saw a silver Airstream caravan which sold mini doughnuts, burgers and chips, but most importantly, it served ice creams.

"Fancy an ice cream?" Jamie asked with a smile on his face.

"Only if it's my treat."

"Go on then," he conceded.

She ordered two plain cones with a chocolate Flake in each while Jamie waited by the railings behind the caravan. Handing over his cone to him she raised her own.

"To my Bill."

"To Bill," Jamie repeated.

They fell silent as the licked their cone, expertly not letting it run down on to their hands. Jamie commented that there was nothing like a plain cone. Teresa agreed wholeheartedly. Once they were all done, they both knew it was time to depart.

"Same time next week?" Jamie said without thought or awkwardness. Teresa was a little surprised, not that she didn't enjoy spending time with him but the fact that he wanted to see her again.

"Absolutely, can't wait," she said.

They exchanged numbers in case the meet wasn't possible for either of them.

"Perfect. See you at the market and remember to breathe, hum or sing."

"I will. Well, I'll try," she said with a semi serious, determined face.

"That's all you can do. Thanks for the ice cream."

Without handshakes, he headed back to work, and she walked further down the Southbank and over the Hungerford Bridge where she got a train back to Greenwich.

Nearing the office, Jamie received a text from his boss asking him where he was. Out of character for his boss, this message put him on edge as he picked up the pace. When we got to his desk, there was a Post-it and an email instructing him to go to the office once he got it.

Under the email was another from Rebecca. Its subject was in capitals and a number of exclamation marks. He did exactly what the short email instructed him to do and went to the bathroom. His boss could see him from his desk and made some gesture that questioned where he was going. Jamie pleaded in silence, indicating a desperate need to go to the loo.

He got into the cubicle and waited. Within seconds, Rebecca barged into the unisex toilets. Jamie opened the door quickly, and she informed him that Jonathan was on some administration blitz and saw that Jamie hadn't attended supervision since he returned back to work. He thanked her, and she left immediately to curb any suspicion. There was no way around this one he thought.

In truth, he had been avoiding supervision which he had never done before. He really missed the input Helen gave to him on his client work. Her insights into the struggles that Jamie encountered through his work were invaluable and only highlighted the importance of having another pair of ears involved when counselling. The bit he was dreading was the other part of the supervision process which was more about how Jamie was feeling, how he was doing and ultimately how he was coping after returning to work, which was the exact reason he had booked clients in at the times he would otherwise have had supervision, adding them on to his list as emergency cases.

He left the communal bathroom and approached Jonathan's office with a fake, carefree abandon which quickly faded when he saw that his boss wasn't alone. Jamie walked in and saw Helen sitting across from Jonathan. He gave a greeting that was a mix of 'happy to see you,' 'it's been ages,' 'really need to see you.' Neither Helen nor Jonathan were actually buying it, and he was told to take a seat.

Jonathan started by thanking the supervisor for coming in, then he turned to Jamie and asked him why he hadn't been to see her since his return when he had instructed him to do so. Looking at both people in the room and knowing that there was no way he was going to fool either of them he became dumbstruck. His mouth was open, and it looked like he was desperately waiting for something to emerge that would make everyone happy and end the meeting. Jonathan began to scribble things on a notepad which Jamie had never seen him do before. Helen also saw it and came to the rescue.

"Jamie, I can only imagine how you are feeling. It is wonderful that you are back to work, but I do wonder if it's too soon. Regardless, you are here, and you've started to see clients again. I know how active you are in our sessions and how you value them, but believe me, you need them more than ever, in fact, I would go as far as saying you will never need our sessions more than you do now. We are obviously concerned about the clients, as you are, but we are also worried about you. Does that make sense?" Helen delivered this in a very soft and thoughtful way.

Jamie just nodded because he couldn't really speak and he also couldn't argue with anything she had just said.

Jonathan tried to place his pen down without making a sound, but they both heard it and looked at him expectantly.

"That's settled then. I see you've no clients booked in this afternoon, so Helen is here to have a supervision session with you where you'll both have your diaries and put in place more regular sessions, understood?" Jonathan was asking, but in truth, he was telling Jamie this was how it was going to be.

"Understood," Jamie complied.

Helen excused herself and said that she needed five minutes. Jamie thanked them both and went back to his desk. Rebecca looked intently at Jamie as he sat there, in shock. She looked around to see if anyone was watching her, then quickly checked in with Jamie by text message. He replied straight away confirming that he was okay. He deleted a few emails and looked at his online calendar. Jonathan had put him down for a double supervision session, which meant a whole two hours of it. The thought of dashing out for a quick coffee and not coming back did cross his mind, but he knew that the next two hours were going to happen and they were going to happen in the supervision room. Jamie left his phone at his desk, filled his water bottle and headed to the back of the office where Helen was waiting for him. Rebecca whispered a 'good luck' as he passed by.

The supervision room was designed exactly like the client rooms except in this scenario, Jamie was on the couch. The rooms were minimalistic with no paintings on the wall, just a floor lamp that arched over the couch and a box of tissues on the arm. Helen put down what she was reading, crossed her legs and sat in silence while she waited for Jamie to sit and begin. He nervously took a drink of water, placed the bottle on the floor to his right and smiled awkwardly at Helen. She didn't reciprocate but had a welcoming expression.

"I feel like it's my first ever session with a therapist and all I really want to say is 'I don't know what to say.' "

Helen didn't play ball and just sat in utter calmness, not really moving and without changing her friendly expression. Jamie decided on how to approach this and began to talk about his client work. He mentioned Dwayne's name and spent quite a while discussing their last session; the passing of Dwayne's dog and how this had impacted on him. Jamie was thoughtful in how he presented his client and was open and grateful for any input or suggestion that he might not be on the right track. After nearly thirty minutes of presenting Dwayne, Jamie finished and waited for Helen. She sat silently throughout, nodding in certain places which wasn't unusual. Jamie always appreciated that she allowed him space whenever he needed to describe and explain what he was thinking on where the sessions with his clients were going.

"I have two questions really Jamie, and I'm not sure how related they are to Dwayne."

"Okay," Jamie said with trepidation.

"You normally have your notes with you, and you don't today, so I just thought I'd ask why that is…"

"And that other question?" Jamie wanted to know what he was dealing with before answering anything.

"Why were you late back from lunch today?"

All the reasons he admired Helen as a supervisor were all the reasons he hated her right now. She missed nothing, and because she had been his supervisor since he started work, she knew him better than Tom or any of his friends.

"I just forgot the files; I can go and get them if you'd like?"

"It's just not like you. I know how meticulous you are about your clients and that you usually take notes from our sessions so, it's just unusual to see you here with just your bottle of water and that sort of coincides with the other question. You're never late, in fact, you're always early and as you would in your sessions if you noticed things about someone's behaviour, wouldn't you point them out?"

Jamie was trapped. Of course, she was right; he would be the first person to be asking those questions, wondering what was really going on.

"Did you meet someone for lunch? Tom?" Helen enquired.

"No, well, yes actually. Just someone I met a couple of weeks ago at London Bridge."

"An old friend?"

"A new, old friend actually," replied Jamie comically.

Helen sat without responding which meant that Jamie had to disclose more.

"It's an odd thing, I was coming through the station a couple of weeks ago, and this lady was unwell, and we sort of got to know each other from there." Jamie stared at the floor because looking at Helen would have made him elicit more information. Saying all this out loud sounded strange, it sounded very un-London-like.

Helen commented on how chivalrous he was and how random acts of kindness were what the city needed. Jamie nodded his head like a child who thought he was in trouble. Helen hadn't changed her posture but had now a quizzical look. He didn't look away but continued with intrigue to observe her seemingly struggle to articulate her next sentence or question. This was a first for him. She always knew the right thing to say but more importantly, when to say it or indeed, not to, but here she was struggling. Jamie wanted to help her because it was starting to unnerve him. He sat up on the chair and took another sip of water.

"Sorry Jamie, how come you met for lunch today if you met her a while back?" she asked with great intrigue.

Jamie wondered how he would answer this without it sounding weird.

"The day we met, we actually met again in the market where I normally go for lunch. It was one of those random moments in life, and well, it happened again."

"What did?" she asked interrupting him.

"We met again, sort of by accident and yeah, I can't really explain it any better than that."

"Okay," was all she could respond with. She began to write a few lines in her book, and all Jamie could do was imagine what it said.

His leg started bouncing up and down with agitation. Helen took note of it by just looking at his leg and raising her eyebrow slightly. He tried his best to stop it, thinking that drinking some more water would distract him. He felt that the session should be nearing the end but because the clock in the room was behind him he wasn't sure and checking his watch in this situation would bring on another set of questions from Helen.

Quietly closing the notebook, she asked him was there anything else about his clients he wanted to bring up today as they had another hour left. Dejected by the time check, for once he wished he had more work to present, something, anything that would fill the hour that stretched before him. He informed her that he was getting back to client work slowly, so that was all he had today.

"So, tell me how you've been, how you've really been since the death of your parents?"

Jamie felt like he'd been shot and was unable to move from the sofa. Shocked by the directness and the preciseness of her words but also the lack of apologising or sympathising that everyone else who knew would always start off with.

"It's been hard, to be expected I suppose but I'm glad to be back to work as that keeps my mind active."

"So, work is a distraction for you? A coping mechanism?"

"No, I didn't mean it like that..."

"What do you mean?" she asked calmly.

"I suppose, I just want to get on with things. Nothing I do is going to change what has happened, and I have a life, a home and a husband, and I just want to get on with that."

"I get that, so how are things with yourself and Tom?"

Jamie thought about how annoyingly good she was at her job.

"It's been tough on both of us. I've told him to treat me the same and not to create any fuss which, for the most part, he has done, but he's very different to me, and well, I think he wants to take care of me and talk about things more."

"And you don't?"

"No, not really," he said defiantly.

"You see this as a good thing, a healthy thing, not talking?"

"What's the point Helen, the result is the same."

"Which is?"

"Talking about it doesn't bring her back."

They both took a second, allowing the emotional echoes to settle down in the room.

"And yet, you have encouraged Dwayne to talk about the loss of his dog. What was the point in that, actually you've spent the last hour or so telling me the point of all of that, and I agree whole heartedly with you. So why are you different? Why doesn't it apply to you? Is it because you're a counsellor and you should be above this?"

Jamie was hurting. He felt like he was being punished by the truth. He knew he wasn't above feeling like this, but there was also part of him that thought that maybe he could do this, that he didn't need help. He was wrestling with anger and vulnerability: professional him and personal him, strength and weakness.

Being an experienced counsellor herself, Helen imagined the struggle inside of Jamie and didn't need to probe him anymore. She set out dates for their supervision and said that she was glad to see him but that she was concerned he had come back too soon. Jamie was expecting to be sent home like someone who had come into work drunk, but this was short-lived as she quickly followed it up by saying she wanted to keep an eye on him and that he should think about how he's coping and not to under estimate the power of his loss.

Jamie thanked her for her frankness but couldn't wait to leave the room. Emerging back in the office, Rebecca directed him to the exit with a nod. She waved her hand that held his coat. On the way out of the building, she told him that she had been glued to the corridor, waiting for him to reappear, knowing that he would need a strong coffee. He was so glad to be out of the office. After getting two flat whites from their nearest cafe, they perched on a window ledge. Jamie was cradling his takeaway cup with both hands, looking directly at the lid. Even though her coffee was still too hot, she sipped away at it to relax. A few silent moments had passed, and after burning her tongue, she had to say something.

"How was it?"

"What, supervision? Yeah, it was fine. She's great, isn't she?" replied Jamie casually.

"Yeah."

More sips were needed as she clocked that Jamie wasn't his usual chatting self.

"How's Pedro, any improvement?" Jamie inquired.

Rebecca was thrilled by the conversation opening up a bit. She began to tell him that things with her new Spanish boyfriend had blossomed and that the cultural differences she thought were an issue, really weren't. As she went into detail, he observed her on the ledge talking but not listening. She was so pretty with her blonde hair, blue eyes and bashful manner. He wished she could be more confident with the men she dated and hoped that she would, one day find the courage to put her needs out there. Some of her red lipstick was on the coffee cup, she had noticed it too and rubbed it away with her thumb.

"Shall we go back?" was what he heard next and it re-engaged his brain to focus on the now.

As they climbed the stairs to the office he thanked her; he had needed that.

Trying to look like they were having a work related discussion, they re-entered the office.

"Jamie, your mobile hasn't stopped ringing," Jonathan announced loudly when he saw his two employees back in the office.

He quickly ran to his desk and saw a number of missed calls from a withheld number and one voicemail. Sitting down, he called to listen to the message. It was brief, but the impact was anything but. He ended the message by pressing the screen with force. He placed both elbows on his desk and covered his face with his hands and whispered to himself "this is never ending."

Chapter 6

A dark and dank October morning meant many things: umbrellas, winter coats and traffic jams, even the bus lanes weren't moving. Tom and Max were comfortable and warm in the back of their taxi. Peering out from their blacked out car they were grateful not to have to travel like the Londoners they spied, who looked miserable waiting for the green man to allow them to proceed. Tom had great sympathy for those who walked, train-ed, Tubed or bused their way to work each and every work day. As a trainee hairdresser, he had to do the very same, six days a week. His route varied slightly as he began to move from salon to salon, always progressing in each location. He worked hard and did extra hours, but he knew it would eventually pay off. The taxi that had collected him from his home that morning would also bring him back after his long day, so knew how lucky he was.

Being younger meant that Max was also less experienced than his boss. He was one of those people who always landed on their feet and without fail got ahead quicker than his peers. He didn't work as hard or for as long as Tom, so was less appreciative of where he was in the world, which sometimes annoyed Tom. Tom couldn't remind him of the difficult days because Max didn't have them. His life started with wealthy parents, and now he had an even richer boyfriend. His phone battery was waning, and it was only 8 am. Tom glanced over and saw his colleague's phone buzz and whirl to notify its frustrated owner he had another message. Tom could see that he was using at least three different hook-up apps at the same time which made it clear to Tom at least, why his battery was depleted. Rather than comment or judge, he pointed to the consul in between the two front seats which had a USB connection for him to keep his personal life going. Max thanked him like he had been hungry and Tom had offered him food.

They were heading to a West London studio to do hair for a music video. Awkwardly they both didn't know the name of the band and were frantically Googling and YouTubing videos once the call had come in. Music videos were exciting work days, interspersed with lots of sitting around until the director shouted 'cut,' when they'd spring into action to either fix or restyle.

Max saw Tom sending a text to Jamie and began to probe. He asked him how Jamie was doing. Tom answered him when the text message was sent.

"I was just texting him there. He's heading back home today. He got a call from the family solicitor because they want to read out the will and put his parents' affairs in order. I was just texting him to wish him luck."

"Did you not want to go with him?" Max pried.

"Of course I did, but he wanted to go on his own, you know what he's like?"

"Big day for him?"

"I just hope he's ok."

Tom's text came through just as Jamie's train began to chug its way out of Euston Station. The Quiet Carriage was always a disappointment for him. It never was what it intended to be. He obeyed the rules with his phone on silent, never answering calls and keeping the volume down on his earphones, sometimes even taking them out and listening to check he wasn't being too loud when he got a strange look from another passenger, but everyone didn't adopt his approach. He always booked this carriage in the vain hope that it would be what it was meant to be and that he would arrive relaxed at his destination, but more times than not, he disembarked stressed and agitated.

The last time he travelled to Ledbury, Tom was with him. They couldn't get a quiet carriage as it was all very last minute. They didn't talk the whole way there or back. A funeral wasn't an event one looked forward to or discussed how excited or otherwise one was about it. Jamie wanted to remain numb, and Tom knew this, so he tried to comfort his husband with his silence.

Jamie spent the three-hour journey trying to read a book, with very little success. His distractions weren't external. He kept reading the emails the solicitor had sent. He couldn't really understand the jargon but knew that he was being picked up at the station and if he needed it, he could get a lift back. He was going to do some research about inheritance or the best questions to ask, but he couldn't muster the energy.

Before his parent's death, returning to his childhood home was done once a year and was as brief as he could make it. Two nights was the most he could bear. He had left the small town years ago. Coming home filled him with dread, so he never wanted to return. He would see classmates who were older, fatter, balder, some with kids some without and he would feel superior, and he didn't want to feel like that. He knew that life choices were for people to choose. He wanted to leave, and others didn't, this was perfectly okay, but he couldn't shake off the notion that he was better than them, even though he knew he wasn't. On previous trips, Jules would be waiting outside Euston in a black cab, where she would take him to Soho, and they would do a shot and a cocktail to somehow cleanse him from country life; the life that might have been.

As the train pulled out of Droitwich Spa, an email came through from Tom. He smiled as he hadn't sent him one of these for quite some time. It was a Gift from iTunes. From time to time they both sent each other the gift of a song depending on what the other one was doing. The first song he had been sent was after the first weekend they spent together. Jamie had travelled to London and stayed in Tom's apartment. On the train back he sent Jewel's *Morning Song*, and on the morning of their wedding, which was the last song he'd sent, he received Bruno Mars' *Marry You*. The short message that appeared before the link to download the song read:

Thinking of you and thought of this song...you don't have to listen to it if you don't want to. Come back to me safe. T x

He saw that this new gift was from a Dusty Springfield album, a song he knew well but didn't own. It was her haunting classic, *Goin' Back*. Tom had a knack of knowing how to musically accompany a scene and its meaning wasn't wasted on Jamie as he immediately downloaded it and began to listen to it on repeat until he reached Ledbury.

The train eventually started to lose speed, and the announcement was made which coincided with an uneasy feeling in Jamie. These feelings always greeted him as he returned home, like the dread he felt about attending a school reunion. His mission for previous trips was to meet the least amount of people he knew as possible, while his mother wanted the complete opposite. They would walk up and down the streets, going in and out of shops. Jamie was convinced she went into as many stores as possible to try and meet his and her friends.

It was a little strange this time that no one was aware he was coming back, apart from the solicitor. His father wouldn't be reluctantly outside in his car to pick him up. When he was alive, he was only there because his wife ordered him. This time, there'd be no fatted calf, metaphorically speaking, ready for him to devour, no awkward hug and kiss as he stepped inside his childhood home. This time a stranger was the only soul in this Herefordshire hamlet that knew he was coming back.

Joe Galloway was the solicitor who had called Jamie and sent him emails to look over before he arrived. He said he would be just outside the station in a suit and bowtie. He certainly stood out as Jamie came through the barriers and ventured outside the small station building. As he approached, Mr Galloway extended a hand and welcomed him home. Jamie didn't want to divulge how he was really feeling and make this seemingly pleasant, older gentleman uncomfortable. The solicitor commented on Jamie travelling light and that his lack of luggage looked like he wasn't staying the night. With an outstretched arm, he ushered Jamie in the direction of the carpark.

Jamie wasn't expecting a Rolls Royce to be picking him up, but he was amused by the very old, beige Mercedes 230E that Mr Galloway opened and started up. It must have been at least 30 years old and when it eventually started, sounded like a Spitfire. He got in and carefully closed the door, trying not to break it. It was yanked into reverse before Jamie had a chance to buckle up. Under other circumstances and with Tom there, they'd be laughing their heads off.

Nothing really had changed as they came down the hill into the town itself before ascending again and taking a left. He noticed no-one and recognised everywhere.

"Would you like to go to the house now or the office? Completely up to you." Mr Galloway asked politely.

"If it's possible, can I not go to the house, if that's not too much bother?"

Mr Galloway's short and courteous reply made Jamie feel that this was a standard request in such circumstances and this relaxed him somewhat.

The car swerved to the left and stopped abruptly outside what looked like a shop front. Mr Galloway got out, and Jamie saw that this was indeed where the solicitors' office was. Trying not to scrape the door off the wall, he eased himself slowly out of the car. The Tudor style shop front was originally black but was now covered in dust. The windows were all intact but were similarly caked in dirt. Mr Galloway ceremoniously opened the door and waited for Jamie to enter. His eyes took a second to adjust to the dim light.

Mr Galloway asked Jamie to take a seat for a moment while he prepared and instructed his receptionist to make some tea. The portly woman removed her thick rimmed spectacles and went to another room. After the old car, Jamie was certainly not expecting modern, minimalist offices. Tom would describe it as 'Old Worldly Charm' while Jamie saw the old world and an exit to the city. Jamie messaged Tom to say he'd arrived safely. From the other room, Jamie heard cups and saucers being arranged, fridges and cupboards being opened and closed. The receptionist came over and asked if he took sugar. Jamie politely informed her that he didn't. Just as she was about to go back to what he thought was the kitchen, she stopped and pointed.

"You're…Peter and Margaret's boy?"

Jamie had never heard himself been described as that in his entire life. The fact that neither Peter nor Margaret were alive, the real answer was that he was now an orphan, but she seemed a rather sweet woman, and he didn't want to make her feel uncomfortable.

"I am, I'm Jamie."

"I'm Grace, Grace Peters. I'm so sorry for your loss. I was in the Church prayer group with your mother. She's a huge loss to us," she said in a thick Bristolian accent while she shook Jamie's hand.

"She loved her prayer group," Jamie lamented.

With that, Mr Galloway appeared from his office.

"How's that tea coming along, Grace?" he enquired but really trying to get her away from his client who looked a little uneasy.

She hopped back to the kitchen without a word. A compassionate half smile appeared on Mr Galloway's face as he courteously invited Jamie into his office. Jamie followed him into an even darker room which housed a serious of filing cabinets and a large wooden desk that had papers strewn all over it. There were two seats on Jamie's side of the desk and a large imposing leather swivel chair on Mr Galloway's, who didn't sit down until Jamie did. New, thicker and darker rimmed glasses were located under mounds of paper which replaced the ones that were on his face. He opened a file and shuffled the papers on the table like he was about to read the news. Jamie was informed that Mr Galloway was the executor of his mother's will and that this was dated 14th August 2016. Inside his head, Jamie was trying to visualise a timeline. That meant that his mother had made this will one week after his father, her husband, had died. In fact, the paper it was printed on looked much crisper and whiter than the others contained in the file.

Grace, without knocking, entered the office with a tray laden with cups on matching saucers, a milk jug that matched the teapot and custard cream biscuits, the sight of them endeared her to Jamie. Mr Galloway politely thanked and dismissed her.

The reading of the will was shorter, with less ceremony than he had expected. In short, Jamie was left everything: the house and contents. There weren't any savings to speak of, and he had already decided that if there were, it would cover the cost of the funerals which he had paid for. Without distress or emotion, Jamie poured himself and the solicitor a cup of tea and sat back with a custard cream in his mouth.

The next decision Jamie had to make was what to do with the house and everything contained within. Jamie was prepared for this part as it had kept him awake throughout the night. He asked Mr Galloway if there was a way for the house to be sold and for the contents to be given to various charities in the local area but most importantly, that this would or could be done without Jamie having to enter the house.

Mr Galloway looked up at Jamie and removed his glasses, cleaned them with a handkerchief from his suit pocket before placing them back with both hands.

"Jamie, I've been doing this job a very long time, and I've seen all sorts of things happen in this very office. I've seen husbands and wives fight over pennies. I've seen families ripped apart by greed when bereavement should've done that. You need to be sure, to be very sure, about what you are asking of me, because there isn't a law that allows you to go back on something like this. Do you want to take some time…"

"Actually, I don't…"

"Actually, can I ask something of you?"

"Sure," replied Jamie.

"Come back to me in one hour to give me your final answer. Go get a tea or a fancy coffee or a bite to eat even, but just think about what you are asking. Now, if you decide you want to go ahead with your plan, then I will do it for you."

Jamie didn't expect this. All he wanted was to sign something and to get on the first train back to London. He knew his mind wasn't going to change, but he wanted to humour this kind man, so agreed to go out and think.

He walked for a bit until he was at the top of the high street. The market towns' main thoroughfare sat between two small hills. As he ambled down with earphones in, still listening to the song Tom had sent, he felt very self-conscious. He thought that the locals were staring at him. He stopped to peer into a shop front only to look at his reflection. The young boy from Ledbury was alive and well today as he scoffed at what he saw. The smart, casually dressed, out of towner with his sunglasses and man bag. He whipped off his designer shades immediately and returned them to their case that was housed in his bag. A double take and then he continued.

He didn't see anyone he recognised, which was a relief. The thought that he might have to make small talk about why he was home or anything else family related had him on tenterhooks. About halfway down he spied a coffee shop and went in. Chuckling to himself he ordered a flat white and was surprised about how perfect it was. Neither expecting to get one nor for it to be up to much. He chastised himself as he left the store for being such a coffee snob. The small beverage served to also warm his hands as he proceeded down to the Market Hall where he had planned all along to sit out his one hour enforced purgatory.

Feeling a gentle tap on his shoulder, he turned and saw the young woman from the coffee shop.

"You left this on the counter, here you go," she said handing him his black leather wallet.

"Wow, you wouldn't get that in London. Thank you so much, I'm not really with it today," he said and regretted divulging this small bit of information to a complete stranger.

"Hopefully the coffee helps. Have a good day."

"You too and thanks again," Jamie said holding up the wallet and then placing it into his coat pocket.

Reaching the Tudor styled Market Hall, he knew that there'd be a seat to sit, think and wait because market day was Tuesday and Saturdays. It was a hall on stilts. Underneath it and on two days a week, various stalls were housed selling fresh fruit, vegetables and other crafts. It was the highlight of his mothers week, where she'd return with a rundown of all the vegetables that were or weren't available on that particular visit and indeed, how cheap or not they were. On more recent visits home he would always accompany her, carrying the heavy bags back to the house. He had gone past being angry at the lack lustre husband his father was, allowing his wife to schlep in and out of town when he had a car and time.

Taking rest on the empty wooden bench, he looked up at the route he had walked from. It was odd, being a tourist in his hometown he thought, as he believed that was how the people who passed by viewed him, a tourist. He took a picture of the town, posted it on Facebook and tagged it along with a link to Bronski Beat's, *Smalltown Boy*. It was a song that he very much related to. His first ever boyfriend, Richard, played it after a marathon weekend of not leaving his bedroom. Those early days of nonstop energy, insatiable lustful appetite with the stamina to match, lazing around naked all weekend, sleeping when not wrapped up in trying new positions. It was after a number of orgasms they decided to order pizza. Eating it, sitting in their CK y-fronts, Richard had always tried to get him to listen to songs he might not have heard of. He played this with the preamble that it sounded like the musical prelude for every gay man from small towns across the world.

Wishing the song had come with a pre-warning, it instantly resonated somewhere deep in his core. Pizza eating stopped, and Jamie had to muster up hidden strength to hold back a brewing tide of emotion. Richard, who was lost in the music, looked to see if Jamie was enjoying it. Being a trainee counsellor too, he was immediately aware that this eighties classic was having an effect on this newbie, this fledging gay. Dropping the half eaten pizza slice he was holding into the cardboard box it was delivered in and swallowing what he was chewing, he wiped his mouth, stood in front of Jamie and extended his hand. Without saying anything, without Jamie agreeing, he grabbed Jamie's hand and pulled him up onto his feet. He manoeuvred Jamie's hand on to Jamie's chest, moving it slightly to ensure it was over his heart. He got his other hand and made him put it around Richard's waist. Richard put both his hands on the band of Jamie's underwear covered waistline and looked at him, waiting for Jamie to do the same, which he eventually did. He then whispered the line of the song "Cry boy, cry boy cry..." The invitation allowed Jamie to do exactly that, but crying wasn't what happened. It was guttural and primal exorcising. He could never cry at home; his father wouldn't have stood for "any of it that sort of thing." At school, he was mocked for quivering lips and the tears that fell after beatings and constant jeering. Dressed only in his underwear, with another man, similarly underdressed, he was being held and being allowed. Allowed to cry, permission to feel and the right to be, and to be without judgement. After the heaving sobs and large tears, he began to smile. Richard let go of him, and together they danced like semi-naked, pagan moon worshippers, allowing the music to move through them and enabling each other to dance like no one was watching.

Laden with bags of shopping, Jamie's arms were beginning to ache, but he knew that all the shops that his mother frequented had been visited, as they waited for a taxi to bring them home. It was an odd sight, the woman with just a handbag and her companion laden with bags upon bags of fresh vegetables and cuts of meat from the butcher. She always offered to carry some, but he would never let her. They had stopped and chatted to nearly every passerby. It looked like she knew everyone. She'd always introduce Jamie as "her son, just down from London" and loved it when they'd show interest in him because that gave her the chance to announce that he was a psychotherapist. His embarrassment was always lessened by the knowledge that she didn't really understand what it was he did.

The last time, before the funeral, he was home, was a month before his wedding. His reason for visiting was to buy his mother an outfit for his big day. The two of them went to a clothes store that had been open long before Jamie was born. Bradley's was that one shop that dots most towns in England, selling both women's and men's clothing, giving most of the floor space to the ladies, with a loyal customer base that shopped for themselves and their husbands in absentia.

Vera, the owner, greeted Jamie's mother with the latest gossip before addressing why they were there. Jamie had thought about pre-warning her not to say the exact reason for the new outfit, afraid she'd be the talk of the town. This was half the truth; Jamie was embarrassed by being outed in his hometown, even though through various social mediums, it was evident he was gay and in a relationship with a man. This didn't bother his mother at all.

"I need an outfit," Jamie's mother said with great excitement

"What's the occasion?" Vera asked nosily.

Inside, Jamie clenched and waited.

"My son is getting married to his partner, Tom," she replied without flinch or pause.

Vera kicked into professional mode and talked about style colours, cuts and finishes. Dutifully, Jamie spent the entire time outside the curtained changing area. Occasionally he would have to get a different size or colour. Without her hair done or any makeup on, his dressed-up mother looked odd, and a little uncomfortable but her face just beamed with pride and excitement.

"Where have you gone?"

Jamie opened his eyes and awkwardly took out his earphones to see the solicitor's receptionist sitting on the other end of the bench.

"Sorry, I must have just dozed off. Early start this morning."

"I bet. You're in London? Your mother would always keep us up-to-date; where you were flying next," she said as she opened up her shop bought sandwich. She offered him half, but Jamie declined.

"How long have you been working there?" Jamie asked.

"Too long," she joked. "He's not a bad boss; he has his moments, like everyone else I suppose."

"He seems nice."

"Have you decided?"

Jamie was a little surprised that she was asking him this question, wondering about confidentially and if she should or shouldn't be conversing like this in such a public space. He put it down to small town rules and that everyone knew everyone else's business or, eventually they would.

"What do you think she'd want me to do?" Jamie asked.

She put the half eaten sandwich in the container and wiped her mouth with a napkin.

"You can't tell him that we talked about this. He'd blow a gasket," she said, sternly.

"I won't," promised Jamie.

"For what it's worth, I think your mother would want you to be happy and to do what was right for you. I think she had lots of regrets in life and that father of yours wasn't an easy man to live with. That said, you were the light in her life, and I would sit at prayer meetings and could see her light up as she talked about you. She wouldn't want a house or possessions to be weighing you down. She would want you to be free from worry. Well, that's what I think." She resumed eating her lunch like she had just talked about the weather.

Sitting up on the bench, he looked at his watch and saw he had about twenty minutes before he could go back to the solicitor's office. The coffee left in his cup was now cold. He stood up to place it in the nearby bin.

"Is it odd, I mean, do many people not want to revisit the family home?

"Nothing's weird when it comes to death, wills and inheritance," she said through a gentle giggle. "Mr Galloway is a prudent man and while he will get a fee if you ask him to sell the house, he does care about his clients and knows that regrets will remain after a house is sold and there's really no going back, unless you buy the house back but by then, homely memories are painted over and lives lived are wallpapered, but no, it's not weird."

"Thanks for your honesty. I've never done this before, obviously, and there's just me to make these decisions, and it feels... very grown up. Sometimes it sucks being an adult. It's times like this you want your..." he stopped mid sentence.

Carefully, Grace finished it "...mother to be around?"

Jamie just nodded and for just a second, felt very young.

"I better make my way back, enjoy the rest of your lunch," he said while also checking that he had his wallet this time.

On the journey back, Jamie knew his mind was made up. He knew he never wanted to come back, that this town held bad memories and small minds and whilst he may have grown up, travelled and expected that the people who made his life harder than it already was had maybe matured with age, he couldn't help but feel loneliness and isolation shackling themselves to him as he exited the train each time he visited.

Approaching the solicitor's office he spied Mr Galloway through the dirty, dusty windows, sipping on his tea while holding the saucer in his other hand. He went to open the door for him and asked him if he wanted a fresh cup. Jamie declined politely as he was led back into the office. They took their respective seats and waited for Mr Galloway to put on his other glasses.

"So, what's the verdict?" he asked Jamie, peering over the top of the black frames.

"I appreciate you giving me time to think, and I have done that, but my mind hasn't changed."

"So you'd like me to put the house on the market after I give it over to local charities to do what they will with the contents?"

"Yes, if you don't mind?"

"Not at all, I'll need you to sign a few documents, and I'll get the house valued and be in touch via email if that's preferable?"

"Email is great, thanks. One thing, can you give preference to charities related to cardiac disease?" Jamie asked awkwardly.

"I'll take a note of that," Mr Galloway said while jotting it down.

Long winded documents were produced and meticulously explained before Jamie was shown where to sign, once he was happy to do so. It took a while for all the documents to be copied and filed away properly. This aged solicitor was in no rush to do so, not for any other reason than to ensure that things were done correctly. Once filed away he came back to his desk and produced an off-white vellum envelope, which was fastened by a paperclip to the back of Jamie's mother's file.

"There's just one final thing today. The only stipulation in your mothers will was to ensure that you got this," he said as he raised it in his left hand.

"What is it?" asked Jamie.

"Inside is an envelope with what I believe is a letter from her. I've put it inside one of our envelopes for safer keeping."

He ceremoniously handed Jamie the letter, and he held it with both hands like he'd discovered the last Golden Ticket, slightly paralysed with disbelief.

"Do you need a lift back to the station?"

"If you don't mind?"

"Not at all. Do you mind just waiting outside while I make a quick, confidential phone call?"

"No, sure, thanks," he said as he placed the letter inside his bag and went back out to the reception area, closing the office door on the way out to give him more privacy.

Grace was back from her break, and she watched as he went to a seat in what seemed to be slow motion. He hadn't noticed she was back as he took out his phone to check the train times. She nervously looked at the office door and back to him and repeated this a couple of times. Appearing to be doing something she shouldn't, she walked quickly over to Jamie.

"Before he comes out, I wanted to give you something. When you left, I went to the Church hall and got your mother's Bible. I'm not presuming your religious but..." she stopped and handed him the worn book which he immediately recognised as his mothers.

"We all keep our Bibles there, saves us carrying them in and out of town." Hearing her boss end the call with loud salutations, she dashed back to her desk.

Jamie quickly put the holy book into his bag as Mr Galloway reappeared.

"Shall we?" he declared as he made his way to his car.

Before leaving the office he turned around and mouthed a "thank you" to Grace, she nodded and mouthed a silent "you're welcome."

He was dropped off in front of the station and after a firm handshake, got out of the old car to check on his train. His phone had told him that the next one was ten minutes away, but the screens inside the station were flashing which didn't bode well. At closer inspection, he saw that all trains were subject to delays or last minute cancellations due to signalling problems in the area. An enquiry at the ticket desk informed him that he had at least an hour to wait. He texted Tom to let him know and saw that the message delivered straight away but wasn't read which meant that his husband was busy.

He slumped down on one of the benches on the platform and went to open his bag a couple of times and then stopped but then started again. Finally, he took his mothers' bible out. The large, black, hardback covered holy book had seen better days. The corners of the cover were more rounded now, and the paper had yellowed with age. He felt it all over with both hands like he was blind. He opened the book and saw his mother had written her name and the date she bought it. It caught his breath, the site of her familiar style. The date didn't signify a particular time in his mind, but it was bought before she was married. Some religious pamphlets fell in front of him. As if they were china plates and he had the ability to stop them from crashing to the ground, he jerked forward to save them. Sorting them like a pack of cards, he saw various religious images, the majority of them were of the Virgin Mary and denoted novena's that his mother attended. Sometimes their Sunday calls would be affected because of these week long novenas. The week seemed like an arduous back and forth to her local Church to pray for souls, the sick and the dead. While not being religious himself, it angered him how physically demanding these weeks of prayer and devotion were, but he knew that if she was doing this, regardless of how much she believed, it got her out of the house and when viewed in those terms, it was a Godsend.

Various other bookmarks were in place as he flicked through like a picture book, immediately stopping when he got to one. There were underlined passages, which he read. Some greeting cards were also used as bookmarks, thanking her for casseroles, prayers and a listening ear. Not needing reminding, but it was nice that people appreciated the kind and thoughtful acts his mother discreetly carried out. The centre of the book fell open due to a large number of inserts. His face became warm and his heart engorged as he recognised his wedding invitation from the envelope. Flipping it around it was confirmed when he saw his own handwriting staring back at him. He looked inside the envelope and saw the part of the invitation that each guest kept, but there was something else. Carefully he pulled out a photograph that had been taken the first time she came to visit them in their new home. The two men towered over her as they stood on the balcony of the Oxo Tower restaurant. It was a fantastically hot summers day, and the photo was taken by one of the staff after she had grabbed her drink and went straight to the balcony to view St. Paul's from such a panoramic vantage point. Big smiles and great memories radiated from the picture but Jamie, sitting on the bench at the train station, never felt so lonely. He gently rubbed his mothers face with his index finger, not to stain or decay her facade. A single tear slid down the image which jolted him to rub it carefully from the photograph and then his eyes. He placed it back in the envelope and with all the other Christian paraphernalia, put it back into her bible and returned it to his bag. He saw the letter he was handed by Mr Galloway and thought he better not read that now, in fact, he was unsure if he was ever going to be ready to see what it contained.

He drank the last of his water and walked over to place the empty bottle in the recycling bin. The board was saying that the next train to London would arrive in thirty minutes while also telling him to be prepared for delays and cancellations. The feeling of annoyance was welcomed as it dampened other emotions that were beginning to overwhelm him. He looked at local notice-boards like he had a sudden interest in the neighbourhood watch program or the local volunteers that met monthly to pick-up the litter from the grass verges around the outskirts of Ledbury. With having read each and every one, he surrendered and sat back down on the bench. Annoyance began to fade. Sitting on the bench, a sensation began to emerge. He was neither thirsty nor hungry, but within this ball of irksomeness, a craving started. He couldn't identify what he was feeling or desiring, but it was beginning to grow. He grabbed his phone and checked Facebook and Instagram, a feeble attempt to distract himself. He called Tom, but he got his voicemail again. His right leg was shaking incessantly like it belonged to the drummer of a death metal band. He noticed he was chewing his gum at a rapid pace on a piece that had lost all taste some time ago. In a move to try to shake it off, he examined the train station board again even though he knew there was no update. Taking out his phone he called Jules to arrange some much needed alcoholic beverages once his train got into London. There was no answer, and in anger, he didn't leave a voice message.

His breathing quickened. He sat, splayed out on the bench, looking intently through his phone book. He came across Teresa's number and for the shortest of seconds he contemplated calling her, but the ominous mishmash of feelings shut that idea down with brute force. He hovered over Max's number. Gritting his teeth, he chastised himself for even thinking about it.

"Get a grip, Jamie!" which allowed a momentary reprieve from the brooding mass that was surging through his body and mind and for a moment he was still. It was as if it had passed.

It hadn't, the foreboding increased and Jamie grabbed his phone, giving into his primal craving and began to download Grindr. He was urging his phone to download the app faster, cursing the local area's inferior connection, thinking it was typical of his hometown to do this to him. Eventually, the download was complete and revealed the black mask embossed in the yellow icon square. His heart began to beat faster as he put in his details and waited to see what guys were nearby. This took longer than normal. Jamie was grinding his teeth with pure frustration. He closed down the app and opened it up immediately, thinking that would speed things up but this wasn't the case.

A high pitched bing was heard, and the announcement that his train was approaching annoyed him. He knew that travelling on the train would mean that for large parts of the journey there would be absolutely no signal on his phone. The app engaged and began to show a grid of other men as the train slowly approached the platform.

"Fuck sake," he said to himself, as he saw that the nearest guy online was over ten miles away.

The train screeched to an eventual halt and Jamie boarded. The silent carriage was just that, with very few passengers and after the customer announcements, the locomotive began the long journey back to London.

He spent half of the three-hour trip hunched over his phone like Scrooge over his accounting books, continually refreshing the app. A few brief conversations were struck up, but as Jamie moved further and further away from them, sitting in the quiet carriage of the train, it ended without a sign-off. Thankfully the seat adjacent to him was free from peering and judging eyes, and it also made having a constant hard-on that more bearable.

When he hit a particularly long stretch of no signal, he threw the phone onto the tiny train table and sat back in his seat as the blood continued to rush through his excited body. Rubbing his fingers through his hair, he tried to engage some part of his brain in a bid to regain order on his current predicament. He looked around the carriage to see who he was travelling with. The carriage was mainly filled with middle aged couples who were reading, sleeping or listening to something. Just at the last set of seats that were viewable, a young man and what Jamie presumed was his girlfriend, seemed to have just arrived in his carriage and were settling in. She was sitting while he remained standing like a gentleman, placing their bags on the rack above. With each bag, the white t-shirt he was wearing hiked above his blue jeans, revealing the top of his underwear band and toned stomach. Jamie's eyes locked onto this view as he felt a surge of energy pulsate through his groin. He noticed that the girlfriend had spotted him ogling her man and that snapped Jamie out of his erotic reverie, as he clumsily picked up his phone and began trawling again. There was still no signal, but he kept the illusion of being preoccupied with something else to ease his embarrassment and the girlfriend's annoyance.

Emerging from a tunnel his phone vibrated and with quick reflexes, he saw a message from Max's phone.

Hi Babe, battery on my phone is dead. Hope today went well. It's been crazy here, and some of us have to stay on. So don't wait up for me. Love, T x

He replied immediately.

Just on the train back. I've been trying to get in touch with Jules to go out for some needed drinks but can't get hold of her. I'm due into

Euston at 7.56 - delayed - don't ask! I'll tell you about my day tomorrow. Don't work too hard. J x

Frustration soared as he noticed that his own phone battery was nearly depleted. He hurried into the phone settings to do everything to make it last, but it was too late as his screen went black. He threw the phone back on the table and seethed. This was just too much now. He needed a hit but of what he could not articulate. The right leg tremor sped up automatically in a vain attempt to jettison his heated desire that oozed through his entire body.

The phone-less part of the journey back to Euston Station felt never-ending. At each station, he cursed the disembarking and embarking passengers for taking too long. Then came the holding pattern into London, where all the trains that had been affected earlier had now converged just outside the capital. Jamie's fists clenched harder with each repetitive announcement that delivered no new news on their predicament. As he neared the station, he packed away his things and stood by the door so he could exit immediately.

Finally, he was released and was the first passenger to emerge. He walked with strides to avoid a pile up at the ticket barrier, but already a queue had formed. The station was booming with noises from trains, mixed with the masses of commuters leaving London. Jamie inserted his ticket which opened the barrier, and as he made his way through, he changed direction to get to the Tube. He saw a familiar face that was attached to a body leaning on a pillar. Across this face was a mischievous smile which made Jamie continue walking for a few steps before slowing down. In the space of two seconds he had an internal debate that raged so hard against each other, but in the end, one side was victorious as Jamie walked over to Max who had seen the messages Tom had sent from his phone.

"You look like you need…"

Jamie interrupted him, "not to talk."

Max just put his arm around Jamie's shoulders and led him through the crowds and out of the station.

Chapter 7

When living in London, the best-laid plans can and usually are scuttled by public transport. Red signals, the wrong weather and driver strikes are things that some of its inhabitants have to factor in before beginning their journey. Jules was not one for pre-checking her route, and on this particular day, she could hear Jamie's constant moaning about her lateness and her inability to peruse travel apps and websites in advance to check for things that could possibly make her late. That all evaporated the moment the Tube doors opened, and she squeezed passed the waiting passengers at London Bridge station. Jules ran because she knew there was still quite a way to go to surprise Jamie on his lunch break, as there were numerous escalators and walkways to negotiate before she saw daylight. At one set of escalators, she contemplated ascending on the left side, which would mean walking in the fast lane, but she took one look at her heels and thought better of it.

Ascending from the underground, stepping off the moving stairs, she trotted cautiously to the barrier which she opened with her phone. Under a sign displaying the various exits, she darted left, then right and stood again in front of the signs to ensure she was going out the correct one. The contrast between her life and Jamie's predictable schedule couldn't have been further apart. They both coveted that part they didn't have in each other, but this also caused arguments which never lasted longer than three minutes.

Red light after red light stood in her way. The crossing to the side she needed wasn't one to take a chance on, as this was an incredibly busy junction leading over London Bridge. She contemplated texting or calling to see where he was, but she didn't want to ruin the surprise. She was trying to make amends for standing him up by buying him lunch, a feat that she had done a few times before.

Eventually, on the same side as the market, she made her way to his favourite sushi store, only to be met by a massive queue. She couldn't see him in front, so she eyed the menu above her. True to form, she knew what he would order for lunch, but she was undecided. By the time she was served, she was still unsure so just ordered what Jamie was having. Near the stores' exit, she picked up some chopsticks, napkins and extra wasabi paste. As she was placing them in the bag, she looked up and immediately tried to duck down so she wouldn't be spotted by the person she was trying to surprise. He walked passed with an old lady she'd never seen before, and when Jules stood up, she saw that Jamie had already bought lunch.

She was gutted and thought he'd only chastise her for being late. The pairing of her best friend and this old lady looked like something she didn't want to disturb. Once she knew they'd left the market, she exited the shop and made her way back to her office with more sushi than she needed. She thought it served her right for letting him down that night and vowed to ring him later.

"You need to stop buying me lunch, Teresa," Jamie said as he lobbed a piece of tofu into his mouth.

"You're grand," she said with her soft Gaelic lilt. "Anyway, it's my way of thanking you. That singing and humming and breathing thing you were getting me to do, well, I've been able to do it a bit more now, and it's great."

He stopped and made eye contact. He was so chuffed for her. "That's fantastic news, well done you!"

They both ate some more and continued on their usual path, comfortable with each other that there was no need to discuss where they were going.

"When did these…funny turns start?" asked Jamie.

Her pace slowed as she gave his question some thought which increased the furrows on her face.

"Not that long ago, maybe a couple of months now."

"And, when was it that…" he paused with hesitation.

"Bill, passed away?" She didn't need to think about this.

"Five years," she answered solemnly. "Why do you ask?"

"I'm just thinking out loud. Force of habit," he said coyly. "Has your GP or your therapist asked you about them yet?"

"My GP said it sounded like a panic attack."

"Sounds like you don't," he said with a smile on his face.

"There were never panic attacks when I was growing up. You just got on with things the best you could. No one paid much attention to head stuff or feelings," she said dismissively.

"It certainly sounds like panic attacks and those exercises, the breathing and singing are ways people try to manage them." He glanced to see her reaction and saw her looking down at the ground as they walked side by side. Aware he might be pushing their casual stroll into a therapy session he looked in the bag for a water bottle. Stopping to unscrew it, she walked on for a bit but stopped when she saw he wasn't beside her. She seemed down, not her usual cheerful self. It was a subtle change, it wasn't like she was being grumpy, but when someone is so pleasant to be around, any slight deviation from this is noticeable. He caught up with her, and they continued on together. Eventually, she resumed talking.

"Funny that these attacks, or whatever they are, started a couple of months ago. I presume you thought they were related to Bill's passing and wondered had they started after he had gone," she said without looking at him.

"It is bizarre but, the mind doesn't always have a timetable for things like this." He wanted to ask more but held back due to her being subdued and the fact that she wasn't his client.

"Can I ask you a question?" she said her officiously.

They moved to nearer the railings of the path to avoid oncoming joggers as the question felt, to both them, needed time and space.

"Sure? What is it?"

"I know we don't know each other that long and well, you seem like you know what you are talking about, if, and I really mean *if* you were my therapist, what would be the next questions you'd ask me?"

For someone who didn't grow up in an era where feelings were talked about, she was looking at him with the hope that he, in some way could help her, like she wanted to learn something incredibly important, something life-saving. Jamie didn't need to think about what he would ask her but gave the illusion of thinking about it thoroughly.

"I suppose, I would ask someone in this situation, what was going on for them around the time of their first attack or had something changed for them in their day to day life or was there a common thread to when these…events took place."

He took a drink of water to allow her space to digest all of that, which she did for some time. Jamie saw her struggle with that old world mentality that was so ingrained in her, that part that told her and her generation that if they had their health they had everything or there was someone who was worse off; endless platitudes that ultimately muted people's emotions, stunted personal development and drove these feelings underground to one day erupt when it all became too much. "Do you have bad days?" she asked without looking at him.

"Of course. Just because I'm a therapist doesn't mean I have the answers to everything. If you ask most of us, we are doing it because we are all a bit messed up and we are trying to heal ourselves," he replied, with his stock answer, as he and his colleagues were asked this question constantly. He didn't challenge her for changing the subject, he knew when to pick his moments and now just didn't feel right.

"Anything planned for the weekend?" he asked.

"Another meeting with my group of ladies. We are still in the midst of organising our Christmas party," answering with little enthusiasm.

"Is it a big thing?"

"Oh yes, all the old codgers in Greenwich might not attend all the meetings and outings, but they all go to the Christmas party. It's not as fun anymore without my Bill, but I still go to support it. I've met some great friends through it, and some of them have also lost their husbands and wives. We form a sort of widowers united and we all dance with each other on the night. It's fun but, not the same. The plans we had weren't meant to be." She looked sad now. "We always joked about getting older. He felt that official retirement age was way too young. When they made him retire from the police, he kept busy doing odd jobs and volunteering. He just wanted to keep active. He said he would slow down on our golden wedding anniversary and that we'd have our first Christmas party dance as bonafide old timers, but it wasn't meant to be, it just wasn't for us." She took a moment before asking him about his weekend.

"Well, it's the first weekend Tom has been off in such a long time, so we are going to a birthday party. Nothing exciting really - a hangover on Sunday probably."

They both chuckled which lightened the mood. She glanced at her watch and told him that he was running late for work. They made plans for the following Friday like old friends, and Jamie dashed back to the office.

Tom and Jamie were late due to spending too much time trying to decide on outfits that didn't clash. The taxi driver sensed tension in the car so stayed uncharacteristically quiet. They both had texted Dan and Brian to apologise and to say that they were on their way. Brian was turning forty but being the type of person he was; a control freak, couldn't have a surprise bash, so organised his own. While they were worried about what they were going to wear, they knew it would be an intimate and casual affair, with them knowing most, if not all the guests attending.

They dashed to the front door and fixed each other's bow ties before Tom rang the bell. The party sounded like it was in full swing and before their hosts opened the door, Tom stole a quick kiss which made them just look at each other for a moment, without noticing the door opening. Dan coughed to get their attention and then suddenly went in to hug and kiss them both in one go, but didn't let go of them.

"M.M.M is here," he whispered.

The newly arrived guests whispered their response in unison, "fuck."

M.M.M stood for the Mancunian Muscle Mary and was an accurate description for Gary who was, as his name described, a muscled man from Manchester. All three hated him but Gary shared a flat with Brian before he met Dan and they continued to see each other even though Brian struggled with his brashness, endless me stories and all the gossip from around town, which they weren't really that interested in anymore.

Tom handed over bottles of wine and Dan continued being host. He looked flustered as he tried to keep everyone's glass filled, really wanting everyone to have a good time but mainly wanting Brian to have a memorable night. They left their coats in the spare room and made their way to the lounge. Brian screamed when he spotted them, placing his glass down and leaving mid-conversation to kiss and hug the boys. Tom winked at Jamie to indicate that Brian was drunk already which made them laugh, but not out loud. Brian put an arm around each of their shoulders and they scanned the room. After one complete sweep of the assembled crowd, Brian relaxed and said he was thankful that they knew everyone, so he didn't have to introduce people all over again.

"Alright queers?"

The three men spun around to see Gary returning from the garden after having a smoke. He was in his signature white t-shirt that just about covered his midriff. He was in good shape, but he was at that point in his life where burning off fat became a bigger chore and one he didn't pay much attention to while all his time was spent on dumbbells. It was air kisses all round as he approached and then excused himself to get some more beer.

The party was catered, with many gym ripped waiters walking around with delicious canapés. Jamie spotted Dan smacking his drunk husband jokingly across the wrist for eyeing up the blonde twink who was serving drinks. He watched the party like it was on TV, admiring what people were wearing, earwigging conversations and reading body language. It never bored him; people fascinated him hence the job he chose. He saw people cringe as Gary approached them. Not everyone at the party knew Gary. Those that did, tried to avoid an audience with him. Jamie wondered did he know how other people felt about him and did it bother him at all. Jamie had, up to this point, escaped a private audience with him.

He went to the kitchen to get some nibbles. As he got himself a glass of water, he saw Tom and Dan outside. Tom tried to hide it, but it was too late. Jamie just smiled, winked at him and headed back to the party. He knew Dan and him had sneaky cigarettes at various points. If Jamie hadn't caught them in the act, he would've smelt too much cologne from him, trying to mask the indiscretion.

"Shit!" Tom said without moving his lips.

Dan dropped the remains of the cigarette on the ground and stood on it without moving the upper part of his body.

"Too late, Jamie saw us."

Dan took the cigarette from Tom's hand and began to smoke the remnants. Dan asked Tom how Jamie was coping.

"I think he's through it now. You know him, he's a hard one to read, but he seems to be getting back to normal, well, who knows. All I know is that we seem to be having fewer arguments and you know us, that rarely happens."

"That's good. It must've been tough on him and you."

"Yeah, he had a complicated relationship with his parents, but to lose both of them in the space of a month, I don't think I'd cope with it too well," Tom confessed, stealing the last drag back off Dan.

"What are you guys going to do about the honeymoon? Not to sound insensitive, but it must have put a bit of a dampener on things." Dan asked, brave now with some vodka in his system.

"I wouldn't say those exact words to Jamie, but yeah, it wasn't the message we were expecting when we landed there, that his father had died. I knew he wouldn't fly back for the funeral; he was more worried about his mother. When we were at the airport in the Maldives, getting our flight to Goa, I said before we boarded that he could go home, that it wouldn't be too late, but he wasn't having any of it. I could see it killed him. He was so angry, he hated his father so much, but all he was concerned about was that his mother would be in so much pain. It was surreal when she died though. We had landed back home and went straight to bed. It was the worst jet lag I'd ever experienced, and then it came. The constant ringing of his mobile, then mine and then the house phone. I remember seeing him clamber over the unpacked cases on the floor as he ran to answer it. I'll never forget seeing him like that. I never want to see him like that again."

"Philip Larken was right, *'They fuck you up, your mum and dad. They may not mean to, but they do,'*" Dan pronounced.

"Never heard of him, but I get the sentiment. To answer your question, I don't think we need to take another honeymoon. He wasn't completely down once he was able to speak to his mother over the phone. His phone bill was colossal when he got back, though that wasn't important."

"It's only money," Dan interjected.

"True." Tom stood on the cigarette butt and clinked glasses with Brian.

"How's young Max? Has he gotten over his bout of calling in sick?" Dan asked with great interest.

"You don't fancy him?" Tom replied in disgust. "Max is Max. Still partying like the world is going to end on Monday. I literally don't know how he parties from Friday to Monday morning and arrives at work on Tuesday like he'd been gardening all weekend."

"As George Bernard Shaw said wisely, 'Youth is wasted on the young'"

"It's smarter you're becoming the more vodka you drink," laughed Tom.

They hugged for the sake of hugging and decided they needed more alcohol.

Before exiting the bathroom, Jamie knew Gary was outside and that he wouldn't have the sense to try the boys en-suite upstairs. He put his hand on the handle of the door, took a deep breath and opened it. He was air-kiss assaulted by the mammoth man who suddenly seemed in no rush to use the facilities, allowing another party guest to go in front of him. Jamie took the first hit.

"So, how have you been?"

Gary took full advantage of this open question about himself and decided to fill Jamie in on all and probably, most aspects of his life: work, gym, sex, drugs, boyfriends and how polygamy was the way forward. There were points through his update that Jamie zoned out and for moments, was unable to hear him but still looked interested. In these all too brief interludes, he felt pity for Gary and how alienating he was, but Jamie thought Gary never picked up on it, that he was immune to negative thoughts, especially about himself.

"I didn't know you and Max partied without Tom?" Gary asked, looking for more information. Jamie was suddenly alert and aware of what Gary had just said, but was floundering for a response.

"I saw you guys in Compton's last week, you don't remember?" he didn't wait for Jamie to respond, "you were fucked drunk, you don't remember me saying hello and trying to get some of those guys from your group's numbers?" Gary was waiting for an answer this time.

"Oh, that night, right. Yes, I was pretty wasted."

"Wasted? You were high man."

Jamie went completely dead pan "Keep it down. It was a one off thing."

"Tom doesn't know, does he?" Gary asked with enjoyment on his face.

"Tom does, and we just don't need to relive all of that, do you understand?" Jamie was trying not to get irritated.

"I get it. I get it. Right, nature calls," and with that, Gary closed the door of the bathroom.

Jamie downed the contents of his glass and exhaled. Tom called him, his head just visible, appearing from behind the door frame of the kitchen. Jolted by this, he hot stepped over as the crowd began to sing *Happy Birthday* to Brian. Tom and Jamie put one arm around each other and sang loudly. After the candle was blown out, Dan started a chant demanding a speech. The crowd swelled in volume until Brian eventually gave in. The crowd hushed while Brian cleared his throat.

"Wow, forty, who'd have thought it? You know I'm not one for speeches, so I haven't prepared anything. I want to thank my darling husband for putting up with me for all these years, and for you for being dear friends to us both. I don't feel forty…"

Someone from the crowd interpreted "you look it."

Brian continued "…fuck off Gary. All I want to say is that time is precious. Spend it with people who make you happy. Here's to the next forty!"

Glasses were raised, the couples kissed and the music was pumped up louder and *Wake Me Up Before You Go-Go* got played. The people who were designated drivers and those less drunk, moved all the furniture to the walls to create space as everyone began to dance. Jamie and Tom grabbed the hosts and created a circle. They danced and recreated some of the scenes from the WHAM! video. The close group were all level in terms of drunk-ness, and while they never expressed their love for each other vocally, however, at that moment, as each of them jumped, swayed and gyrated, they felt it. Jamie looked at each of them and felt this profoundly, how these people had become his family and were the only family he had left. He kissed each of them on the lips and huddled them together for a group hug. This delighted Tom, to see Jamie like this. Seeing him smile and to be his silly, loved-up, drunk self was something he thought he'd never see again. When he saw Jamie's eyes well up, he pulled him closer and without saying anything hugged him tight and tenderly, kissed his forehead as he let him go. Tom knew he needed that moment to compose himself. Jamie never felt so lucky to have him.

The music slowed and quietened as the group became less mobile and took to sitting, chatting and making cups of tea. Dan commented on how times had changed while he stirred a cup of hot chocolate. Slowly, the taxi's began to arrive and eventually it was just the four of them splayed out on the couch. Shoes and bowties off with gaping shirts. They were exhausted but thankful.

"Anyone for one final drink in Halfway To Heaven?" cackled Brian, recalling how they'd end their nights out in Soho when they were much younger.

"No fucking way. I'll stick to my hot chocolate," Dan protested.

"When did we become this old?" Tom asked.

"And boring?" Jamie added.

There was no need to answer because they were happy that their night ended at home, with beds waiting upstairs, a hot drink and some paracetamol in their system. The thought of having to dash across the road from Halfway To Heaven to McDonald's and then to clamber onto the last train home from Charring Cross station seemed incredibly unappealing to each of them, as was the prospect of cleaning up the house in the morning.

Jamie began to fall asleep on Tom's shoulder.

"I'm going to take Sleeping Beauty upstairs," Tom whispered.

He stroked Jamie's face gently, and in silence, they got up and stumbled upstairs. Tom followed behind to ensure Jamie didn't fall backwards. Collapsing onto the bed in the spare room, Jamie struggled with his boots and skinny jeans, but with Tom's help, they eventually came off. The bed was cold so they snuggled in as tightly as they could with Tom behind Jamie.

"Goodnight my love," Tom whispered into his husband's ear.

"Do you think I should've spent more time at home?" Jamie asked in a whispered slur.

With his mind not being entirely clear, Tom wasn't sure what he was being asked, so he didn't respond.

"When we got back from the honeymoon, do you think I should've stayed with her, do you think she'd still be with us?"

Tom was unsure if Jamie was aware that he was speaking or that it was some sort of drunken speech he'd forget in the morning. What he did know was that he was now in a minefield and not having a clear head put immense pressure on him delivering something honest without causing an explosion, but Jamie just continued.

"I think she died from a broken heart. I could've saved her you know, if I'd only I had gone home."

Stillness enveloped the room. What had been said was like a shot of espresso for Tom; his eyes were wide open, but he wasn't moving. Jamie's eyes were closed with a tear trickling down the bridge of his nose. With his mouth opened he began to snore subtly. Tom was never so relieved to hear his other half snore. Even though Jamie had quite a bit to drink it was heartbreaking for Tom to think that he thought like this. Would he bring it up in the morning or at some stage in the future? He knew that this would not be a conversation Jamie would want to have, and since they've had fewer arguments of late, Tom wasn't keen to revisit them. For now, all he could do was to gently kiss the back of Jamie's neck and hold him. Soon after, both men were fast asleep.

Tom woke up and saw a glass of water and some pills laid out on a bedside locker. Jamie was nowhere to be seen, but he could be heard talking to Dan and Brian downstairs as they cleared glasses and plates. The smell of bacon wafted up the stairs and sitting on the edge of the bed he popped the pills and the entire glass of water without taking a breath. His head hurt, and his mouth felt odd. Then he remembered he had smoked and had been caught. Looming from the fog of last night were the words that Jamie had uttered in his half sleep. There was no doubt in his mind that he was not going to bring it up. He remembered the strict instructions Jamie gave just after he calmed down from initially hearing about his mother's passing. It was a sobering moment that he'd never forget, seeing his husband in that much pain, sat on the floor trying to ensure that the tsunami of sobs and tears didn't breach. Jamie wouldn't let him hug him at first. It wasn't until Tom took the phone out of his hand and placed it on the receiver which triggered the flood. He sat in silence on the floor with Jamie for over an hour and held a broken man. His first coherent words to Tom was a stark warning not to pander to him or treat him any differently because that was what he felt he needed to get through. Jamie made him promise that he'd do it. Tom agreed in the moment and under emotional duress but found that this left him feeling utterly useless.

With a splash of cold water to his face, a brave facade emerged, and he decided to get on with the day. In the kitchen, he saw three men devouring bacon sandwiches. Jamie heard him at the door and sprung into action, ushering him to a seat, pouring coffee and fixing another bacon butty. Headaches all round led to a quiet breakfast table. Dan cleared the plates and tried to fit them into the already rammed dishwasher. Tom was impressed that they'd managed to do so much while he was still asleep. After devouring the sandwich, washing it down with three cups of coffee, he got up, hoovered, and when all the others had retired to checking their phones for any embarrassing social media posts from the night's antics, he mopped the floor, ending up marooning himself on the sofa with Jamie.

Hours later they both were woken by a McDonald's bag wafting in front of their faces. Dan and Brian had sneaked out and got their usual hangover cure.

Clear heads were restored once more, and Jamie and Tom eventually were in a taxi back home. George seemed ambivalent about their return and just sauntered upstairs to lay on their bed. Tom checked the automatic feeder had worked, which it had. His feline friend was being stroppy for being left in the house on his own. One by one they emerged back in the living room in their tracksuit bottoms and hoodies, slumping on the couch and semi-watching the TV they missed while dozing off.

In a lucid moment, Jamie opened his eyes and saw George had mellowed and had graced them both with his curled up, sleeping presence. Lazily he thumbed his phone to see what was happening in the world and saw that he had unread WhatsApp messages. He opened them and saw they were all from Max. Looking over, he saw Tom fast asleep, so he opened them. Max was still partying, and in-between invites for Jamie to join him were photos of what his weekend looked like. He could make out that Max was hosting another party and it seemed like it had triple the number of people in it, compared to the time Jamie was there. One selfie alluded to Max being naked apart from some knee high gym socks. He looked really sweaty with his hair dishevelled and his eyes indicating he had more than vodka in his system. The scenes from the party were in stark contrast to Brian's birthday bash and even to the scene of domesticity he was in at that current moment. Silently, Jamie took a selfie of his hooded face and one of his sleeping husband and cat. With a one word message, Max replied almost instantaneously.

Wrecked.

A much-anticipated knock came from the door. Jamie ran to answer it and was never so glad to see their pizza delivery guy. Money, tip and pizzas were exchanged. Returning to the sofa at the same time was Tom with large glasses of coke. Jamie had a pizza slice in his mouth before he sat down. Their *Strictly Come Dancing* marathon could resume as they tried to catch up on the previous night before the Results Show was aired.

"So, I've been left the house and a small amount of savings which will pay for some of the funeral costs," Jamie said without warning.

Tom stopped chewing and was transfixed on Jamie as he declared this while fast forwarding the interview part of the TV show. Tom didn't make a sound thinking that in doing so might elicit some more information. Jamie pressed play, placed the remote control on the coffee table and drank some coke, before sitting back on the sofa. Tom hadn't moved a muscle but realised his silence wasn't working.

"Okay," was all he was brave enough to say. He resumed chewing, a decoy to show semi-interest in the conversation.

"I told the solicitor, I didn't want to go back to the house and that all the contents were to go to local heart charities."

"That's very generous of you," Tom cautiously commented.

A whole dance, judges comments and scores went by. Jamie grabbed another slice of pizza and with one bite looked at Tom.

"Do you think I did the right thing? I'm no good with these sort of things. I just couldn't go back there. There's nothing there for me now and going back seemed too hard and pointless, maybe."

Tom felt like Jamie was permitting him for the first time to talk to him about his parent's death and there were so many topics he wanted to discuss but knew that he couldn't. He could only comment and address the one being presented to him.

"There's no right way of doing it, and usually people in this situation have siblings or other family members who have gone through it before. I honestly wouldn't know the first thing. Was the solicitor helpful?" Tom risked a question.

"He was. Eccentric, but helpful."

Tom could sense the wall reassembling, and his window of opportunity to speak freely was closing. He scoured his thoughts to make a final statement, something that would leave a chink.

"Well, I don't need to say it but, you know I'm here if you need anything." Tom eyes flicked right and left to see if this had registered a reaction.

 Jamie got up and grabbed his empty glass. He went passed Tom to go the kitchen. When he was behind him, he went over and kissed Tom on the head.

"I know. Want a top up?"

"No thanks. Actually, I think we need milk for the morning, so I was gonna pop 'round the corner. See if we need anything else?"

Jamie checked the fridge and said that milk was all they needed. Reluctantly, Tom put on his trainers and donned a coat before leaving. Now alone, Jamie went to their bedroom. He sat on his side of the bed and reached down to the bottom drawer of his locker. He pulled out his mother's bible and the envelope, still unopened that Mr Galloway had handed him. Sitting back with pillows to prop him up, he carefully opened the holy book and looked at the pages that were marked with a number of multicoloured woven bits of material. To his heathen eye, the marked pages followed no pattern. He slowly flicked through it, reading some underlined sections but apart from these, the only distinctive feature was how worn the book appeared, indicating the frequency of use. Gently he closed the book and brushed it with his hand.

Picking up the envelope, he fingered it with closed eyes. Spinning it between two fingers, he looked at it with indifference. His phone vibrated indicating a call coming through. He saw it was a FaceTime call from Max. He answered it. It was dark, and there was only the slavish thumping of a disco beat, and occasionally, Max's face would appear when the light was bright enough. Jamie turned down the volume on his phone and just watched. When Max's movements slowed, it was possible to make out men's legs, torsos and underwear, but little else. Suddenly the mass of men became smaller as Max appeared to leave the room. Under a lamp, he appeared ghost-like, not just because of the extreme light but how drained he looked. They tried to communicate that they couldn't hear each other via various hand signals. Max appeared frustrated and ended the call after kissing the screen. Instantly Jamie sent a text.

Couldn't hear a word. Chat soon. J

The message sent as Tom arrived back. He quickly but carefully returned the bible and envelope to where it had been hidden.

Chapter 8

"You don't look well," Teresa said, watching Jamie turn down the offer of some lunch while cradling a large takeaway cup of coffee.

"It's been a hectic week, do you mind if we just skip our usual walk and just plant ourselves down here?" he said, pointing to a vacant bench inside the market.

Teresa nodded, complying in concerned silence, sitting only after checking the bench was clean and dry. She gazed into the bag of sushi and wondered about how long it might keep for, as she too wasn't all that hungry either.

"How's the Christmas Party plans coming along?"

"It's all pretty much organised. The date has been set, the menu has never changed, and the band have been replaced by my iPod. We couldn't afford the band this year." There was a real sense of disappointment in her voice.

"That's a shame, nothing like live music. And when is the big day?"

"It's always on the second Saturday of December at the Greenwich Dance on Royal Hill."

"I know where that is."

The conversation dried up, but neither of them were bothered. One sipped coffee; the other ate and they both watched all the goings on around them. Teresa was glad Jamie wasn't asking her questions about her weekly session, and Jamie was glad Teresa never pried too much into his life.

"Too early to talk about outfits for the big night?" Jamie asked her.

"Something free flowing and comfortable. Long gone are the days of high heels," she laughed out loud which cheered Jamie up.

He peeked into the bag and helped himself to some sushi rolls. As he chewed, he asked her had she had any more panic attacks this week, deliberately calling them that. She didn't flinch when asked and reported a week free from them, so there was no need to "hum and breathe", as she called it. They were both chuffed with this piece of news. Jamie knew that this wasn't the end of them but put it down to a good week. He didn't want to tell her, as he felt it might in some way take away from what she appeared to view as a significant achievement.

"I was looking back on my diary..." she started.

"You keep a diary? That's a great thing to do," interrupted Jamie.

"Well, I think so too, but I was looking back and looking to see when these...panic attacks started," Teresa said, feeling slightly uneasy about using such a therapeutic term

"They seemed to have started in and around May of this year. I've even looked back at old diaries, and there doesn't seem to be anything like what I was describing to you. I now put a little sad face at the top of the page on the days that I have one. It makes it easier for me to count them now."

Jamie commended her. "What month did Bill pass away, if you don't mind me asking?"

"November."

"His birthday?"

"August," she said with a warm smile and sad eyes.

They looked straight ahead at a group of business men who breezed into the market, apparently finished for the day. Their ties loosened, jackets across their arm and sleeves rolled up. These men were craving beer and sustenance and weren't quiet about their needs.

"Young bucks," Teresa said sympathetically.

"I'd use other words, but there's a lady present."

As they looked on, Jamie noticed a familiar face trying to avoid the rowdy men. He tried to look away, but she eyed him just before he did. Like an awkward teenager, he waved, and half smiled. She waved back with subtle confidence and made her way out of the market.

"A work colleague?" enquired Teresa.

"Sort of. That's my supervisor, Helen. I've got a session with her this afternoon."

"You have sessions too?" Teresa sounded intrigued.

"Well, all therapists should be seeing a supervisor frequently to ensure they are working well. It gives another perspective sometimes on the work we do."

"That makes sense. I wonder if my fella goes? Actually, I don't want to think about him?"

"I won't ask then," putting his hands up in surrender.

His watch told him that it was time he got back to the office. They managed to get through all the food she'd bought.

'Same time next week?" they said in unison.

Jamie was not looking forward to supervision. He got another coffee to go and made his way back to the office. Remembering to take his notes this time, he went and sat in front of Helen. Immediately he was a little startled by Helen starting off the session, which in their history had never occurred. She began talking about the busy market. He small talked back about the best time to go before all the lunch breaks start and the best places to eat. He didn't know why he was feeling nervous about this informal introduction to the session, but then she therapeutically pounced on him.

"Was that..." putting on her glasses and looking at her notes, "Teresa, you were with, in the market?" She removed the glasses and looked expectantly at him.

He felt ambushed and angry, and she could tell this from his body language. She, however, remained her calm, stoic self and Jamie knew that she could sit there for the next ninety minutes and not say a word, but she was expecting a reply. Thinking like a therapist, he thought that going on the attack would surely backfire, even though he was mustering up all his strength not to lash out.

"Yes, as a matter of fact, it was Teresa," he said as calmly as he could.

It sounded calm to her, but Jamie wasn't convinced because he felt his voice was shaky.

"How is she?"

Again, his mind was clambering for answers to why she was asking about Teresa and what it had to do with her, it wasn't like this was on work time.

"She's fine," he replied simply, like playing a trick chess move.

"Jonathan and I are obviously in communication about certain aspects of the staff's performance, and as you are aware, some things will remain confidential. He did inform me that you took a day off last week to go back home and that you called in sick this week, which is very unlike you. How was that for you...going home? I can't imagine it was easy."

Jamie peered at his notes and would have loved just to discuss the clients he saw over the past two weeks. He still wasn't seeing the amount of clients he had been. Jonathan wanted to gradually ease him back in. So Monday's were the only day he saw people and the rest of the week was administration and audits. He knew she would report back on anything that might indicate that him seeing his usual caseload would be too much. He was in a bind.

"No, it wasn't the easiest of trips. My mother's solicitor needed me to sign a few things and to hear her will."

"Must have been hard going back to your childhood home, obviously from working together for some years, I know that it wasn't always a welcoming space for you."

"I have told Tom and no one else, that I didn't…I couldn't go back there. The solicitor was kind enough to arrange to handle the sale of the house. He gave me an envelope which I've yet to open." Jamie felt like he had run a marathon, so he slumped into the sofa.

She jotted a few things down before closing her note book and placing it on the table beside her.

"Jamie, I admire you as a person and as therapist. You know you do great work here, and you will continue to do great work, but I would be lying to you and be doing you a great injustice if I wasn't to say what I'm about to say." She looked at him for some sort of acknowledgement.

He just closed his mouth and sat up.

"I am concerned about you and how you are dealing, or not, with your recent bereavement. I can see that your client work is not suffering which is a testament to your dedication to the young people you work with but I am worried that this won't last and that ultimately...well, I'm afraid that it will just become all too much and I can see Jonathan signing you off work for quite some time, which I know would be the last thing you'd want right now. You think you need to be here to be distracted from what has happened..."

"I'm coping Helen, can't you see that?" Jamie pleaded.

"Actually Jamie, I don't. You are in some way splitting yourself, putting all your pain and sadness to one side and bullying your way through your day to day, hoping against hope that you'll escape, that you won't be affected by this massive emotional bomb that exploded in your life. You fear it will consume you and that you'll lose yourself, your sense of purpose. You feel you should be better than this, that you, *you*, a therapist no less, should not be up to your knees in the quagmire of something so trivial as grief."

He had never seen her like this before, but knew she was absolutely correct and she knew, he knew but was unable to respond.

"I'm on your side, Jamie."

"I know that..." his lip began to quiver and for the first time in his three years with Helen, he reached for the box of tissues. Like any good therapist, Helen remained in her seat and observed with compassion. Jamie appeared lost as he covered his face with a handful of tissues. For the briefest of moments, he allowed himself to hear the truth and to, unfortunately, feel it. It was worse than he had imagined and feared he would drown, that his distraught self was so burdened with the pain of loss that he couldn't fight his way up for a breath to allow him to think clearly, to function at work or to nourish his relationship with Tom.

More tissues were required, and his nose needed blowing. With each of these, Jamie began to become calmer until he sat up, red faced and said, "I'm ok now."

"Are you telling yourself or me?"

They knew it was rhetorical.

"It's ok to feel like this...to feel. Why don't we end it here and lets meet next week, how does that sound?" she asked.

"Sounds good."

Grabbing his notes, he stood up and was about to make his escape when she delivered her final volley.

"Just one more thing. I think we need to address your relationship with Teresa, but let's do this next week. That ok?"

Nodding like a chastised child, Jamie walked briskly to the staff toilet and assessed any signs of his crying. He threw some cupped handfuls of cold water on to his face, attempting to cool the redness and to remove any proof. A few paper towels to dry it all off and with a double take in the mirror, he appeared, to himself at least, normal. Gingerly he walked back to his desk. Thankfully Jonathan was off today as he had imagined seeing him in his office with Helen, getting all the in's and out's of their session. At his desk, he stared blankly at his emails, consciously blurring his vision, he didn't know what to think.

His phone vibrated on his desk. For less than a second he refocused and saw that Jules was calling again, but he just let it ring out.

The remainder of his working day was far from productive. Thankfully the office was quiet due to members of his team using up their annual leave before the year ended. In between the brief periods of inputting data and updating spreadsheets for his audit, he frantically checked Facebook, his personal email and Instagram, so much so that things weren't happening quick enough for him and he soon became frustrated by the lack of stimulus. He had turned his phone off twice, not to curtail his distraction but to see if his phone needed refreshing due to seeing nothing new in any of the apps he was always checking.

Turning around to check the clock, he was annoyed that it only said 4 pm, like it was the clock's fault. With that, his phone beeped to announce a new email. He snatched the phone and saw that it was from Galloway & Co. and the email was entitled *Update*. Jamie read the brief but very polite email from Mr Galloway. His email style was from an era of plush paper and gracious fonts. His opening line softened him slightly.

Dear Mr Anderson, I hope this email finds you well…

The email was just a few lines informing Jamie that he had contacted some of the charities, who were touched by his kind offer of allowing them to take what they could sell, auction or use. Being the officious gent, he went on to say he had given priority to charities that had a specific remit around cardiac issues and attached a timeframe for these charities to visit the property. Jamie was relieved to read that Mr Galloway had informed the organisations that these were to be treated like anonymous donations, and there were to be no public notices of thanks, alluding to the address or family name, but stated that if Jamie wanted the family name to be associated that he was to let him know. Jamie replied with just a *Thank you.*

When he had engaged his senses, the office sounded different to him. Looking around he realised that he was the only person left, even their dedicated receptionist had gone. An uneasy desire for something began to rear its head within Jamie's mind. Before it's hold became too intense, he unsuccessfully tried to trick it by focusing on the mound of printed spreadsheets that lay across the keyboard on his desk, but this unnamed hankering stood its ground like the stronger contestant in an arm wrestling match; toying with its weaker opponent, putting the squeeze on and then relenting, giving its weaker counterpart false hope before slamming their feeble hand to claim dominance. Defeated, Jamie sent a text, received an immediate reply and then left the office.

"Someone's had a head start."

Shot glasses were raised, downed with ease and slammed back on the counter of The Village bar. He certainly did have a head start because after leaving the office he bought a flagon of vodka and poured it into a diet coke bottle to consume on his tube journey into Soho. Being a Friday and post work, Soho was filling up quickly. Everyone was trying to take full advantage of happy hour. It was odd for Jamie to be there so early. Back in the day, The Village was a quick stop off point on his pub crawl of Soho. It was usually two drinks while watching the Go-Go dancers do their thing on top of the bar. Ordering another round, he spied an unoccupied table and suggested they sit.

"You didn't take long to reply," Jamie commented while trying to force his wallet into his front pocket.

"Well, I thought I'd never hear from you again plus, I just had enough of work today," Jesus replied in a confident tone, his eyes never straying from Jamie's.

This didn't go unnoticed, and Jamie was transfixed by the powerful stare. The slight lisp that rounded off the soft Spanish accent tingled the fine hairs on Jamie's arms.

"Well, I'd a rough day too and just needed to let my hair down. I hope you didn't have anything planned?"

"Not really. Max is out somewhere, and we had a loose arrangement," he said with a wink as he downed a shot that had been brought over to their table.

Jamie felt uneasy knowing that Max was around and wondered if Tom was also out with him. He looked around the bar to check, but it was clear he looked panicked.

"What is the deal with you?" Jesus asked without a hint of discretion or embarrassment. Being unsure what was being asked, Jamie tried to fob him off with a confused look, followed by a shot.

"I mean, we met at the party and then we had drinks, and I took you back to my place, where you freaked me out, by the way, that's why I called Max, and then nothing until an hour ago. I just don't get it."

Jamie admired the cocksureness that Jesus possessed. There was no rudeness or aggression, just an honest curiosity that seemed to puzzle the Spaniard. A part of Jamie wanted to be uncharacteristically open with him. The other part wanted to brush off the awkward previous meetings.

"You texted to arrange to meet sometime, so I texted, and we're now meeting up." Jamie hoped that would put an end to his questions.

Jesus decided to drop it. He went up to the bar to order cocktails and left Jamie at the table. Not enough alcohol to not feel self-conscious sitting at a table in a gay bar on his own, he pulled out his phone. No messages or missed calls, he was unsure if this was good or bad news.

Discreetly, he popped a mint from his pocket. Jesus arrived back and announced he had bought Porn Star Martinis. After trying them and agreeing that he liked them, Jamie began to ask Jesus more about him and what was it like being a doctor in the present state of the NHS.

Jesus painted a bleak picture of long hours, diminishing resources and his desire to leave the insane workings of A&E. Jamie found him engaging, insightful and imagined that he was a good doctor, kind and competent.

"I hope you don't mind me asking, but how do you juggle work life and..." Jamie hadn't the courage or vocabulary to continue.

"Work life and...?" Jesus tried to help him out, even though he knew what he wanted to ask.

"You know!"

"Party?"

"Yes, 'Party,' how does that work?" Jamie checked his face to see if he had in some way offended Jesus because he sat still and looked pensive.

"I see it as part of being gay and being gay in London. I work really hard, and I need to play hard, so once I stay in control, then it's cool."

He felt envious but not wholly convinced by his answer and didn't want to challenge it.

"Are you single?"

Before answering, he took his time to take a drink from the delicate cocktail glass, licking his lips and fixing his gaze on Jamie again.

"My boyfriend lives back in Spain."

Nothing else was added, and Jamie couldn't believe that there was no further explanation.

"How long have you guys been together?"

"Three years. He's also a doctor but couldn't get a job here, so we see each other when we can."

Jamie was intrigued and leant forward to pick up his glass. He felt he needed to ask the next question and take a drink straight after to appear to be casual and non-judgemental.

"So you guys have…you know…an arrangement?" Jamie drank immediately and hoped that the cold cocktail would dowse the embarrassment of using the word 'arrangement.'

"Arrangement? How very British of you," Jesus jested. "We love each other, and that's all that matters. I have fun here, but my heart is in Spain."

While his English was excellent, Jesus' answer sounded foreign to Jamie; it sounded like he was talking about chores, errands, laundry, things that didn't matter.

"And what is your…arrangement?"

"I'm married."

With that Jesus' phone lit up and with a quick glance, he informed him that Max was two minutes away.

"Does he know where we are?"

"Yeah," replied Jesus while showing Jamie that they used the *Find My Friend* app on their phones.

As he downed his drink, he saw Max, thankfully on his own. His confidence was unmissable as he strode over like he owned Soho. He waved and went straight to the bar with Jesus. Jamie fidgeted with his phone and tried to start a message to Tom but couldn't send one. The internal dialogue was full of energy, justifying the need to be out and to be drinking because of the day that had just been. The counter arguments had less heft and at this point of the evening, sounded less convincing and void of fun. Interrupted by a tray of shots descending on the table, he put the phone back in his pocket. Max placed a shot of Sambuca into Jamie's hand, remained standing and toasted the weekend. The overpowering aniseed taste had to be washed away with the remainder of his cocktail as he struggled not to cough in front of anyone. Jesus' phone lit up again. Jamie could see it was a FaceTime call. He excused himself and went on to the street to take it. Max informed him that it was Jesus' boyfriend.

After he took his coat off and checked his reflection in the mirror, Max sat down and began talking about the week he'd had and how much he needed to unwind. Jamie already knew how busy their week was because Tom too was struggling with the amount of work, but kept saying that if he started turning things down, it would mean his competition would be asked, so it was good business to keep saying yes. Jamie thanked Max for meeting him when he came back from visiting the solicitor, but Max wouldn't hear any praise, seeing it as a random act of kindness.

He began to tag himself in on Facebook, and Jamie asked him not to tag him. Max complied as he tried to take a photo of his drink. Looking outside onto Brewer Street, he watched Jesus FaceTiming, his boyfriend. It jarred with him that it looked normal, that they seemed to be having a normal conversation. Jesus saw he was being watched and with that, ensured he wasn't in view of the camera and gave Jamie a quick wink and pursed lips, which made Jamie look away.

Max saw this private moment and just sucked on his straw with a self-satisfied expression.

"That night I picked you up from the Euston Station was such a laugh. All my usual gang had plans, and I just thought, after reading your messages to Tom and him telling me about what you had to do back home, I thought...why not? Did you get home ok?"

"It was fun. To be honest, I don't remember much which was exactly what I needed," Jamie said with uncertainty. Out loud, it sounded reckless.

Max heard the inner judgment in Jamie's voice, so he tried hard to look serious and asked Jamie was there any update on his parent's house. He filled him in on the email he received earlier. Max asked him how much the house was worth, which summed him up. It was the first time Jamie had even considered the house value or that he'd receive this as a lump sum.

"So what's the plan."

"Plan?" Jamie replied innocently.

"Yup, the plan! Where to next?"

"I don't know."

"What are you in the mood for?"

Jamie knew what he was being asked, but the wink from Jesus sobered him up slightly. He was feeling tired now and the old gay that he felt, wanted to get some greasy takeaway and a train home. Max could see a less jovial Jamie, so he immediately intervened.

Standing up, he put his hand on Jamie's shoulder, told him to hold that thought and then disappeared to the bar. Jamie thought the sensible thing would be to pack up, grab his coat and leave. Peering at his phone, he saw a missed call from Tom and a text from Jules, which was just a waving emoji. At this point, he knew he was on the edge of going home and the point of no return.

Max arrived back with too many shots for the number of people at the table. He placed one of these in each of Jamie's hand and sat down to do the same.

"Fuck life. Let's party," he yelled.

Downing the shots, one after the other, Jamie careered past the point of no return. Jesus returned to see what was happening and caught up by matching their shot tally.

They went from gay bar to gay bar, covering the length of Old Compton Street. They were gluttons throughout Happy Hour. Jamie wasn't thinking passed what was in front of him: Max, Jesus, men, beards, stubble, skinny jeans, bears, twinks, drag queens, bar men, shots, spirits, Jägerbombs, crowds, bouncers, lights, music and nothing else. An assault on his senses which he could tolerate. Negative thoughts couldn't penetrate, permeate or pester. Spilled drinks or 'No Happy Hour' were the low points of the evening.

Max had to pull Jamie out of the Admiral Duncan, because he had put an endless stream of change into the jukebox and even though the whole bar was dancing to the songs he'd selected, Max knew they would have been there all night because he had selected at least four Madonna albums in their entirety.

The three men held each other up as they made their way through the crowds, the taxies and rickshaws. Eventually, they ended up at Ed's Diner, and in a moment of feeling less drunk, Jamie took on the responsible role and ordered the other two to stay outside while he went in and got them some food.

Emerging sometime later, he saw them both being propped up by street bollards. He gave them various bags, unsure what he was giving them, but ordered them to eat up and to drink the milkshakes, proclaiming the benefits of Ed's at a time like this. Jamie found his own bollard to keep himself vertical and ate while squinting, keeping an eye on the other two.

To their surprise, they began to become more upright and alert. Napkins appeared, and Jamie collected the groups rubbish and looked for the nearest bin. On his return, he saw them walking back up Old Compton Street. He was flagging a little and was hoping to be going in the opposite direction, to the train station, so he ran after them.

Max broke off and went to the left while Jesus was amidst a group of strangers. As he approached, he was able to make out that these strangers were club promoters trying to entice him into G-A-Y Bar. Jesus loved the attention from these young and beautifully presented young men. They were giving him half price passes and kept telling him it was a Lady Gaga night. Sobering up, even more, Jamie was conscious that he would be the oldest person in there and just wanted to go home.

Max reappeared and grabbed both of them away from the promoting and the leaflets. As they huddled, Max produced a bottle of diet coke, three plastic glasses and three white pills. Jesus held two and Jamie reluctantly held the other. He divided out the diet coke as evenly as he could. They all drank some and swallowed a pill each, and both of them pulled Jamie into G-A-Y bar.

Just as Jamie had expected, he seemed to be the oldest person there. Jesus went to the bar and Max spent some time pointing out patrons who were older, trying to prove a point. There were hardcore Gaga fans, who must have spent weeks on their tribute costumes. Suddenly Jamie felt different. A rush of energy exploded inside of him. The club seemed brighter, and the colours began to merge and blur. Jesus handed Jamie a drink, and the touch of his tanned hand sent surges of electricity up Jamie's arm, down his chest, soaring through his thighs, racing down to his toes before ricocheting back up and exploding in his groin. The crowd went hysterical as *Telephone* began to play. Jamie drank the contents of the plastic glass in one go and grabbed his two accomplices by the hand which magnified the effect on the colours, the lights and the skin to skin contact. He dragged them to the only space big enough for the three of them to dance and by the time they got there, all three men were in the same place, the same space and were in sync. They danced like a six armed creature. Their bodies were entangled with no holds barred on where each other's hands were placed. The unspoken rule was that they needed to be close, their hands needed to touch. Their breaths on each other's face and neck felt like seductive fire that turned each of them on so much at times they felt they were going to climax.

The song ended, and Jamie had the back of Max's sweaty head in his left hand and Jesus' in his right. They were all out of breath. Jamie looked at both of these men; their proximity was intoxicating. He could smell and feel both their colognes anointing his lungs. He licked sweat from his lip and could feel that he was aroused. Suddenly Jamie's grip on his friends loosened, and he stumbled back. The other two found this hilarious and for a moment so did Jamie. The ground started to feel unsteady, and Jamie tried to counterbalance and stay up right, sending the other two into convulsions of laughter, with tears streaming from their eyes.

Like a light going on, Jamie wasn't finding it funny and the vivid scenery blackened for seconds at a time. Viciously, he rubbed his eyes and opened his eye lids with his fingers. The periods of blackness increased. His heart became louder and stronger while more sweat appeared on his brow. Falling back, his hands became contorted, and he began to fit. Jesus slapped Max across the face to stop him from laughing and ran to his aid. He screamed at Max to get water while he cradled Jamie's head ensuring it didn't hit any hard surfaces. A few clubbers stood and watched while Jamie shook unpredictably. Max arrived with two-pint glasses of water. Jesus poured one over Jamie's scarlet face and told Max to hail a cab. He argued that they should call an ambulance, but Jesus said he could handle it. Max disappeared downstairs, and Jamie's body became limp.

Bouncers arrived and were compassionate enough to help Jesus carry Jamie down the stairs. He informed them that he was a doctor and that a cab outside was going to take them straight home. The crowds parted as the burly security guards approached. Miraculously for a Friday night, Max was waiting outside with a black cab. He was arguing with the cabby to hold on, that this was an emergency. On seeing the procession, Max opened the door to allow the bouncers to place Jamie gently inside. Jesus got in and rested Jamie's head on his lap. Max clambered in and gave the driver his address.

Chapter 9

It was that time of year when shops were torn between seasons. Should they just embrace Christmas and reveal their festive fronts and start cranking out all those tunes we love or, should they just hold back and wait for Halloween to do its thing? All the stores on Regent Street seemed to have had the restraint to hold back on the tinsel and glitter. Most were keeping the autumnal colours and pumpkins front and centre however when Tom popped into a small corner shop to pick up some headache relief; he was greeted with advent calendars and shelves full of tins of Roses.

He popped two pills with some water and made his way to meet Jules. He desperately needed her help. The Jamie he knew and loved had gone. What remained was a husk of a person, who slept in the same bed as him, who nodded and answered monosyllabically, who went to work occasionally and sometimes he came home. Tom had tried to be the supportive husband and to do what was asked of him, but there seemed to be no end in sight, and he was guiltily feeling depressed himself.

Contacting Jules felt like cheating. With every character that he typed, he felt he was doing something wrong. He knew it was a risky move, knowing how close they both were. Contacting her to meet meant she could've told him, and that would've backfired spectacularly, but he felt he had no other options and in his opinion, things couldn't have gotten any worse. He hadn't slept much, on top of a busy day at work, trying to finish as early as possible while rehearsing and re-editing what he had planned to say, thinking of every possible way it could be misinterpreted by Jamie, which didn't help his already throbbing head.

He walked into The Wolseley and saw that she was already there. He wanted somewhere Jamie wouldn't bump into them, so he decided on the opulent surroundings of one of London's favourite eateries. Jules and Jamie had been spending more time together over the past month, ending up with Jamie getting home very late, calling in sick to work and sometimes not coming home at all. The last place he'd start or even end up drinking was here. Work had been very sympathetic towards Jamie and his behaviour. According to him, this was the only perk of working for a charity dealing with mental health.

The courteous maître d' took his coat and led him through the restaurant. The sight of Jules without his husband in tow looked out of place to him. As he approached the table, she wasn't sure about staying seated or standing up. She had the look of someone who wasn't comfortable with this clandestine rendezvous either. He bent down and kissed her on both cheeks before taking his seat. Menus were perused while drinks arrived at the table. They both weren't hungry but were glad of the alcohol. The waiter took the menus from them and left to attend the other diners.

After the pleasantries, their day and journeys there, they sipped wine, like mirror images of each other. Tom was building up to broaching the subject with her. He took a large gulp and just went for it.

"Jules, I'm not sure if you know why I messaged you. Obviously, it's about Jamie..." and with that, he broke down while trying desperately to be as discrete as he could to hide his embarrassment and tears from his fellow patrons.

Jules, sat forward to touch his knee and tried to comfort him. Diners close by were looking from the corner of their eyes but eventually went back to their meals. Jules pulled some tissues from her bag and placed them on the table in front of him. Clumsily, he dabbed his face with them.

While he tried to compose himself, she tried to think had they ever, in their history, met without Jamie. They enjoyed each other's company, but they weren't constantly texting or calling. She had always been supportive and respectful of their relationship, trying to avoid all the tragic melodrama that can occur with fag hags when their fag begins to date. Tom loved how both Jules and Jamie were so close, how they were there for each other through thick and thin and how they both hated anyone branding her a fag hag.

Tom removed his fingers from his closed eyelids after a large intake of breath. Opening his eyes, he mouthed "sorry" in silence. She waved her hand to indicate she wasn't bothered. He placed his finger on the base of the wine glass as if to move it to an exact spot on the table.

"Take two…bugger it, sorry Jules, I had a whole speech worked out because I didn't want to put you in an awkward position, being his friend and all that. You know I would never want to come between you two. He loves you dearly, and well, I love you for that. He has really needed you, and you've been there for him. It's all I want for him." He stopped to take a breath.

Jules looked uncomfortable and fixed her dress to appear calm.

"It's just; you know what he's like. All along he's wanted us not to mention anything, and that life should continue as normal, and maybe I don't understand all this stuff but nearly three months in, I'm not sure he's getting any better. I actually think he's getting worse. At home, we're like two bumper cars. I try desperately not to collide with him, but there are times when I think he actively wants me, just to somehow hurt or punish him. I know you guys have been meeting up way more often after work than you normally do and I'm not one of those partners that shun that. I'm just not sure if it's helping. In all the time I've known him, he's never missed work and never went in with a hangover. I think it's becoming a real problem."

Jules tried to say something but was politely cut off straight away.

"I know how that sounds Jules, but believe me, I'm not blaming you or even angry at you. I just want him back," Tom said all this through a measured mouth, to allow only words to be released. It shut instantly to retain any emotion.

Jules looked even more awkward. Her facial expressions showed inner turmoil which Tom understood and admired.

"Tom, I don't know how to put this, and I too feel like I'm in an awkward position here but...I haven't seen Jamie for nearly two months. Actually, the last time I saw him was the night you arranged for us to meet him after his first day back at work. He's not replying to any of my calls or texts."

"What?"

"I haven't seen him or heard from him since the night I stood him up. I thought you were meeting to sort out some kind of intervention, to get us in a room together..."

"Then who?"

"Who?" Jules repeated without thinking but quickly understood.

The waiter was making his way over to see if they needed anything else, but she discreetly signalled to him that they were okay regarding food and drink, while everything else was far from being okay.

Tom's head was in his hands, his two elbows on the table, staring into his wine glass. Jules looked around while drinking, unsure how to proceed and what to say. He spoke, but she couldn't make out what he said, and rather than asking him to repeat himself, she sat up in her chair.

"Where has he been?" he said, suddenly looking at her.

She was caught between being really concerned for Tom, her best friend and not wanting to get him into any trouble. She was sure Tom wasn't aware of the visit to A&E.

"I don't know, Tom," was all she could offer.

His phone beeped and buzzed, and without looking at it, his heart sank. She saw the change in his demeanour as he struggled to remove the phone from his pocket. Without him looking at it, he showed her his phone. She thought this odd but went with it and looked. She covered her mouth with her hand as he checked the message himself.

Just with Jules now. Men trouble again. Don't wait up. J x

They both sat back in their seat and stared at the table. Inside, Jules wanted to run out of the restaurant, locate her friend and somehow simultaneously strangle and hug him. Any suggestions or words of advice would seem to implicate her friend in all sorts of trouble and upset Tom even further. She cared for both men, but her loyalties lay with Jamie. She wondered what her friend had been doing and whether he was in trouble, serious trouble. Tom's mind was churning out possibilities which helped to divert the absolute dreaded feeling that was drilling a cavity into his chest. This felt like a break-up, cheating and lying all fighting with compassion, concern and grief, some sort of emotional Rock-paper-scissors. Who would trump who?

"What are we going to do?" asked Jules.

"I am going to have to do something," he said sternly, but not actually directing it to her. "Listen, I'm sorry, but I'm going to have to go."

"Sure," she said, secretly relieved.

"Please, don't contact him. I know you're his friend, but it wouldn't help. Promise me," he pleaded.

She nodded her compliance as he left money for the bill. Tom began to put on his coat when Jules reluctantly asked him something.

"Out of curiosity, does Jamie have any remaining relatives or an older friend?" she asked. He stopped zipping up his coat and peered at her with intrigue.

"Why do you ask?"

"It's probably nothing."

"Jules!?" he pleaded.

"No, well, it was one day I went to try and surprise him for lunch, and I saw him walk off with an old lady, and I've never heard him speak of anyone that matched that description."

"Did he see you?" he asked with haste.

"No, they were so enwrapped in the conversation it seemed a shame to disturb them, and he looked…" she stopped.

"What? How did he look, Jules?"

"He looked peaceful, like the old Jamie. It was just nice to see," she reluctantly admitted.

He thanked her curtly and departed with a brief kiss on the cheek.

Glad he had left, she sat back in the chair, relaxing her shoulders while she took out her phone. Unlocking it, she scrolled through some previous messages from Jamie as pangs of guilt gnawed her for missing the signs. The last month of communication from him had been mainly texting apologising for missing her call because he had gone to bed early. There were missed calls from him during her work day, when he would know she was unable to answer, followed by a message saying that he had tried to call her.

Finishing the glass of wine and placing it back on the table she became paralysed by the dilemma. Should she text her friend and warn him? The waiter came to enquire if she wanted another glass. Nodding, she accepted a much needed second white wine. She didn't know what the right decision would be and the only person she could turn to who had the ability to think from a different person's perspective was hurting, grieving and was limping through life and she, supposedly his best friend, was blindsided by work and other seemingly non-important problems to stop and think that this was all seeming too fishy. How would she explain to him that she knew what Tom now knew?

The next afternoon, an alarm began. No one was awake to turn it off. George had been sound asleep on the bed but being violently awakened by the noise, bounded onto the floor and went to his bed on the landing, near the radiator. Slow movements could be seen underneath the duvet. These became more frantic as the duvet became entangled with legs and arms. Finally, a single arm appeared and grabbed the phone to silence it. As the arm struggled to put it back on the bedside locker, it knocked over a large glass of water and some headache pills onto the floor. Jamie managed to peel the duvet off him to assess the mess. He hadn't the headspace or energy to deal with this first thing, so he let his sweaty head fall back on the damp pillow to assume a type of foetal position.

A couple of hours later and with George curled up beside him, Jamie opened his eyes slowly, adjusting to the light penetrating the wooden blinds in his bedroom. Closing one eye he gawked at this phone and saw that he had muted a reminder which he had set the previous day:

1:00 pm Teresa - Borough Market.

Jolted by the sight of it he clumsily clawed through his phone to see if he had Teresa's number. On arriving at her name, he remembered that they had exchanged numbers, but neither of them had contacted each other yet, assuming that they'd just see one another at the usual time and place which had worked, except for the last three weeks. Cowardly, he began a message on his phone, stopping and starting it, then deleting, throwing his phone on the bed before picking it up and starting again.

Hi, Teresa, it's Jamie here. I'm so sorry I missed you today.

He stretched out on the bed. George gave a disapproving meow due to his sleep being disturbed, again, before jumping off the bed. Jamie heard an unusual noise, so he rolled over and peered to where the sound was coming from. He saw George licking up the water that he had dropped earlier with the pills, now half dissolved, on the floor. He leapt out of bed, shooing George before running to the bathroom to retrieve a towel to wipe up the mess. Nearing the bathroom, he saw the spare room door was slightly open and peered in. He could tell from the way the bed had been left that Tom must have slept there. An immense feeling of dread began to pester him as he closed the door slowly, resting his throbbing forehead against the cold spare bedroom door.

Entering the bathroom to find something to wipe up the spillage he noticed only his toothbrush in the holder and that Tom's wash bag wasn't there. Dread became panic as he ran to their office to see if Tom's suitcases were there, which they weren't. Dashing back to the bedroom he slipped on the wet floor, falling back and banging his head. Letting his body go limp, he closed his eyes.

Another reminder from his phone began to pierce through his throbbing head. He began to search for his phone. On finding it, he squinted through half open eyelids and saw that it was reminding him of his 2 pm supervision appointment. He looked at his goose bumped skin and only registered that he was freezing cold from laying on the wet wooden floor for the last hour. Creakily he managed to get himself sitting on the side of his bed where he checked his phone for some clues. He was able to ascertain that he had texted his boss a lie at 4:27 am, that he was up all night with a vomiting bug. He could see he had got home by taxi. There were 23 missed calls from Tom, the last one was at 11:34 pm, and that's when he must have sent the final text.

Worried out of my mind. I don't know where you are, but I need to go to bed as I have an 8:30 flight to NYC in the morning. PLEASE text or call me.

No initial. No kiss.

The floor was dry now, due to him having laid on it, wearing only his underwear. He decided to have a shower so he could warm himself up quickly. He grabbed two more paracetamol from the bathroom cabinet and placed them in his mouth. When he got into the shower he opened wide and allowed some water in so he could swallow them.

Standing in the shower, surrounded by steam, he was empty. He had no thoughts and no feelings. He was motionless as he allowed the water to wash over him like he was a powered down android. It was George's rapid and repeated soft pawing of the glass that reanimated him. He switched off the shower and dried himself while George sat on the toilet like he was keeping a concerned eye on his owner.

Clothed, he made his way downstairs. Pangs of hunger greeted him as he opened the fridge to find something to eat that required minimal effort and preparation. He saw that Tom had made dinner the previous night and had carefully cling-filmed a plate of it for him. He pierced the film with a knife and microwaved it. While it whirled around, he got out his phone and saw that his WhatsApp message to Teresa hadn't been replied to. Oddly, it hadn't even been delivered. He sent a short, apologetic, information-light message to Tom ending it with an appreciation for his shepherd's pie.

Binged into action by the microwave, he uncovered the hotplate and was hit by warm, succulent aromas. He devoured the meal with a large glass of milk, sitting at the dining table. It was a lonely scene, dining alone. Between mouthfuls, he was still, and the house was silent. He felt he should have been worried about something, but he lacked the knowledge of what it could be like he had been cryogenically frozen for years. With an empty plate in front of him, he stood up and went to put it in the dishwasher. The sight of Tom's coffee cup, a single side plate that he used for his toast, one butter knife and one tea spoon opened up something in him where he began to feel regret.

He closed the door on the dishwasher and looked at the world clock on the wall and figured out that there was no point in calling Tom as his flight wouldn't land for another couple of hours. That left him some time to try and make amends elsewhere. Grabbing a pen from the coffee table, he ran back upstairs to the office, pulled out sheets of paper from the printer and sat down. It was strange; he hadn't written a personal letter since he was in primary school and wondered did people still write their postal address at the top right-hand side or was that deemed old fashioned. It was all emails and WhatsApp messages these days, so he couldn't really tell. Sucking on the end of the pen, he felt that since it was a personal letter, that maybe he should refer to his primary school days and do it the way he was taught.

With his address written and the date underneath, he began to pen a letter to Teresa, apologising for not meeting up over the past three weeks. It was short because he didn't go into the details of why he reneged on their weekly chats. As he signed the letter and reviewed the page, the sentiment he was trying to convey didn't permeate enough.

With that, an idea came to mind. He opened up his laptop and while waiting for iTunes to load, grabbed a blank CD from one of the drawers in the desk. He found the track he wanted, burnt it to the CD and put it into an envelope along with the folded letter.

He peered out the window of their small office to find that it was dull, windy and very wet. His heart sank a little, but he had enough energy to fight through those feelings as he put on a woolly hat, his winter coat and gloves and decided which umbrella to take from their collection by the front door.

On the wintery streets of Greenwich, he was feeling upbeat and proactive, something he hadn't felt for quite some time. The weather wasn't bothering him as he dodged puddles and other pedestrians with their umbrellas. He sort of remembered where Teresa had lived but was pretty sure he wasn't taking the most direct route. Once on her road, he looked out for the inviting duck egg blue front door, which he eventually found.

Under the cover of the overhead canopy, he put down his umbrella, rang the door bell and gave his brolly a good shake. On hearing footsteps coming to the door, he ceased shaking the wet umbrella and did a quick check that he was well presented. Something didn't seem as it should because the door opened uncharacteristically fast and a strange woman appeared from behind it. For a second, Jamie thought he had the wrong house. It was too late then.

"Oh, sorry. I was looking for Teresa," he said very apologetically.

"No, you've got the right house. Can I help you?" said the strange woman, who seemed irritated by this disturbance.

"I was wondering if I could speak with Teresa?"

"May I ask who you are?" she asked officiously.

"Oh sorry, I'm Jamie, Jamie Anderson," he offered his hand but midway, she opened the door in silence and signalled for him to come in.

Once inside, he wiped his feet furiously on the mat and left the damp umbrella by the door. Looking around, he saw that she had already gone into the kitchen, so he followed her in. Surprised there was no sign of Teresa, he looked around at the woman.

"So you're the famous Jamie?" she eventually said.

Jamie smiled and shrugged off the praise.

"You're the man my mother has been going to meet instead of the counsellor that I've been forking out a fortune for."

Jamie tried to politely interject, but she silenced him with a look.

"You're the man that allowed her to stand for hours in the cold, waiting for you to show up and didn't!"

She was angry now, and Jamie found himself in something he wasn't prepared for. He had quickly deduced that this was Teresa's daughter but was unsure where Teresa was and if was she ok.

"Is your mother in?" he asked meekly.

"My mom is in the hospital with pneumonia, thanks to you!"

"I'm sorry but…"

"But what? What possible excuse can you come up with that makes it okay to prey on an old woman's vulnerabilities and then allow her to stand out in the pouring rain waiting for you to peddle your wares, or do you get off on letting old ladies down?"

It was angrier she was getting and Jamie raised both his hands like he was facing a shotgun, trying to calm the situation down.

"What are you after? Are you one of those sick men who prey on older women, befriend them, work your way into their lives? Was it the house? Get your name on the will somehow?"

On hearing this Jamie erupted.

"And who the fuck are you to preach to me about elder abuse? What kind of daughter are you to remotely arrange therapy sessions for their grieving mother like it was some sort of spa day and not have the common, actually, the daughterly decency, to go along for the first session or at the very least, visit her from time to time? Or are we just too busy making money and hoping that lack of contact and communication with her only child will send her to an early grave and she'll get the house in Greenwich and whatever lump sum Mummy and Daddy put by for their spoilt wretch of a child?!" Jamie was red faced with spittle hanging from his mouth. He stopped because he had run out of breath.

There was a moment where neither of them spoke. Jamie was panting and he rubbed his wet lips with his fist, waiting for her volley but it didn't come. Instead, he witnessed this angry woman shrink in front of him. First, she grabbed the counter top for balance; then her sullen face morphed into devastation. She slid down the kitchen cabinets, on to the floor, where he saw her body convulse as she forced her tears to stay put. Jamie slowly walked towards her.

"Just breathe, don't hold them in…just breathe," he said very calmly.

She resisted for a few seconds but on having to breathe or pass out, she inhaled and on exhaling came tears and hard sobs. He looked around the surrounding worktops and found some kitchen roll. He ripped a few sheets and handed them to her. Reluctantly she took them and hid her face while drying it at the same time. Jamie stood close by in silence.

Eventually, he could hear regular breathing in between sobs and this increased over time. She wiped her face with her hand but didn't stand up. Jamie felt out of place towering above her, so he slid down the kitchen cabinets, a few feet away from her and became still again.

"I'm sorry," Jamie said softly, "that was harsh. I'm sorry."

She didn't respond and he was unsure if she'd actually heard him through her sniffling. She raised her head and looked at the clock on the wall.

"It's very easy to pass judgement on something when you've only heard one side of the story," she said.

"What do you mean?"

"To be fair, most of what you just said is true, well, except for the bit about the house. Yes, it's a great house and being in Greenwich it is worth or will be worth something when it is sold. But things since my father's death haven't been great. I was very much a Daddy's girl. He adored me. I was his world. It was how Daddy's are supposed to be and being grown up now; I see that not everyone was as lucky as I was. Don't get me wrong, I had a great relationship with Mum too, but there is a very special bond between a father and his daughter. When I found out he had...passed away, I was in work. I dropped everything and got a taxi here straight away. It was surreal being in the cab. I felt panic because I wanted to get there as soon as I could. On the other hand, I didn't want to arrive at the house because that would've made the news somehow real. I prayed for the first time in years for it not to be true that somehow my mother got it wrong but...it was...he was...gone."

"Death in a family is tough. Everyone is hurting. The people you usually go to for help can't because they are also in need."

"Tougher when someone blames you for it."

"Who? Your mother?" asked Jamie incredulously.

She just nodded to confirm. "My husband and I bought properties, renovated them and sold them on. My Dad would insist on working at these houses because when he retired from the force, he struggled with doing nothing. We employed him to do the painting and decorating, anything he could do, he would, but we always paid him for it."

"Great to have something like that when someone retires, especially if they enjoy it," Jamie added.

"He did. He'd send me photos of the walls before and after and it reminded me of the time I'd bring home my good test results to show him how well I'd done. After the funeral, we had a little gathering at the house. When it was just my husband, myself and Mum and we were getting ready to go home, I went into the sitting room. She had had a few glasses of wine; she's not a big drinker at all. I was just going to see if she needed anything or if she wanted me to stay. She was in the good sitting room looking at a photo of him. She looked so small, so lost..." she began to sob a little but coughed to try and shake it off. "She started to say that if I hadn't been working him so hard in his retirement that he'd still be here. They had planned to slow things down once retirement came so they 'could travel a little, dance a lot and enjoy not having to work.' Thankfully my husband had heard this and was silently ushering me out of the room. I wanted to lash out, but I knew she was hurting. I wanted to comfort her because her husband, my father had gone and I understood her pain. Instead, the last thing she said when I was leaving the room was 'I hope you're proud of yourself?'"

Jamie wasn't expecting to hear this. The parting shot from Teresa filled the room while they remained low on the ground like the words were harmful to inhale. He was trying to marry up the story to the Teresa he had come to know and like, but as her daughter said, there's always two sides to every story. He wasn't doubting her and felt guilty that she had to go through this and that his outburst resulted in her having to retell it all to a stranger.

"I don't know what to say," was all Jamie could come up with.

"There's nothing to say. Things have never been the same again and it's never been spoken of since. That's the reason I've kept my distance. It's hard enough having to come back, knowing that Dad isn't here but when you are being blamed for something, actually blamed for his death, why would I come back? I still care about her; hence I was sending her to therapy after the GP had called me saying he was concerned about her and that she might be suffering from panic attacks. I'm not that heartless, you know?

"I understand."

She gazed at the black and white photographer that hung on the kitchen wall. It was her parents' wedding day.

"You know they would've been fifty years married this year."

With that her mobile rang. Stretching out her leg she removed it from her trousers. It was a call from the hospital. Jamie saw a worried look develop on her face as he overheard her being told that she was going to be kept in for a few more nights and that she needed a few personal items. She was very polite on the phone and double checked with the nurse who had called that she had remembered the list correctly, which she had. She stood up, a little creaky from being on the floor for some time, and informed Jamie that she had to leave. He got up too and said that he understood and apologised again.

"For what it's worth, I didn't know your mother wasn't attending her appointments. I'm a therapist myself and she was telling me she was going, which I encouraged her to do. I meant her and mean her no harm and I'm not after money or anything like that."

Making his way to the front door, she followed in silence. He let himself out, and while she held the door open, she stood and looked. She wasn't sure what to make of him. Pausing on the front porch, with his back to her he pondered for a second.

"Will I tell her you called?" she asked with softness in her voice.

"Would you mind?" Jamie turned around. "Actually, could you also, maybe, give her this? It's a letter and a CD." he said as he handed it over.

She took it off him and looked at it oddly.

"I'm Lily, by the way," she said, extending her hand.

"After your mother's cousin?"

"Yes, how did you...she told you then?"

"Just a guess. Take care."

Closing the door, she thought about her interaction with the stranger in her mother's house. Lambasting this 'Jamie' hadn't panned out the way she had planned. Without thinking, she placed the envelope on the nearby table and ran upstairs to her mother's bedroom. In a dated overnight bag, she neatly packed a nightdress, toiletries, her mother's bible and rosary beads along with a phone charger and her iPod. It was oddly satisfying for her to be handling these intimate items like she was doing something familiar and important. Looking around the room was a trip down memory lane, seeing all the photographs and the costume jewellery all laid out on ornate holders in front of a mirror.

She went and sat on her mothers' side of the bed and carefully picked up a photo of her, her mother and father that was taken at the ice cream parlour in Broadstairs. She remembered she was around six at the time and it was such a beautiful day. Smiling with tears falling on the frame she caressed it tenderly in her hands and then held it to her chest for a brief moment.

She coughed to try and snap herself out of the nostalgic trip and checked her makeup in the mirror. Before zipping up the bag she scanned the room, wondering was there anything else she needed to bring. Nothing else was added to the bag and as she fastened it, the sight of the iPod made her chuckle to herself as she still couldn't believe how tech savvy her mother was for a lady her age.

Descending the stairs she saw Jamie's envelope in the hallway. There was no one around and she wasn't going to lie and say she wasn't intrigued by it, but he had mentioned a CD and thought that if she opened it, she could upload it onto her mothers iPod before giving it to her in the hospital.

She dropped the bag on the table and examined it. It was a normal burnt CD in a plastic case. On the front of it he had written, in black marker, *She Misses Him on Sunday the Most by Diamond Rio.*

Inserting the CD into her mother's dated laptop, she then connected her iPod and waited. As it thought about working, the envelope was beside her and she just couldn't stop herself from wanting to read what this strange man had written. Peering inside she saw two sheets of paper. She delicately pulled them out and just as she began to read the first page, the laptop began to play the single track that Jamie had burned on the CD. She listened and read. Helpfully, Jamie had printed out the lyrics on the other sheet of paper. The song told the melancholic story of a widow thinking of all the things she did with her husband when he was alive in their very ordinary day to day existence.

It took one verse and chorus before Lily was on the kitchen floor, sobbing for the second time that day. The computer was on her lap as she held the pages to her chest listening to rest of the country song. When the track finished, it took her a few attempts of trying to catch her breath and coughing before she could do anything. When the song was uploaded, she stood up, closed down the computer and put the iPod back into the bag. She gently folded over the two pieces of paper and inserted them, along with the CD into the envelope. After catching a glimpse of herself in the mirror, she had to reapply some of her makeup. Waterproof mascara was the last thing she thought she would have needed. It was a novelty for her, applying makeup in her childhood home. She liked it, it made her feel whole, connected somehow.

A final touch up of her lipstick, a closer inspection and she was ready. Grabbing the bag, she stopped in the middle of the hall to compose herself. There was no sound apart from her breathing. With closed eyes, she tried to breathe slowly in and out for about thirty seconds before leaving and locking the duck egg blue coloured door.

Jamie sat in Noodle Time on Nelson Road. This was their place to go to when both of them were too hungover to cook. Dining alone, he began to run over the chat's he had had Teresa in his mind, he remembered about how they came to know each other. Incredibly, in a city often too busy to care, they met each other in a moment of urban serendipity. Using the calendar on his phone, he worked out that they must have met at least seven Friday's in a row. He struggled with not becoming her therapist but he couldn't help wonder that the reason for the panic attacks she described had something to do with the fact that she would've been married to Bill fifty years this year, something she and her husband had talked about and had planned for. Even though he had died some years ago and it might have appeared to her, her family and friends that she was coping well with it. However, he believed that entering the marriage milestone of fifty years alone, without Bill, was like revisiting the grief and loss all over again.

After paying for his meal, he exited the restaurant. The cold air hit his face. The warm food inside him had a calming effect as he walked home. He was keen to get back and charge his phone to see if Tom had replied.

He plugged it in the instant he was inside. George was circling and rubbing off his leg making sure Jamie knew that it was dinner time. Without thinking, Jamie sorted out fresh kibble and water to appease the hungry cat because he was aware that not doing so immediately would mean a constant barrage of meows.

The phone beeped to announce it had power which promoted Jamie to leap over to the kitchen counter and check were there any messages. There weren't any from Tom. His message had been delivered and had been read. Jamie thought it strange and put it down to the faff of getting through security and then meeting up with his driver and checking in. He didn't send another one and just left it charging on the side while he made himself a cup of tea.

A night in on the sofa was initially very appealing to him. A warm brew with some digestive biscuits and George curled up nearby as he caught up on the shows he'd missed over the past couple of months. All of this was interspersed with trips to view his phone, ensuring it wasn't on silent and that it had full signal until it was fully charged and on the arm of the sofa. With each hour that passed, Jamie's relaxing evening became more torturous for him. The lack of response was now nothing to do with getting through a busy airport or checking in to the hotel. This was so out of character for Tom and indicated that something was up. Something was really up. He knew that Max wasn't with him on this trip because he was spending time with his boyfriend who seemed to be home for the first weekend in months, so he couldn't text him to find out what was going on.

Eventually, the TV shows came and went without him actually watching them. He was running through the scenarios in his head while keeping an alert eye on his phone with every update and email that came through, hoping against hope that it would be a message from his husband.

A vibrating noise woke him suddenly. Opening his eyes, he saw George purring heavily and kneading his stomach, his cute and unsubtle way of telling him that it was time they went to bed. He jerked his head to check the time on the wall, which also said that it was bedtime. Gently, not to push George off, he raised himself off the couch. George's job was done and so he bounded upstairs. Still no messages from Tom. Angry by the lack of contact and feeling like he was being punished, he turned the TV and all the lights off before going to brush his teeth and wash his face.

The house seemed more silent than he had ever experienced it, as he stood in front of the mirror waiting for his electric toothbrush to tell him he had done a good job. He looked and recognised it was him but there was something he was unfamiliar with. There were no physical changes, spots or marks. No weight gain or weight loss. It scared him slightly, so he decided to spit and rinse before the brush had instructed him to and switched the light off, so there was no more reflection. He kissed a curled up George who assumed his place on their bed. As Jamie slid in, George looked up as if he too was expecting Tom to walk in and get underneath the duvet.

Jamie grabbed his phone for what he hoped would be his final check before he woke up. Alas, no messages from Tom, but he did see that he had checked in to the Ace Hotel a couple of hours ago on Facebook. He hovered over the LIKE button and gave in in the end and just liked it. He also decided to send him a text:

Hey you, just in bed. Hope the flight was ok. Chat tomorrow? Love you, Jamie x

He didn't put the phone on silent but turned it upside down. As he turned around to get comfortable, hoping it would be for the entire night, he found that George was now curled up just below Tom's pillow as if to offer him some comfort on the night ahead. He kissed George again and tried to fall asleep.

Chapter 10

Alone on a bench in the market at lunch time, Jamie began to eat. Amidst no contact at all from Tom, he managed a healthy week of homemade dinners, DVDs with no alcohol or illegal substances and lots of early nights. Work had been bearable, and they seemed glad that he'd been in every day so far. It was a long shot, but he was hoping that Teresa would gently walk up and take a seat by his side. He thought about texting Jules, but decided against it, passively hoping that she'd surprise him with a lunchtime visit. However, this was a solitary hour. He was trying so hard to relax and not over think things. Most of the time it worked, but as it drew closer to going home, this became more difficult. Tom's flight got in that morning, so he had that to deal with when he got in. He missed him terribly, but he knew that he had used up whatever levels of compassion someone could have for a loved one and that a difficult conversation was on the cards. There were a couple of times where he wanted to contact Max but decided against it, thinking that he didn't want to intrude on his time with his boyfriend. He looked lost and alone on the bench, looking around, hoping someone would show up.

He put all his rubbish into the bag, drank the last of his water and walked over to the bin. As he put the bag in, he looked around one more time and disappointedly, he went back to work.

At his desk, he checked for any work emails and then checked his phone. Neither one had anything new for him to read. He began to sort out which files he needed to bring into supervision which didn't take that long before sitting in front of his screen staring at the clock and waiting until the exact moment he needed to go.

Four minutes later, with thirty seconds before his computer told him it was 13:30, he got up and walked to the supervision room. Helen was there, ready and waiting for him. Jamie sat down and got comfortable. There were the usual greetings back and forth and then Helen asked him how he had been after the previous session. Jamie tried to be honest and said that he was eventually glad that she was upfront with him and that he had thought a lot about what she had said.

She interjected and asked had he met anyone for lunch. He knew she was wondering had he met Teresa, so he was glad to say that he had lunch alone. She gave a smile that indicated she was pleased with his answer. He didn't say anything else about Teresa because he had taken from her comments at the previous session, that meeting up with her probably wasn't the healthiest of things to be doing.

With a false sense of progress, which was helped by Jamie not being completely upfront about why he hadn't met Teresa for lunch, Helen suggested that they leave the personal stuff to one side and spend the rest of their time looking at the client work he had brought in with him. Jamie, relieved by this suggestion and feeling slightly guilty that he seemed to have lured his supervisor to think he was probably doing better than he was, grabbed the first set of notes from the pile and got straight in with presenting them and what he thought might be the reasons for their referral.

The ninety minutes flew passed, and he managed to squeeze all the clients into the session, where he got some great suggestions from Helen. Feeling energised, he headed back to his desk to write up some notes which he would need when seeing the clients again.

With no contact from Tom, the rest of his afternoon dragged. He was hoping that a text would come through asking him to choose what type of food he wanted this evening, and even though he didn't sleep great the previous night, an impromptu drink in Soho with Tom, sounded so appealing. As he filed away his notes, his phone vibrated. Nearly jumping out of his skin he stretched over to grab it to see that it was a message from Max. He was just checking in, wondering how he was and if he needed some fun later. He said that Tom would be so jet lagged from his trip that if Jamie wanted to get out of the house for the night to call him, that he'd be out anyway. Jamie let the phone fall on purpose in sheer frustration.

The anticipation of arriving home to an angry husband became too much for him as he knocked on Jonathan's door. He asked him if he could go home early and make up the time next week. His boss was too caught up with their accountant to ask questions and just flippantly agreed. He packed up his bag and dashed to London Bridge station.

Once at the right platform, he texted ahead to say he was coming home slightly earlier, hoping to start the flow of communication and give him a heads up on how angry Tom was going to be. There was no response when he boarded the train as it made its way on the short journey to Greenwich.

When the doors opened, Jamie felt less enthusiastic, and the sight of no new messages on his phone filled him with terror. He was in a dervish of thought, and someone nudging him to get passed was the only reason he got off, as it snapped him out of the endless possibilities going around in his head.

With each step home, he went from thinking it was a good idea not to have bought flowers and wine to thinking the complete opposite. Turning up his cul de sac, his phone began to vibrate in his pocket. He yanked it out with hope only to see another message from Max telling him he was in The Duke of Wellington and that if he wanted to, he could join him. He told his phone and Max to 'piss off' out loud as he fumbled with putting it back in his pocket.

A few strides later and he could see their black front door. Nothing was unusual with the outside of the house which was unnerving, even though he wasn't sure what he was expecting: removal vans, a signs to say the house was for sale or a different door which he didn't have keys for. He walked on, trying to get away from these intoxicating, persecutory thoughts and eventually reached the front of their house. Inserting the keys, he opened the door and instantly knew Tom was home. It comforted for second and then scared him. He dropped his bag at the door and hung up his coat. There was a shuffle from someone sitting at the dining table, so he decided to face the inevitable. Walking in, he saw a different Tom sitting at the head of the table. Wearing a black shirt and more stubble than normal, this Tom looked angry, foreboding and exhausted. Jamie's first reaction on seeing him was to send him to bed; he looked so unwell. Before anyone spoke, he noticed that on the table in front of Tom was his mother's bible, the envelope that was left for him in the will and the remainder of the PEP medication that he was given the time he was in A&E.

Jamie's insides collapsed and the colour drained from his face. He was scrambling to say something, but he couldn't come up with anything that would make this, whatever this was, better for either of them.

Tom looked directly at the items in front of him and focused on these for a few seconds before slowly focusing on Jamie. He knew he needed to get through this for both their sakes, he felt he owed Tom that at least.

"I think you should sit down," Tom said.

As Jamie sat, Tom got up and went to the wine fridge and pulled out a bottle of white. He fetched two glasses from the cupboard. Standing behind Jamie, who had complied and was sitting down, he reached over to place a glass in front of him and the other, close to the containers of PEP. With a bottle opener, he pierced the cork and screwed it before easing it out. Jamie felt like he was watching this in slow motion. He just wanted this to be over.

Calmly, Tom poured some wine into Jamie's glass and before sitting down, poured himself quite a large serving. He replaced the cork carefully, putting the bottle on the table and sat down. They both drank a little and looked at each other, wondering should either one of them begin to speak.

"I think it's time we actually spoke about things."

"I think so," replied Jamie.

"There are some things we need to talk about, and we are going to talk about them. The first item on my list is the old woman you have been meeting up with."

Jamie was stunned by this being the first thing Tom wanted to discuss. How much did he know? He took a large drink to prepare himself and sat back in the chair.

"Obviously Max had mentioned he had seen you with an older woman and at the time I didn't really think about it. Then, last week I met up with Jules," he looked uneasy about mentioning this meet up.

Jamie felt a stab of betrayal but realised that his husband and best friend meeting up behind his back paled into insignificance, so he didn't lash out.

"Before you get annoyed at her or me, we were just really concerned about you. However, she had said that you hadn't been in contact for months. You weren't returning her calls or texts and haven't met up in ages. A while back she tried to surprise you on your lunch break, and she saw you leaving Borough Market with, what she described as an older lady. I don't usually ask this, but is this someone you know through work? I thought it was just young people you saw?"

"Her name is Teresa. I met her one day at London Bridge station where she was having a funny turn and we just sort of met up after that. I know it sounds weird but she's going through some stuff, and I was maybe, trying to help her."

"Jamie, I cut hair, and I don't claim to be some sort of genius, but I'm not an idio. Why do you keep meeting up with her? She is not a client."

"I know she's not."

"She is not your mother, Jamie. Your mother is gone." Tom drank some more and watched what he had said take effect. He could tell Jamie was fighting with wanting to be dramatic and scream that he was being ridiculous, but he was also trying not to get emotional. He had had enough of not talking about Jamie's grief because it was affecting both of them now. There needed to be no more avoiding the subject, but there was a part of him hoping this wasn't too much too soon.

"I know she's not my mother. I just thought..." Jamie was interrupted by Tom.

"You just thought that if you could help this little old lady, it would make you feel better for not being there for your mother? For not being a better son? Or not going home more often? Take your pick, Jamie?"

Jamie was completely winded by the pinpoint accuracy of his hairdressing husband. While they jested in the past about Tom just cutting hair, he never thought less of him for doing what he did. If Jamie wasn't hurting, he would have been so impressed, even proud of Tom. He was indeed correct, but it was weird to have someone tell him out loud what he'd been lying to himself about. Jamie had always tried to shove this to one side of his mind, putting his chats with Teresa down as something entirely philanthropic. Now it was out there, he could deny it, but what was the point? His current location was rock bottom. It was all going to come out tonight. Looking at his glass, he found his chest begin to pulsate while his face became hot. He grabbed both sides of the chair he was on and held on tight because Jamie thought he needed to clasp on to something solid. He hunched forward with one sudden movement. Tom watched Jamie convulse in front of him. Without making a sound, he got up and placed his left hand on Jamie's back and told him to breathe. Jamie shook harder still, and Tom could see his neck turning scarlet.

"Breathe. Don't hold it in."

With that Jamie, complied and began to cry with rasping sounds exploding out of him. The floor underneath him was wet with tears, spit and snot. Tom didn't grab tissues or hold him close; he just kept his hand on his back as if this aided in the expulsion of Jamie's emotions. His hair became sweaty with the sheer physical exertion of expelling what he had invested so much time and energy trying to keep quiet and secret.

"She's gone! I can't believe she's gone!" Jamie cried out.

There was nothing for Tom to say because it was sadly true. He felt a bit cold not offering some words of comfort, but he also felt that Jamie needed this.

With time, his sobbing slowly lessened. Tom eventually grabbed some kitchen roll and handed it to him. He blew his nose hard and rubbed away residual tears from his eyes before sitting up again. Tom kissed him on the head and said he needed to go to the toilet and that he'd be right back. As Tom turned to head upstairs, he spotted George for the first time, sitting on the chair at the end of the table looking concerned at his owners and feeling like he did, a bit useless.

He quickly went upstairs to use the loo. It was also an opportunity for him to take a breather. He wasn't used to seeing Jamie or indeed anyone that upset and while he was holding it together downstairs, he was frightened of what he had heard coming out of the man he loved. It was as if someone had just told him for the first time that his parents had just died. Amidst all Jamie's grief and sadness was Tom's anger. The lies, the reasons for Jamie to have been on PEP and the hurt he felt that Jamie couldn't talk to him about any of it. Washing his hands, he felt he was psyching himself up for round two. After drying his hands, he just stood in the bathroom to compose himself before he went downstairs.

As he approached the last few steps, he noticed George was returning from the front door. Dashing to the kitchen, he found Jamie and the bottle of wine missing. Tom quickly ran outside. The street lights had come on, but he couldn't see any sign of him. He put both hands on his head and turned around slowly in disbelief. George rubbed up against his leg, and immediately Tom picked him up and took him inside. Scrambling for his phone he speed dialled Jamie, but it went straight to his voicemail. He kept trying, but the result was the same. He called the local taxi firm who sent a car ten minutes later. Tom instructed the driver to go to the train station and to do a loop of Greenwich. The driver looked at the distraught man in the back of his car and silently did what he had been asked.

The short drive to the station was spent looking on both sides of the road. As they approached, he told the driver to wait as Tom hopped out of the car and dashed across the road to loud, angry horns from oncoming traffic. Racing onto the platform to frantically look for a familiar silhouette, he saw two trains; one was just departing for London, the other was going in the opposite direction. The station was a mix of commuters returning home and revellers heading into London for a night out. He tried to get through the crowds of people, and when he couldn't, he tried to jump up for a better view, but it was fruitless.

Heading back, hoping the driver hadn't sped off, he called Jules, who didn't pick up. He left a voice message telling her as calmly as he could that Jamie had gone missing. In the car, he felt like he was losing his mind and while waiting at a red light, he went through his phone. He knew Dan and Brian were out of London. Finally, he spied Max's number and out of sheer desperation, called him and instantly regretted it because all he heard from the second Max had accepted the call was the roaring sounds of someone scrambling to get out of a bar. Max was shouting down the phone at him to hold on. The car stopped and started as it negotiated Friday evening traffic.

"Okay, I'm here. You ok?"

"Sorry to bother you, Max, but...Jamie's gone missing!" Tom finally broke down. The taxi driver sneaked a quick peek at the grown man crying in the back of his car.

"Don't panic. I'll get an Uber to yours right now," and hung up.

It was comforting to know, and it did calm him down. Tom spent the next thirty minutes slowly edging around a bustling Greenwich town centre. He was moving from the left to the right side of the car, checking every person passing, every shop and restaurant until they were back at his house. The taxi driver asked if he wanted to go around again, but Tom just enquired how much he owed. He paid and thanked him for his patience.

No one, but George was home. No missed calls or messages. Facebook revealed nothing of note, no clues. Searching the Police website, it informed him that missing persons don't become an issue until they have been missing for twenty-four hours.

With the battery on his phone running low, he dashed upstairs to grab his charger and returned to the kitchen table with his laptop, using it as a hub to view all potential communication portals.

An hour had passed. Countless calls to Jamie's phone made Tom think that he had turned his off. His empty glass of wine wasn't replenished, believing that coffee was what he needed. He was making a third espresso when there was a loud knocking on the front door. This frightened the already agitated cat that was patrolling the kitchen, only stopping the circular walks to pop up onto the table at various moments as if to check in on Tom. He ran to open the door and as he did Max burst in. He knew that his colleague had plans to be out in Soho but was a little shocked how sober he appeared. Max gave a perfunctory hug while walking through the house and taking off his coat. He wanted to show that he was there to be of help.

Having been to their house many times, he went straight to the coffee machine and made himself a strong one as Tom filled him in on the what he had done so far which only amounted to constant calling and a slow taxi ride around the area. After having some hot coffee, Max turned around to see Tom hunched over the laptop, which his phone was connected to. In front of him were an empty espresso cup, one empty glass of wine, a bible and pill jars. Max realised that a significant conversation was had and now understood why Jamie might have felt he needed to get out of the house.

Awkwardly, Max took a seat opposite Tom. In a rare occurrence, Max was lost for something to say as he began to rethink his presence at this sensitive time. Tom tapped at his phone and used speed dial to call Jamie for the umpteenth time and for the umpteenth time it went straight to voicemail. Behind the computer screen, Tom burst into tears and held his weary head in his hands. Silently, Max watched and drank. Having never seen Tom like this before he was struggling with constructive platitudes to deliver, but felt that this would just annoy rather than sooth.

Finally, after a brief cry, Tom's head was up, rechecking his laptop and phone. As if he'd forgotten Max was there he looked up and felt like he needed to say something but was interrupted by another knock at the door. They immediately looked at each other. Max quickly got up and went to see who it was. Tom stayed in the kitchen with his hands over his face praying that he would hear Jamie's voice. No sooner had Max opened the door when Jules burst through. Tom leapt out of his seat and met her half way where they just embraced. There was nothing for them to say because they both loved him, they both knew he'd been hurting, and they felt like they had let him down, but they were also aware that he wouldn't have let them help.

When the embrace broke, Tom filled her in on what was happening as they made their way to the kitchen where Max was now on his feet and on his second coffee. He singled to her to see if she wanted one, but she declined. She placed her coat on the back of a kitchen chair and sat next to Tom at his laptop. She suddenly spied the PEP pills in front of them and was struck with panic. She wasn't sure if Jamie had fessed up to their A&E visit a couple of months ago or had Tom discovered them and confronted her best friend with them, demanding some sort of explanation. She looked at Max who knew exactly what she was thinking but was in the same position of not knowing what was or wasn't said, so he just discretely shrugged his shoulders.

George began to meow, and it took a number of them for Tom to realise that it was dinner time. Jules sensed his agitation and said that she would feed him, as she knew where everything was. She grabbed the bag from on top of the fridge to find it near empty. Tom told her that there was another one in the shed. She asked Max if he could come with her and to take his phone to use as a torch. The sentence hadn't finished before Max was by her side. They went straight across the small path to a wooden shed, lit up by his mobile.

"What does he know?" asked Jules.

"I don't know. They were just on the table when I arrived, and nothing's been said. Should we say something?"

"I don't know. I don't know what Tom's been told. We don't want to make this worse for them."

"What could be worse than this?"

"True."

They knew they didn't have much time to talk or Tom would be out helping them find the cat food which was their whole purpose at present, to be as helpful as they could.

"I think it would be better coming from you," Max said as he grabbed the bag of kibble.

"Why me?"

"Just, you're his best friend. You were at A&E."

"You were the reason he was in A&E, do you not think you should be telling him?"

No decision was made as they reappeared in the kitchen and filled up George's food and water bowls. Once that was all done, an awkward silence emanated from the two house guests. Max eyed Jules and nodded for her to start. She shook her head and volleyed it back at him. Tom noticed it this time.

"What's up with you two?"

The pair didn't know where to look or what to do.

"If either of you two know something that could help me find my husband, I'd really appreciate hearing it."

They could tell he was losing patience. Jules lost due to the sheer awkwardness and wanting to help. She sat down in front of him and tried to process her thoughts. Tom watched her; he just wanted someone to tell him something.

"Okay, I don't know what's been said or how much you know. Has Jamie explained these to you?" she said, pointing to the two pill containers on the table.

"I was hoping he would but, we never got round to it. I found them in one of his drawers along with these."

She swallowed hard but knew she was going to have to tell him and hoped that it wouldn't destroy either of the men involved.

"A couple of months ago, around the time you were at Paris Fashion Week, you remember Jamie stayed at mine after you guy's had a falling out?"

Tom nodded rapidly wanting her just to keep talking.

"Well, that weekend Jamie was rushed to A&E because he was feeling unwell and because of the circumstances, they gave him P E P just in case something happened." She hoped that he would just accept this and continue calling Jamie or checking the internet.

"Unwell? Circumstances? What the hell do they mean?"
She was struggling now and began looking to Max for some help, but his body language emitted nothing.

"He collapsed at a party, and an ambulance had to be called for him. Circumstance, well, he was at one of Max's parties, and the doctor thought his drink was spiked." She just let it out because she wasn't good at lying and because Jamie was missing.

Tom's gaze fixed on Max who looked worried. He waited for him to say something.

"Someone at the party put some G into his drink and I didn't know that at the time, so I offered him a drink which had G in it and, well, you know what a lightweight he is when it comes to drinks and not having had G before and I suppose there was too much in his system he, OD'ed on G," Max tried to sound blasé, but it jarred with what he had disclosed and made him look callous.

"What are you telling me? Why was Jamie at your place, at one of *your* parties?"

"You guy's had a fight, and he texted me, and I thought he needed some fun after all the stuff with his Mum and Dad, you know? I didn't mean for this to happen. It was just…"

"Just what!?" Tom demanded.

"It was one of those things," even Max wasn't buying that and immediately regretted it.

Nobody uttered a word while both guests watched Tom try to compute what was being disclosed.

"Was he raped? Is that why they gave him these drugs?"

"No, they were over-reacting. He had blacked out and wasn't able to do anything but made his way out of the apartment and on to the street." The more Max spoke, the more he regretted every word because telling the truth was not painting a picture Tom wanted to hear, but Max wasn't registering this until he had said it and observed Tom's face, because to Tom this sounded horrendous and other worldly, but to Max whose weekends were a chemical haze, it was part of his life.

It felt like an intermission, no one said anything, and everyone in the kitchen needed some time. Jules felt some relief that the truth was out there and knew that she hadn't done anything wrong. Tom's brain was in overdrive, with images of scenarios and possibilities. He wondered how bad Jamie had been feeling and angry that he wouldn't allow anyone to help and he was petrified about the possibility of more stories. Max wanted to leave or have a stiff drink. He would've been delighted with both.

"Max, I want you to be completely honest with me, okay?"

Max just nodded rapidly.

"I met up with Jules the other week because I was worried about Jamie. I thought that they were meeting up more frequently than normal for after work drinks, but it transpires that that's not the case. On the nights that he was supposed to be with Jules, was he with you?"

Eventually, Max gave a single nod.

There was relief and anger in equal measure in the room.

"What have you done to him? What have you done to my Jamie? Why would you do this to him? He's not one of your randoms. He's a good person with a good home and people who care about him. Why would you toy with someone who's hurting like he is?" Tom was angry, and the litany of questions gave no illusion that these weren't rhetorical.

The usually quick witted Max was mute as he thought about each of the questions, but this wasn't fast enough.

"Well!?" Tom shouted.

"He was just so sad that night in Soho, and I just felt that he could do with some light in his life."

"Light?! You've got to be fucking joking."

"He wasn't talking to you, to anyone about this stuff and I thought he just needed to forget it for a while. We've all been there," Max said scanning the faces of the two people in front of him, hoping that one, but mainly both, would concur.

"We've all been there? Can you hear yourself? You've not been there. You're a privileged, upper-class homo, with a rich sugar Daddy for a boyfriend that you see every couple of months. You spend your weekends off your tits, not caring about those you are with. Where and when have *you* ever been there?"

Jules agreed with what was being said but was uncomfortable about how angry Tom had gotten and began to feel sorry for Max.

"Well? When?!" demanded Tom.

When Max wasn't forthcoming, Tom just continued.

"Exactly! Never! You've had it so bloody easy and yet you treat others with so little regard. You've never had to deal with anything difficult, nothing like this. People are just pawns to you!"

"I just wanted to help. I understood what he was…"

"Oh fuck off Max, were you going to say that you understood what someone else was going through? That'll be a first! Was his pain a little like when you didn't have enough to go shopping with…Daddy didn't send you enough money…eh?!"

Jules could see a different expression developing on Max's face. He was on the back foot with no comebacks. She had never seen this cocksure man like this before.

"I was just trying to help him. It had helped me forget stuff…"

"Forget what? Daddy not…"

"Leave off, Tom. I know you're mad but just…"

"Just what? Hit a nerve have I? What have you tried to forget? You're pathetic!"

"That I'm HIV positive!" Max screamed.

No one knew where to look or what to say. Tom's anger dissipated and he felt ashamed. Jules looked at Tom, urging him to say something. With both his hands down by his side, Max's face exploded into one of emotional carnage. It contorted and became red, his lips were quivering, and his body shook, but he just stood there. It was uneasy to watch because he wasn't hiding his face or drying his tears. It was like he felt that nothing at all was happening to him when his face said otherwise. Afraid that he was unable to stand up while in this state, Tom dashed over to embrace him. Max didn't put his arms around him and just allowed himself to be held.

"That's why you were missing work, calling in sick all those months ago. Why didn't you just say something?"

There was no response, and Tom knew that there was no response needed. He knew Max so well. All the stuff he had spouted out in anger, which he instantly regretted, were all the things that he knew Max was unhappy about: wealthy parents, Sugar Daddy, no real love, just money. All these things fuelled his hedonistic weekends.

"I promise you, nothing happened with Jamie," Max eventually said. "I knew that he didn't want to talk and I know what that feels like so I suggested some, momentary forgetting. Yes, we were at places where sex was happening, but I always put a little bit too much G into his drink which just put him to sleep. It was a real pain actually because I had to spend the rest of the night looking after him." He pulled back from Tom's embrace and looked him in the eye. "Nothing happened. I promise. I wouldn't do that to you two."

Tom didn't need to question him further because he believed him. When they were away on work trips, the stories of their domestic life garnished jeers from Max, but he knew that secretly it was all he ever wanted, to be loved and to have the mundane amazement of true love.

He took Max's face in his hands.

"You better be linked to a hospital and that you are taking meds, or else!"

Max stood up straight and saluted him. Tom kissed him on the forehead and hugged him again. Still mid embrace, a knock was heard at the door. They both immediately looked towards the noise. Jules ran to answer it, followed by the two men.

"Oh, I'm not sure if I've the right house. Is Jamie in?"

Jules opened the door further so Tom and Max could see that it was the old lady Jamie had befriended. Jules looked at Tom for guidance on what to do.

"I think you should come in," Tom said gently.

The group all moved towards the kitchen. Jules offered Teresa a seat as the rest stayed standing. Tom introduced himself and the two others.

"I'm Teresa; I'm a friend of Jamie's, well, at least I think I am. We met under odd circumstances, and we've been chatting ever since. Are you expecting him home anytime soon?"

"Teresa, Jamie is missing. He's been dealing with a lot of stuff recently and well, he just ran out this evening," Tom said, trying to stay calm. "I keep calling him and checking online, but his phone seems to be switched off."

Teresa looked genuinely concerned which seemed odd to the other three.

"Oh, I hope he's ok. He's been ever so good to me. He sent me a lovely letter and a CD, and I was returning the favour. I miss our chats. We'd meet once a week when I was supposed to be seeing some highfalutin counsellor which my daughter was paying for. I got more out of talking to your Jamie. You see, I lost my husband a few years back, and I realised, with Jamie's help, that I hadn't really dealt with it and he gave me a few ideas on how to survive it all. I'll be forever grateful to him."

The three were enthralled by her soft Irish accent and the heartbreaking story. They knew Jamie was a good person, so it didn't surprise them at all. It was just hard to hear how wonderful he was at sorting someone else out when he needed to do that for himself or to allow someone to do it for him.

Tom's phone lit up, and he grabbed it with great haste.

"He's posted something!" he exclaimed as he tried to get his phone to load. "It's one of his photos with a song link that he usually posts."

"What is it and what's the song?" asked Jules.

"I don't recognise the photo and song is "Gone" by Madonna. Don't know it either. Happy Madonna or Sad Madonna?" he asked Max.

"Sad," Max said reluctantly.

The three looked at the photo for clues, but it didn't look like anywhere they knew.

"Can I have a look?" asked Teresa.

As if she'd been part of their group for years, Tom showed her the photo that Jamie had posted on Facebook.

It was around eight in the evening when a taxi pulled up outside Tom's house. A group of four exited in a hurry and piled into the car. Tom sat up front with the driver, while Jules and Max sandwiched

Teresa in the back seat. The driver knew the destination, but Tom requested that when he could, for the driver to go as quick as possible.

Nobody had said anything for a while. Tom and Jules were praying that Jamie would be ok and that Teresa knew exactly where they should be going. Max was just happy that the focus wasn't on him anymore, but he was feeling lighter having told someone about his new HIV diagnosis. Teresa was sitting quietly in the car, enjoying being part of this young group of people. Jules caught a glimpse of her content face and felt that someone should fill her in a little on what's been going on.

As if she was a mind reader, Teresa casually broke the silence.

"So, is somebody going to tell me what's been going on?"

Tom turned around to look at the sweet old lady. He glanced at Max who shrugged his shoulders and then at Jules who gestured for him to start talking. Tom turned around a bit more to get comfortable, as he faced backwards and began to tell Teresa about Jamie's parents' passing and how he hadn't been dealing with it. His heart was melting anyway in the telling of how hard it had been for Jamie but what he wasn't expecting was seeing the eyes of this stranger glisten with tears as she sat, looking so small between Jules and Max, listening to what he had to tell her. Jules handed her a tissue from her bag, and she nodded with a smile, which made a large tear fall before she had time to wipe it.

The traffic was typical of a Friday evening, and Teresa could see that Tom was getting anxious. Tom tried to be as polite as he could when he asked how sure she was about where they were going. She was adamant they were heading in the right direction.

After hitting most red lights en-route, they were as far as they could go on four wheels. They launched themselves out of the car and stood to wait for Teresa to get herself out and show them where they had to go. It was dark, and Jules offered an arm for her to link, which Teresa accepted gladly. Following her lead, they found themselves on the banks of the Thames. Max and Tom looked up and down the pathway but found nothing. Turning around they saw Teresa begin to walk up a jetty and it clicked that that was where Jamie had taken the photo from. Jules let her walk on, and as they both approached, she suggested they give Teresa some time. Huddled together, they watched Teresa walk to the end of the pier, where it looked like she was talking to someone.

"Fancy meeting you here," she said with cheer in her voice.

Jamie looked up from where he was sitting, a little shocked and annoyed that she was there.

"How did you…"

"There are three unofficial detectives who care for you very much, who did all the work."

Jamie peered over the railings and saw Tom, Jules and Max all waiting in the cold. He had finished the bottle of wine but was still holding on to it.

"I've messed everything up, Teresa."

"Oh no you haven't. What you haven't done is told me anything about what you were…are going through. Now, I could be a little mad at you, but then, if we'd been talking about you I might not feel a little better about what's been going on for me. I am still mad, but I'm not going to hold it against you."

"I just wanted it to go away and hoped that I could skate through my days not having to deal with it."

"It doesn't work like that, and you know it. Wouldn't it be awful, that when people we really loved and cared for left us and it had no impact on us? Like they meant nothing. The memories would fade faster, and we'd never learn from their passing."

"Learn what? How shit it is?"

"How precious time is and to try and make the best of the time we have. This isn't going to make the pain of grief go away, nor should it. There's a saying back home, 'It's the living that have to resurrect themselves, not the dead,' and it's so true. Our loved ones are gone and in no pain. We owe it to them to live on. You also owe it to those lovely people who are freezing over there, who care so much for you and don't really care what might or might not have gone on."

"I wish I'd done more, you know?"

"Hindsight is the best view. I bet she was as proud as punch of you and like any mother, wanted you to live your life as best you could. It's the inevitable burden of the parent to have to deal with a childless house, seeing their children a couple of times a year. That's the order of things."

"It just hurts so much sometimes."

Teresa put out her hand to encourage him to stand up. He knew she wouldn't be able to pull him up, so he got up himself and then held her hand. She took the bottle and placed it on the ground. Leading him to the railings, she let go of him and put both her hands on the cold black metal barrier. He looked at her with amusement as she altered her posture, so she was standing upright and began to breathe in and out. Her eyes were closed, and Jamie knew she was right but didn't want to admit it. Quickly peeping through one eye, she saw he wasn't copying her. She exaggerated the posture and her breathing even more and then began to sing *Across the Universe*.

She repeated the chorus once before Jamie matched her stance and posture. He began to sing, and as he sang each line, tears just poured down his face. He let them fall afraid that now they were flowing they might stop. They repeated the chorus a couple of times, and they both came to a natural ending. Teresa placed her hand on his back and checked he was ok. The lights of London made the track of tears shimmer on his cold face. He smiled and embraced her.

That was the cue for the others to make their way down the pier. They all collided into a giant group hug. Jamie held Tom, squeezed him and without words, communicated all that he needed to say at that very moment with a promise to do things differently in the future.

Chapter 11

Three weeks until Christmas and one day after the staff party, the office was looking festive with all the workstations tinsel trimmed and a few members of staff with Santa hats, but energy levels were low with hangovers still been tended to.

There were no clients booked for the day which was always a sensible thing to do for both clients and staff. Jamie was in the counselling room and found himself for the first time waiting on Helen. He had a lot to talk about in the session and was keen to get started. Five minutes had passed when Helen burst into the room apologising for the delay, telling him that someone had thrown themselves on the tracks which held up the whole Northern Line. They commented on this time of year being very tough on lots of people. The expectation of family get togethers, peace and love to all and not to mention the financial strain, can just be too much for people. It was a conversation both of them had quite a lot being in the business of counselling. They were the vessels in which was poured festive stress and seasonal despair every year they had worked.

He checked if she needed a minute to get settled, but she declined by whipping off her coat, throwing it on the back of the chair and sitting down, poised for action as she cleaned her glasses. The pregnant pause was the signal Jamie needed to launch into his clients' notes. Thankfully caffeinated, Jamie was getting through quite a few clients that he felt needed extra input. They thrashed out many possibilities and a few new angles. Jamie wrote these down, while Helen wrote shortened reminders for herself of what was being planned and discussed on each of the clients that were being presented.

After the last case file was placed on the top of the others, they knew that the client work was done and it was time to discuss other things.

"So, how have you been?"

Even as a counsellor, it was odd to have this simple yet pointed question directed at him. He took a minute to think. He started off by telling her that he was doing okay. That for the last number of weeks he had found going back to therapy himself a beneficial process. His new therapist, which Helen had recommended, was working out quite well and it was interesting having a female counsellor for once. She wasn't letting him away that easy and remained silent after all the talk about the new counsellor. He knew what she wanted, and he told her that he had reconnected with Jules and that they were now trying to meet at least once a week. He recognised in himself a pattern of shutting people out when he was in pain and that he gave her permission to call him on it and to pester and nag him. Similarly, with Tom, they had spent time talking and 'not talking'. Seeing what his splitting off of his grief had done to the people around him, he was no longer allowed to 'not talk' about things. They now had an agreement that there would be 'no talking' after therapy sessions unless Jamie wanted to share and if Tom wanted to check in on him, he was allowed to defer for one day only. Jamie chuckled at the prospect of his husband giving him twenty-four hours to have some space before he could ask again how he was doing. It had worked out well and gave them both space and permission.

Helen looked pleased and commented on how well Jamie had done amidst the difficulty that the year had thrown at him. In a cautious tone, she encouraged him to continue with therapy for longer than he thought he would need it and that it was of utmost importance that he just be mindful of himself.

This was the last time that they'd see each other before Christmas. Typically, there were no exchanging of gifts or cards, as is the circumscribed relationship between supervisor and supervisee. They wished each other all the best for the holiday season and the New Year while Jamie arranged the stack of notes he needed to take back to his desk. After they had scheduled their next appointment, he began to make his way out of the room. Just as he was about to close the door, Helen turned around in her chair and looked slightly awkward. This stopped Jamie in his tracks because to him; she looked like she was going to say something.

"You should consider buying yourself something for Christmas this year, something to celebrate and remember that you got through this one and that you're still here."

Jamie knew what she meant. It was something he used himself when talking to clients, that they should reward themselves for still being here after horrendous experiences and upbringings. Having it said to him made him feel proud that he was indeed still here, still breathing and getting through. The pain of his loss and regret was still there too, and there were days when it would ambush him. Equally, there were days when it was nowhere to be found. There was just no predicting it and he was now okay with grief's guerrilla tactics.

"I'm actually picking it up on the way home this evening," he said with a smile.

"Good for you!"

There was very little work being done in the office. Coffees were still being drunk, and Krispy Kreme's were being eaten, all in search of the sugar rush and caffeine hit to get them through the last couple of hours. Rebecca put a doughnut into his mouth as he walked by with the notes in his hands. Being festive personified, she had an elf hat and jumper with a tinsel scarf. No hangover could curtail her Christmas cheer, but it wasn't going down well with everyone, and there had been requests for her to turn off the Christmas playlist she insisted on playing for the entire day.

Jonathan, in jeans and a jumper for once, came out of his office and began to put on his coat and scarf. He announced that everyone was to go home due to the lack of productivity. He jested that there was no point in anyone being in the office. He didn't have to say it twice, as everyone scrambled for their winter jackets and accessories and exited feeling the warmth of the bosses generous festiveness.

Being the last to leave, ensuring all lights were off, and doors were closed properly, Jamie stepped out, and the cold December air nipped at his face. With his head down, he made his way to the station. Before taking a right on to St. Thomas Street, he could hear a choir singing carols from inside the glass atrium of Borough Market. On approaching the Shard, he saw a wonderfully stylish display of Christmas lights. It had been a good day, and he was allowing himself these moments of cheer and contentment without judging them or thinking too hard, afraid that they'd waft away. The station was awash with Christmas jumper wearing workers mixed in with tuxedoed men and ball-gowned ladies making their way to their office parties. Another choir greeted him at the station. He placed some change in their bucket and dashed for his train.

He didn't take his usual route home as he had to pick up his Christmas gift to himself. He was told that it was ready for collection and as he entered the store on Circus Street, it was all wrapped up. After the payment was made, he strolled home with a large parcel under his arm.

Their house stood out with its white lights ablaze. George was at the window and once he had spotted Jamie, jumped down to greet him at the door. Thankfully, the Christmas tree was still standing. There had been a few years where George's curiosity got the better of him, and he climbed the tree only to topple it over. He stood innocently inside the front door. Jamie bestowed lots of unwanted affection on him when all he wanted was his food bowl to be topped up. He placed the package underneath the large illuminated Christmas tree in the living room. The house felt warm and welcoming.

Tom was on his last trip of the year with work but was due back around 4 am. Their annual Christmas bash was the next day. It was always the same theme: 'Informal Party. Formal Dress.' They loved hosting it, and everyone looked forward to dressing up without the commute, the noise or lack of places to sit and chat. The preparations would take most of the following day, and as Tom wasn't getting back until the morning, Jamie had a night to relax after the busy week.

He finished yesterday's lasagne, poured himself a glass of wine and threw himself on to the couch. Music was playing throughout the house, so there was no need for TV. With George preening himself after his dinner, he pulled down one of the checked blankets that draped the back of the sofa, threw it over himself and dozed off.

He woke up an hour later with George snuggled in beside him, still fast asleep. He checked the time and tried to sit up without disturbing the cat. The lights on the tree were gently blinking on and off. The new package underneath the tree stood out. He never enjoyed opening presents from people, much preferring giving them. This was running through his head as he tried to work out if he could open his own present to himself now rather than in a couple of weeks time. He decided that he could. He went down on his knees, shuffling over to the tree and carefully placed it on his lap. It was wrapped beautifully in brown paper and tied up with red string. Carefully, he loosened the string and began to peel off the paper. It caught his breath. Imagining something and then seeing it for real can go either way, but in this case, it looked better than he had thought.

Both house occupants were startled by a knock at the door. George looked annoyed as Jamie went to see who it was. The spy hole was all fogged up so he couldn't see out. He opened the door to find Max standing there wrapped in a large scarf and an oversized woolly hat on his head.

"Hey! One of Tom's clients dropped off this F&M hamper, and I couldn't be bothered dragging it along tomorrow night, it would ruin my look. Do you mind if I come in, it's freezing?"

Max walked in and was charmed by the quaintness of what he saw. The lights, the tree and decorations everywhere. Jamie offered him a drink, and he accepted a glass of wine. There was lots of small talk: work, Christmas plans and shopping.

"So, how have you *really* been?"

Jamie looked at him oddly. He was shocked by Max, of all people asking him this. He told him that the day he had, had been a good one and that was all he could really think about. Bad days were still on the horizon but that he felt prepared for them. Jamie returned the question and Max looked uncomfortable as he drank the rest of the glass. Rather than breaking the silence, Jamie just filled up their glasses again and waited.

"I'm okay. I had my follow-up appointment at the hospital today, hence why I'm not in New York with Tom. My bloods are fine. The numbers are good, and I'm remembering to take my one pill a day."

"That's wonderful. Imagine, one pill a day?"

"I only have to go there now twice a year to pick up my prescription. It all feels a little too easy, doesn't it?"

"I'll be honest and say I don't know very much but that seems great, twice a year, one pill a day. You don't seem convinced."

"Convinced? I'm convinced I'm a fucking gay cliche. Hairdressing Homo with AIDs," Max said half in jest and half in anger at himself.

Jamie gave him space. He'd never seen Max like this before, vulnerable. Where was the handsome, confident, sharp tongued man?

The guy who walked into bars, where both sexes took notice. Always dressed impeccably, a good job and a fantastic home. To the outside world, one would think that he should have nothing to be down about. This was just a fleeting thought in Jamie's head, but he knew that all those things meant very little when a crisis hits. He knew that Max's phone would be full of one night encounters, some without a first name, maybe just some memorable physical characteristic, all ready and willing to meet for fun, escape down the rabbits' hole, only to emerge on Monday morning.

"You know, you're the only people in my life who know this? Well, you lot and the doctors at the clinic. You'd think that being part of a community so ravished by this, people would be more compassionate?"

"You haven't told anyone else?"

"No way! There are guys I meet up with from time to time and the stuff they say about this one having it or that one having it and how they'd never want to be with them and all the usual bullshit about drinking out of cups and kissing; it makes me sick. Idiots. The thing is, they could be in the same boat if they bothered to go and get tested."

"All you can do is focus on yourself for now. Don't worry about them. There will always be idiots. Even hairdressing, homo idiots."

That cracked a smile. Jamie left the table for a second to get something from under the tree. He handed Max a beautifully wrapped gift. He looked at Jamie strangely as he opened it. He saw a DVD entitled *Jeffrey*.

"If you're going to be a tragic hairdressing homo with AIDs, at least learn some better lines."

With no gift for Jamie, he just thanked him as he opened the card attached. To his surprise, it wasn't a Christmas Card. Instead, it was a simple white card with a large 'Thank you' embossed on it.

"You don't have to read that now," Jamie said awkwardly.

Max read it anyway as Jamie sat watching him. When he'd finished, Max looked gobsmacked.

"I really mean it, Max. I appreciate what you were trying to do for me. I did need to forget what was happening, what I was feeling and meeting up with you for our 'not talking' sessions was a beautiful distraction."

"I hear a 'but' coming."

"But, all the problems were still there on all the other days we weren't meeting up, and in fact, more problems were added to the pile. For what it's worth, in your situation, there are days when you won't like yourself and want to run away, to drink something, to shag someone and sure, it will feel okay for a bit, but the icky feelings will come back. Just remember, that icky feelings don't kill, they're just uncomfortable and not nice. Find something else in those moments, call me, Tom, go to the cinema, do something to distract you for a bit. Sorry, I don't want this to be a therapy session, what I'm trying to say, is 'thank you' - I mean that."

"Icky? Icky feelings?"

"Piss off."

They both raised their glasses and paused trying to think of something witty to toast. Finally, Max said, "To icky, homo feelings!"

They clinked glasses and downed what was left. Max had to leave because his boyfriend was due back for the entire Christmas break. He told Jamie that he was planning on telling him everything. As he fastened his coat, he saw the half opened present beside the tree. Jamie saw him looking at it and asked if he wanted to see it. They walked over, and Jamie took off all the wrapping this time.

"Jesus wants you for a sunbeam? Have you found Christ?" Max mocked him.

"My mother could only have wished. No, it's her bible. I got it mounted and framed."

"That's sweet, sort of, in a hippy Christian sort of way."

"I'm not religious at all, but it's just something of hers. She used it a lot."

"I can see. Why that page?"

"Read the underlined bit at the top."

"'He will wipe every tear from their eyes. There will be no more death' or mourning or crying or pain, for the old order of things has passed away.'"

"Revelation 21:4," Jamie said in an authoritative voice.

"Very nice. Where are you going to put it?"

"I haven't decided yet."

Jamie carefully placed it on the coffee table and escorted Max to the front door. He opened the door, and for a second they didn't move. Max looked at Jamie and without discussing they embraced each other. There was no back slapping or quick releases. So much had happened between them, good and bad without any real conversations. Both their struggles were immense and very personal, and somehow they made a stab at trying to get through them. Regardless of the outcome, here they were. The embrace communicated real emotion and admiration, there was no need for anything else. Eventually, it ended, and Max walked out silently while Jamie watched him until he couldn't see him anymore. Closing the door, he spied George heading upstairs. Jamie thought that was a wonderful idea and joined him.

The next morning Jamie awoke to find both George and Tom all cuddled up on the opposite side of the bed. He tried so carefully to get out without waking them, but George's ears pricked up and before Jamie could leave the dark bedroom, George was prancing down the stairs awaiting his breakfast. He looked at the sleeping Tom, still undisturbed by his movements. He loved how he could sleep through most things and that no matter what position, he always looked so handsome in slumber.

Cat fed, coffee made and radio on. It was truly Christmas, with every other song a yuletide classic. Amidst refills, Jamie gathered all the glassware they owned and began systematically putting them through the dishwasher to ensure they sparkled. The wine fridge was stocked, the oven cleaned and playlists edited. On his way back from opening the door to the postman, he spotted a Post-it on the wall near the stairs. He went in closer and instantly recognised Tom's handwriting.

I think it would look great here x

Jamie had also thought that this spot would be perfect for his mothers' framed bible.

The food for the party was delivered and not breaking with tradition; the plan was to serve finger food that could be cooked all together at the same temperature. When they used to have a dinner, they felt it too stressful and difficult to do while all dressed up so it was Jules' idea to move to drink and party food and no-one had complained.

Party preparations done, he sat down in silence, the only time for the next twenty-four hours the house would be that quiet. Scanning the living room for things that he'd forgotten to do he saw all the Christmas cards they had received so far and thought that people didn't send them like they used to, preferring to send online messages and texts. He loved Christmas cards, and it dawned on him that this year would be the first without one from his parents. He knew that his father had no input when it came to things like cards but it was always nice that his mother insisted on getting a card that said 'To My Son & His Boyfriend.' He knew that if she were alive it would have been 'To My Son & His Husband', and sad feelings bled into his morning. Other firsts already broached were his Christmas visit home, and his mothers visit to see the Christmas Tree in Leicester Square. They hadn't gone unfelt but rather than pushing them away, Jamie had allowed himself to be sad and spoke to Tom and Jules about those wobbly moments. They never lasted long, but he knew they would come and return next year, but he hoped they'd be less potent.

Tom eventually woke up and required copious amounts of coffee to get him anyway excited about their party. After numerous cups, Jamie ordered him to go and shower and get ready because he was afraid he would sneak back into bed and wake up the following day. After doing what he was told, Tom came back downstairs in his fitted dark suit, crisp white shirt and his red bowtie with white polka dots. Jamie was stopped in his tracks at the sight that was standing on the bottom step. Tom knew a compliment was coming so he just got in there first and told him that it was his turn to get ready. They kissed as they passed each other.

Less than an hour later, Jamie appeared in a grey suit, white shirt and a blue bowtie with white polka dots. Tom had just poured some Prosecco, and they clinked glasses and as if on cue, Jules was knocking at the door. She looked stunning in her little black dress with killer heels. They both kissed each cheek as she entered, laden down with presents and more bottles. Brian and Dan had bumped into Max at Greenwich station, so they arrived together, and with the music on, the party was underway. Brian and Dan had come in their usual classic black tuxedo, and they were busy arguing with Max, saying that the white tuxedo that he came in was really an affront to the classic black tux. Jamie loved the banality of the topic and the mock arguments they were coming up with. He thought they all looked dashing with their gelled back hair and shiny shoes.

Tom had the oven on and was arranging the food on the racks and then setting the timer. Food was always his department and drinks was Jamie's. He ensured everybody's glass was constantly topped up and when he had a quiet moment, he would perform clandestine shots of Ouzo, Sambuca and Jägermeister when Tom wasn't looking, with the rest of his guests.

Taking a moment from his hosting duties, Jamie grabbed Jules and sat on the couch. He had seen her using her phone quite and bit and knew that things weren't going well with her new boyfriend. She blocked his line of questioning and said she would only answer his questions if he talked about how he was doing. Without hesitating, he began to speak of the last month since that fateful night by the Thames. She knew he wasn't there to harm himself and that he just needed some space, but she told him that she was really worried. He spoke about this being the first Christmas and how annual reminders, some he was prepared for, would take his breath away but that he saw it all as part and parcel of what was ahead of him.

She was so proud of him and grabbed and kissed him on the lips. As their lips parted, she looked right into his eyes and warned him that if he ever didn't reply to her that she'd burn all his Madonna memorabilia. They downed their glasses which signed the deal.

Tom announced that the food was warmed and that everyone could help themselves. The group all made their way into the kitchen, passing plates down the line as they waited to serve themselves. For a few moments, as people began to eat, all that could be heard was the Christmas playlist. Rather than sitting at the table, the group hung around the festively lit kitchen, eating in silence, contemplating second helpings.

Having wolfed down his plate, Tom opened another bottle of Prosecco in a hurry and went around the room, filling every glass and then coughed to get everyone's attention.

"Right you lot, quiet down. First of all thanks for coming to our annual Christmas bash. We love to see you all dressed up and fingering small food while sipping on some bubbles." He walked over to Jamie and put an arm around him. "This year has been, well, it's been a year that we've gotten through, and it wouldn't have been possible without all of you. So, without getting too sentimental, cheers and here's to another three hundred and sixty-five days, spinning around the sun."

Glasses were raised, kisses, hugs and squeezes were exchanged with everyone there. Max was convinced that someone would spill some sauce on his white tuxedo and decided that air kissing was the safest option. The music was turned up louder, and everyone went in for more food.

An hour and many glasses later, shoes were off, jackets were draped across chairs and bow ties were undone. The group were all on the couches waiting for the presents to be opened. George sat on the stairs, annoyed that his owners insisted on him wearing a festive collar. Jules was nominated to be in charge of handing out the presents. Their Secret Santa presents had to be under twenty pounds, and there had been many years when peoples budgets were used very imaginatively.

Reluctantly Jules walked on her knees, sat by the tree and looked at the gift tags to decide who was first. She saw her own wrapped present and decided to give the first gift to Jamie. The tipsy group cheered and those near the coffee table, drum-rolled. As they looked around the room, the noise petered off when they noticed that Jamie wasn't there. Tom shouted up the stairs and told Jamie to get his ass down, or he'd open his present. A few awkward looks were exchanged between the group. Tom heard nothing from the bathroom. He peeled himself off the couch and ran upstairs. Everyone else just looked at each other. They could hear him calling out and no reply. Tom ran back downstairs, faster this time.

"He's gone!"

It was bitterly cold, and Jamie regretted not taking an overcoat, he thought his suit jacket would suffice. There really wasn't a chance for him to start searching for a coat as he made his exit while everyone crammed the dishwasher and retired to the couch. He felt he'd done well throughout the day but as it went on and after Tom's speech he began to feel overwhelmed. Jamie knew he had to do this and even though he had promised not to keep any secrets, what he was about to do was surely going to garnish a lot of criticism. He had put his phone on Airplane Mode once he knew exactly where he was going and standing outside, the photo's on the internet matched the sight before him.

A group of men laughed loudly as they smoked on the street. He could hear music inside. They looked at him standing on his own, all dressed up and thought he looked out of place.

"You've got a few more years before you need to be in here young man!" an older, red faced elder said to much laughter from his friends.

A quieter and more sympathetic member of the group asked if Jamie wanted to come in out of the cold.

"I was just wondering if I could pop in for a minute to see someone?" Jamie asked politely. They all agreed that this wasn't a problem and Jamie squeezed passed them. He checked his reflection in the mirror and fixed his bowtie, ensuring his jacket was buttoned properly.

As he pushed through the inner door, he was hit by a wall of heat, light and sound. It took him a few seconds but his eyes eventually adjusted and he gazed around the decadent ballroom. Large circular tables and chairs were dotted around the walls, allowing the beautiful wooden dance floor to be as uncluttered as possible. The massive, slowly rotating glitter ball shot beams of light and twinkled with every turn. Jamie felt like he had been transported back in time.

"Aren't they a little old for you?" said a familiar voice.

Jamie turned around and saw Lily, in a full-length ball gown, smiling wryly.

"Lily? So lovely to see you. Having a good night?" He scrambled for something to say as he wasn't at all expecting to see her here.

"I don't think I should be enjoying myself at a party like this, but I don't think that's the point really. The main thing is that she is," she nodded to Teresa who had her back to them as she stood listening to a group of ladies chat and laugh.

Seeing Teresa again struck up warm feelings for Jamie. While he didn't expect to see her sitting in the corner on her own, he admired her get up and go attitude as she stood there in her evening dress, her arm around one of her girlfriends, listening to the rest of her group gossiping about something.

Jamie suddenly moved closer to Lily and began whispering various instructions in her ear. It wasn't until near the end of these that Lily's poker face relaxed. He sent a group message and his location before he handed it over to her.

The smoking gents reentered the room and headed straight to the bar in one moving mass. Waiters had begun collecting the dessert plates along with the cups and saucers. Jamie spotted the source of the music and felt sad that there wasn't a live band playing as it actually would have added so much to the gathering. The hall's stage was draped with a red curtain as if it was embarrassed that an iPod was providing the musical entertainment.

Inhaling deeply while silently psyching himself up, he walked slowly to the other side of the room. He negotiated a path through the chairs, tables, bags of presents and fast paced waiting staff and eventually he was a few feet away from the group. He stopped. His head hung low as he tried to muster energy and courage which were failing him now. He glanced around and saw Lily was in place. He looked nervous to her but urged him to go on, which Jamie used to continue walking.

Finally, he was standing behind Teresa. For the first time in weeks, he heard her lilting voice, and the furrows on his face softened. Most of the group she was with were focused on the lady who was talking, regaling them on a recent trip to her GP. The ailment didn't seem too serious as they were all laughing. Someone who was sitting directly across from Teresa spotted Jamie, and her non-laughing face got Teresa's attention. The lady nodded to her to encourage her to turn around. Jamie spotted this and quickly turned to Lily and gave her a thumbs up. Instantly the music stopped to a few gasps of annoyance and then a slow, soft guitar strum could be heard through the speakers. This took Teresa's breath, but she continued to look behind her where she saw Jamie looking rather nervous. He extended his hand.

"May I have this dance?" he asked with a smile.

She couldn't speak because her eyes were welling up and lip movements would somehow weaken the dam she was hoping would keep her emotions in check. Instead, she just nodded, and Jamie led her slowly to the floor. One of the ladies from the group told the one who was talking to shut up and pointed at the odd sight of the strange young man taking their friend for a dance.

They made their way to the centre of the dance floor. Jamie gently turned to face her and put his right hand behind her back, while he held her right hand in his left and began to sway to the music gently. The song was Neil Young's *Harvest Moon*, and while some of the dancers were puzzled by this un-festive classic, they soon were taken over by the gentle rhythm and resumed their dancing.

During the first verse of the song, they said nothing as he felt Teresa sob gently into his chest, while still keeping time and moving gracefully with Jamie. The smoking group from the bar were now silent and focused on the unlikely couple in the middle of the dance floor, while her girlfriends were on their feet looking on. As the chorus began, Teresa moved slightly back and sang it out loud not caring about tears and makeup. Jamie sang along with her. He carefully twirled her, and this provoked her to giggle. They resumed their hold and continued to dance being flanked by more couples joining them on the floor.

In between their fellow dancers, as they moved around the floor, Jamie caught a glimpse of Lily wiping away tears from her smiling face. He hoped that Teresa could see it too. He didn't know if her beaming face was because of seeing it or just the fact she was hearing and dancing to her song. The disco ball shot brilliant white lights in every direction around the room from above. The shiny floor gave way to ease of movement as they carefully placed their feet and glided effortlessly, making the most of the space they had.

They knew the last chorus was coming up. She stepped back, and they held each other's hands and sang it to each other, reconnecting for the final few bars. Once the song had concluded, there was a deafening cheer from one corner of the room. Everyone looked around and saw that their Christmas party had been crashed by strangers. Jamie saw Tom, Jules, Dan, Brian and Max with Lily, clapping loudly and cheering on. Jules and Lily were desperately looking for tissues as they both hadn't worn waterproof mascara.

"Thank you! You've made an old woman very happy. How did you know about the song?"

"A guess."

"But how?"

"When I was in your house, it was the album that was standing on its own, on display with the lyrics framed just above it. I take it, this was his plan, that you were going to dance to it at parties like this one, once you had reached your Golden Wedding Anniversary, which would have been this year?"

Teresa didn't reply. Instead, she squeezed his hand and silently mouthed another thank you which made Jamie think he was indeed correct. They walked off the dance floor to join their friends and family. Lily embraced them both and asked everyone what they were drinking. Dan and Brian headed straight to the dance floor with Jules, while Max looked awkwardly around wondering where his night had gone wrong and why he was at an old aged pensioners' Christmas party.

Tom took Jamie's hand while Teresa put her arm around Tom which started a group hug. They looked at the busy dance floor as the revellers danced to Wizard's *I Wish It Could Be Christmas Every Day*. Tom saw Lily struggling with lots of full glasses, so he dashed up to help her.

"I've missed our chats," Jamie said.

"Me too."

"It's been a mental couple of weeks, and I'm supposed to be focusing on myself and sorting my head out, so I haven't been avoiding you."

"I thought that might be the case, so I haven't gone to the market for our Friday walks for a while now, thinking you'd text me when you might want to do it again. Too cold anyway," she joked.

"That dance wasn't a freebie by the way."

She looked puzzled as he led her to a corner of the room where there was an empty round table. They both sat down beside each other and Jamie reached inside his jacket pocket where he took out a slightly battered envelope. He gazed at it reverently.

"What is it?"

"This is a letter that my mother left me in her will, which, I've never opened. I've been too frightened to open it because after this there is no more...no more contact. Every night I go to bed and can feel it sitting in the drawer calling out to me, and each morning I want to forget it exists, but I know I can't."

"You want me to read it?" she asked gently.

Jamie just nodded, and he saw the envelope been taken from his hand.

Carefully she opened it and pulled the single sheet of paper from within. She checked, with just a look, to see if she should proceed. He nodded again, looking petrified.

14th July 2016

Dear Jamie,

Death does odd things to us. I've just buried your father, and it's spurred me to sort out our will and write this letter because once you're gone, you're gone.

If you are reading this, I have gone too, but I know you will be okay. You've always been able to keep yourself safe and out of harm, but I know that came at a cost.

When you told me you were moving to London, I knew it was the right thing. You were never going to settle here.

I hope you know that my decision to not attend your wedding has haunted me every day. I regret it more than anything. I can't blame

anyone, other than myself, for that – but please know, I so wanted to be
there.

I wish you a long and happy life with Tom. You chose well.

Grieve if you need to but know this, I'm so proud of you so just
let me be and remember I'll be watching over you and praying for you.
Love always,
Your Mum x

Nothing was said because there wasn't anything that would add to that moment. Teresa kept looking at the page until she gently folded it and placed it back in the envelope. Handing it back to Jamie, she saw his doe eyes full to the brim with tears but he wasn't distraught, he appeared to be content. He just put the letter back in his jacket pocket. WHAM's *Last Christmas* was turned up loud, and they looked at each other.

"Let's dance!" Jamie said, grabbing her hand to lead her to the dance floor.

———————

The G Club Book Club

Facebook

Please go to The G Club Facebook page and share your thoughts.

Twitter

If you are on Twitter, use the Hashtag **#GClubBook** to spread the word and see what others thought.

Instagram

Take photos of you reading the book using the hashtag **#GClubBook**.

Spotify

Go to www.paulmadden.info to find a Spotify Playlist and listen to all the songs mentioned in the book along with other tracks that set the tone of the story.

25451211R00192

Printed in Great Britain
by Amazon